Offender of the Faith

Offender of the Faith

An Alex Warren Murder Mystery

Zach Abrams

Fiction titles by Zach Abrams

You can buy Zach's fiction books at Amazon by linking to:
Alex Warren Murder Mystery series:
Made a Killing - http://mybook.to/madeakilling
A Measure of Trouble - http://mybook.to/ameasureoftrouble
Written to Death - http://mybook.to/writtentodeath
Ring Fenced - http://mybook.to/ringfenced
Source - http://mybook.to/source
Twists and Turns - https://www.amazon.co.uk/dp/B00818C16O/

You can find out more about Zach's publications from his Amazon page at http://author.to/zachabrams

Chapter 1

The gloved hand was steady, confident and sure. Controlling a razor-sharp blade, it smoothly sliced through skin and flesh. Barely a drop of blood spilled as deft fingers carefully probed and peeled back surface tissue to expose vital organs.

As if watching a road crash, Alex squirmed, with his eyes locked on the unfolding scene.

"I really enjoyed the lasagne and I'd like to keep it down. This isn't really the most appropriate after dinner viewing," he complained, his tone unable to disguise his distaste.

"Alex you're a six- foot- four, fifteen stones brute of a man not a six stone weakling. I didn't have you down as being squeamish. It's not as if you don't see plenty of blood and guts at work." Sandra shook her head. "Change the station if you have to."

"Precisely my point. We need to deal with more than enough death and mutilation on a daily basis; it hardly makes the most entertaining recreational viewing. I'd much rather see a good drama or even a mediocre sit-com."

With care, Sandra lowered herself onto the couch next to him, leaned across for the remote and scrolled through several channels before settling on a repeat showing of a *Big Bang Theory* episode. "Is this more to your liking, oh great master?" she asked while cosying in close, smiling contentedly.

"Perfect," Alex replied, circling his right arm around her shoulder while tenderly stroking the distended bump of her formerly trim abdomen. He then added, "First class comedy; we want to ensure this young lady is given the best start in life."

Sandra laughed for only a second before a frown darkened her face, "Will you be really disappointed if we have a boy?"

"Of course not. I just meant…" Alex started to reply but any reassurance he was planning was interrupted by the shrill ring from his mobile.

It was now Alex's turn to frown when he glanced at the screen before swiping to accept the call. "Yes Phil, What's up?"

"Evening Boss. Sorry to break into your free time."

"I guess it must be something serious. Okay, forget the pleasantries and let me know what's happened."

"Yes, Sir. Unexplained death, almost certainly murder. Not far from you, Waverley Gardens, just off Minard Road."

"You're right. It's only a five-minute walk from my flat. Just as well I don't need to drive as I've had a glass of Rioja with dinner."

"I'm sure it beats the drivel they call coffee from the office vending machine and I suspect it's not too safe to drive after drinking that stuff either," said Phil.

"Too bloody true, but that's hardly the point. What more can you tell me?"

"Yes, Sir. Young Asian girl, late teens maybe early twenties, battered and strangled or so it seems. We've still to get the doc's opinion to confirm the cause of death. Boyfriend came home from work and found her lying there. So he says. He called it in."

"Any sign of sexual assault?"

"Can't say for sure yet. She wasn't naked or anything like that, but her clothes look badly crumpled. We didn't want to disturb anything until Scene of Crime have checked everything out. They're on the job now.

"What about the boyfriend? Where is he now?

"Sanjay's talking to him. From what I could tell, the boy seemed really distraught, so either he's innocent or a bloody good actor." He looks to be a similar age and he's white. This could be a delicate one because of the multiracial aspect so we thought we'd better let you know A.S,A,P. Sanjay's taken charge so far. He asked me to fill you in."

"Thanks Phil; you've done the right thing. Give me the flat position and number and I'll be with you in a few minutes."

Alex noted the information then disengaged the call. Turning to Sandra he asked, "I take it you picked up on that?"

"I caught enough to know Phil called, there's been a major incident and it's put the knackers on our carefully planned, nice, cosy evening," Sandra answered.

"Sorry, Love, you know what it's like?"

"Yes, I think I've been in the job long enough to understand how duty calls." Then glancing at her bump, Sandra added, "If it wasn't for this little one confining me to six months' desk work, and now maternity leave, you'd have had to tie me down to stop me being involved."

Alex nodded gravely, "You can't be too careful, particularly after the miscarriage last year. I know being restricted must be really tough for you, but it won't be long now, only a couple of weeks hopefully, and it will be worth it."

"I know, I know. We've talked it through a thousand times, but it doesn't make it any easier. There's nothing I want more than to have a healthy baby, our baby. I know I have to be careful, but it's hard having to sit around doing nothing."

"You're not doing nothing," Alex said but seeing the look on Sandra face, he knew better than to offer more platitudes. "Listen, I'd better get going."

Sandra stood to see Alex out. Moving down the hall, she caught a glimpse of herself in the mirror sitting above a photograph of her and Alex when they'd started dating. The contrast was startling. Over recent months, she'd let her hair grow out of the page-boy style she'd previously favoured and added highlights detracted from the severe jet black. Having a naturally slim, slight stature, the large baby- bulge made her look misshapen. Sandra frowned and ran her fingers through her hair. "I'm not surprised you can't wait to get away from me. I'm fat and ugly."

"Don't be ridiculous. I think you're gorgeous and you're not fat. You'll get your figure back in no time after the baby's born. Alex pulled Sandra into a brief hug, his arms straining to fully encircle her.

"I thought you promised never to let anyone come between us," she joked before adding, "I'm really okay. I was only feeling a bit sorry for myself because I'm bored and frustrated waiting to get past this stage, but I'm really happy too, if that makes any sense."

Alex smiled, pecked her cheek then slipped on his jacket, "I'll be back as soon as I can," he said, then he sidled out of the door.

* * *

Skipping down the stairs, Alex barged through the security door and was outside in the street before he registered the inclement conditions. A chill in the air, together with a blustery wind, carried cold penetrating rain in a near horizontal direction. Alex shuddered, pulled his jacket close, before starting to jog, his long legs covering the distance to the crime scene in little time, without breaking sweat.

Taking the steps two at a time, Alex entered the close. The door was already propped ajar. T he uniformed officer who'd been left as sentry was standing further inside, protecting himself from the elements. Recognising Alex, he snapped to attention, "Sorry, I didn't see you approach, Sir. I'd been checking out back."

"And you are?"

""I'm PC Black, Sir, Stuart Black."

Alex removed his jacket and shook off the excess moisture. "Well PC Stuart Black, precisely what did you find in the back court?"

"Nothing, Sir."

"Nothing? Can you not tell me when the bins were last emptied? Were there any footprints? Could the back door have been used as an escape route?" Alex quizzed.

"No, Sir," I didn't see anything.

"Right, Constable. I don't believe you were out back, not unless it was for a sly smoke. I think it far more likely you've been skulking about in here, saving yourself from the cold and the wet."

Tall, skinny and gawky, he gave the appearance of an overgrown schoolboy, and didn't seem too much older. Stuart Black was unable to meet Alex's gaze. He stood, dejected, his head slouched forward, staring at his own shoes,"

"Well?" Alex pursued.

"I'm sorry, Sir."

"Too bloody right you're sorry. Sorry you got caught out, more like. Now listen to me and listen good. I don't have a problem with officers taking care of themselves, not as long as they're still doing their duty. But one thing I won't stand for is being lied to. If I catch you at that game again I'll have your balls on a plate. Is that understood?"

"Yes, Sir. Sorry, Sir. It won't happen again," the boy stammered.

"Okay, now tell me what's happening?" Alex demanded.

"Yes, Sir. The body was found in flat 2/2, that's at the right-hand side on the second floor. Sergeant Guptar is up there talking to the husband. The techies got here some time ago, and Doctor Duffie's arrived not long before you. DC Morrison is there too."

"Fine, I'll go and check for myself." Alex made his way up the stairs, confident that the constable had learned an important lesson.

* * *

Alex bounded up the two flights and recognised the shape of Phil, swathed in crime scene coveralls, waiting at the front entrance. Seeing his attire, Alex chuckled inwardly. Although, at thirty-five, Phil was only a few years younger than himself, Alex considered he gave the impression of being an overgrown schoolboy. It wasn't only his adolescent sense of humour, his chubby face looked younger than its years and he appeared to handle everything with an exaggerated enthusiasm.

"Any more to report?" Alex enquired.

"Not much, Sir. We've not been given clearance to poke about yet. Do you want to come in? I've a suit here for you."

While Alex covered up, Phil informed him of what they'd learned so far. "No sign of forced entry. The flat's owned by George Radford, a private landlord, he's registered and seems to be reputable. The tenancy started more than three months ago and Kevin McGowan, the boyfriend, is the only tenant on the lease. Since moving in, he's shared it with the victim, Keiran Sharma. It's a big flat for just the two of them, particularly as they're fresh out of university; both are aged twenty-one. I'll give you the layout. Through the entrance, there's a large square shaped hall, with all rooms off. Running clockwise, first there's a bathroom and then a sitting room, open-plan to a fitted kitchen with a scullery off to the side. There's a couple of cupboards and then there's two bedrooms off to the right. The first is enormous and was where they slept; it has a large double bed and various other items of furniture. Then last, a small double used as a study with a convertible sofa."

Alex nodded, "Yes, a lot of these flats are this shape."

"The body was found lying on the bed. There's bruising to arms and face and particularly to the neck; I reckon the windpipe's crushed.

"Has she been moved?" Alex asked.

"Not as far as we know. McGowan says he came home and found her like that. He claims he didn't touch her. He saw her, realised she was dead and came straight back out to call for help. Uniforms arrived within ten minutes and called us in, maybe an hour ago now."

"Anything else?"

"Yes, before we arrived. he'd knocked on the neighbour's door, through there," Phil pointed to the first door on the landing. "A single lady lives there, elderly. When she saw the state he was in, she asked him in. Sanjay's talking to him now, in there. He has Mary with him taking notes. Donny's got uniforms checking all the other doors in the close and next door as well, to see if anyone saw or heard anything or had anything else to tell us."

"Did the boy speak to anyone else before you got here?"

"Not that we know of; he said he hadn't when we asked."

"Right, I'll see how Sanjay's doing first. By then Duffie might be finished with the body and the techies may be a bit happier for us to wander around. You come with me."

Chapter 2

A blast of heat hit him, and Alex stepped back in surprise when the door was yanked open by Edna Gallacher. It was clear she'd been standing waiting at the door because he'd barely had the chance to lower his hand from pressing the doorbell.

Small and rake thin, a shock of pure white curls crested the lady's wizened old face. She peered at Alex's warrant card before pointing to a closed door. "They're in there, sitting at the kitchen table. They said they wanted me to give them some privacy. You'd better go on in."

"Not just yet," Alex replied. "I'd like to ask you some questions first, if I may. Is there somewhere we can sit? Tall and muscular, Alex was a big man in any circumstances, but by contrast, standing next to the old lady, he appeared to be a giant.

Mrs Gallacher shuffled forward and led them through to her formal lounge. The room could have been taken straight out of the nineteen-fifties. It was adorned with a fuss of heavy, dark brown furniture and covered in a profusion of ornaments. Everything looked old and worn but there was a pronounced and pleasant odour of beeswax polish and not a speck of dust to be seen anywhere.

Accepting her invitation, Alex and Phil sat down on a heavily-stuffed, deep buttoned sofa and were surprised by the comfort.

"Would you like me to make you a cup of tea?" she asked. Although appalled by the circumstances of their meeting, Mrs Gallacher was hospitable and appeared pleased to have company.

"Thank you, but no," Alex replied. "We won't keep you long and we have a lot of other things to take care of.

She nodded slowly then lowered herself into a matching armchair, before looking up expectantly.

Trying his best to put her at ease, Alex noted her personal details and asked about her circumstances, confirming his suspicions that Edna had lived in this flat for most of her life. A widow and now aged eighty-eight, this had been her first and only home after she'd married, some sixty-five years ago. She'd raised her children here, although both boys had grown and married, before emigrating to New Zealand. Besides Christmas and birthday cards and an ever-rarer phone call, she'd had no contact with them for decades.

"Now how well did you know your neighbours, Kevin and Keiran?"

"Och, they were a lovely couple, much nicer than the last tenants who stayed there. They were so much in love. They put me in mind of me and my Charlie when we started out. Full of the joys. They were very good to me, too. They had me in for tea every week and they were always checking if I needed shopping or anything" A darkness fell over Edna's expression and tears started to flow. "Kevin was so upset when he came in. He said she was dead. Is that true? What could have happened? Was there an accident?"

"We don't have any answers yet. We're trying to put the pieces together. Now, can you tell me if you saw or heard anything unusual this evening?" Alex probed.

"No, nothing, not until Kevin came to my door. Of course, my hearing's not what it used to be. Unless the telly's up really loud, I can't make out a thing. I always worry that it might be disturbing my neighbours, but nobody's said anything. Anyway, I rarely hear anything from outside. That nice 'Care and Repair' man from the Council even attached a light thing to my entry-phone so I'll know if anyone comes to door."

"I see," Alex replied. "Can you tell me if you ever saw or heard any arguments between Kevin and Keiran, or by them with anyone else for that matter."

"No, never a cross word, not that I ever saw. Mind you, there was the one time, Ian Fulton caused a bit of a fall out. He's the idiot who stays on the ground floor. He had a moan at Keiran for leaving the back door open when she was taking out the rubbish. Then he started shouting at her saying she wasn't wanted here. He didn't want the smell of curry coming near his flat, and he went on at her about what she was doing with a nice Christian boy,. and saying she should go back to her own people."

"When was this?"

"Och, that was months back, not long after they moved in. It only lasted a minute before Janet, his wife, came out and gave him such a mouthful. Keiran was upset though and went running up the stairs, streaming with tears."

"And you saw all this happening?"

"No, no. It was Janet who told me all about it. I never breathed a word to Keiran as I didn't want to upset her more."

Alex got to his feet; Phil was quick to follow. "I think that will be all for now, although we may need to speak to you again. Thank you for your help. I'd like to go in and speak to Kevin now. If you'd please wait in here, we'll let you know before we leave. Is there anything you need from the kitchen in the meantime?" The response was negative, and Alex and Phil made their way out to the hall.

* * *

"Hi Boss, I'm glad you're here." Sanjay stepped into the hall and closed the kitchen door behind him to have a private word with Alex. "I'd like your take on this. There are a number of things that just don't add up. Shall I fill you in before you talk to him?" As he spoke, Sanjay removed his thick black glasses and took out a tissue to clean them. Unadorned, his face lost its normal impression of severity as the little man craned his neck to look up at Alex.

"No, thanks. I'd prefer to hear it first hand to form my own impression. If you can take me in and introduce me then I'd like you to interview Ian Fulton, the guy on the ground floor. Apparently, he had a spat with Kieran some time back, not long after they moved in. Possibly a bit of racial tension there, so I'd like to see how he takes to you."

Kevin raised his head when Alex opened the door. Supervising him, Mary sat impassively. Kevin seemed unaware of her, her stocky frame and rosy cheeks, a benign presence sharing the same room. He'd been sitting facing her, with his elbows on the kitchen table, holding his head in his hands, a blank stare facing downwards. As he looked at Alex, a glimmer of hope flashed in his eyes, as if he expected to be told it was all a mistake and he'd only had a bad dream. He had the look of the cartoon character, *Oor Wullie,* with a pale face and ginger hair sprouting in all directions, dishevelled from his hands trying to contain his grief. He had an untidy look, his suit was creased and the top buttons of his shirt were open with his tie draped askew.

"I'm DCI Alex Warren and I'm leading this enquiry," Alex introduced. "I know you've been through this already, but I need to hear it from you myself."

Kevin exhaled deeply. "What do you want to know?"

"Let's start with this morning. Take me through everything that's happened today."

Kevin looked puzzled. "What does this morning have to do with anything?"

"Please just bear with me. It helps put everything into context."

"Okay," Kevin briefly shook his head, appearing unconvinced."My alarm went off at 7.30 a.m. I got up, showered, cleaned my teeth, dressed, had breakfast and went for the bus."

"Let's go back, please. I need more detail. Your alarm may have gone off at 7.30 am but when did you wake? Were you already awake, and what about Kieran?"

Kevin's face flushed. "What the fuck's this all about?"

Alex said nothing, instead looking fixedly at Kevin's face and let the silence build.

"Kieran had the day off work. It's the second anniversary of when we started to go out and she wanted the time off. She planned to make us a special romantic dinner. I was to bring the wine. I bought a bottle of Prosecco on my way home. I left it on the table."

"Kieran drank alcohol?"

"Yes, although she was raised a Moslem she hasn't practiced any religion since she started university."

"Sorry, go on"

"We both woke before the alarm. Kieran went to shower first, and I followed afterwards, then got dressed."

"Had you been intimate?"

"Why do you want to know?"

"We don't know yet if there was any sexual motive to the attack." In a very matter of fact tone, he continued, "We need to know the last time you had sex together to help us interpret any forensic evidence.

Kevin winced then sat back, the words striking him worse that a punch. "Yes, we'd been intimate," he whispered. "Afterwards, we had breakfast."

"What did you eat?" Anticipating another question, Alex pre-empted, "We'd like to know everything Kieran ate today as it could help us establish the time of death."

Kevin looked as if he might faint. "Coffee and toast, that's all. We treated ourselves to a Tassimo machine last month and we've been trying out all the different flavours together. If I remember correctly, we had a Mochiata with Caramel this morning - it was awfully sweet. I had toast and butter, I think Kieran had a scrape of marmalade." Overpowered by the memory, together with the current predicament, Kevin's eyes filled with tears and they started running freely. He swabbed at them with closed fists.

Seeing paper kitchen towel on a work surface, Mary ripped off and handed him some sheets. "Would you like a glass of water, or a cup of tea, maybe?"

Kevin shook his head and dabbed at his face with the towel.

"After breakfast?" Alex prompted.

"I went for the bus. We kissed 'bye' in the hall and I said I'd be back around six; then I left. I walked round to Pollockshaws Road and caught a 38 bus into Hope Street, then walked to my office in Waterloo Street. I arrived just before nine."

"What time did you leave the house?"

"I'm not certain but it must have been around eight-twenty."

"What's your job?" Alex asked.

"I'm a Trainee Solicitor."

Alex raised an eyebrow.

"I work for McPhail and Morgan, have done since I graduated last year. It's mainly conveyancing I do, although they're giving me a general training with some family law and commercial and legal aid work."

"What about criminal law?"

"I studied it for my degree, but M&M just do bits and pieces. It's not our speciality, but sometimes existing clients have an issue which they bring to us."

"And how was your day."

"Nothing really out of the ordinary."

"You had your special dinner to look forward to?"

"Well yes. I was planning to go straight home but then I had a message from Billy Marshall. One of my mates from Uni but he lives in Aberdeen now, so I've not seen him for ages. He asked if we could meet for a jar after work. I explained I had plans for this evening, but I could maybe manage a quick one."

Alex nodded.

"I texted Kieran to say I might be a little bit later and I worked through lunch to make sure I got away sharp. I went to meet him in Wetherspoons as arranged and got us in a couple of pints, but he didn't show. I was really pissed, because I'd explained I didn't have much time. I finished my drink and tried calling him, but it just rang out. So, I downed the other pint, no point wasting it, and headed for home. I picked up the wine and flowers from Sainsburys in town, on my way and caught the next bus."

"Which Wetherspoons was it?"

"Corner of George Square."

"Did you see or speak to anyone who can confirm any of this?"

Kevin thought for a moment. "The pub was quite busy for that time of day, but no, there was nobody there that I knew, not that I can remember."

"And how were you feeling just then?"

"I dunno. I wanted to be home. I was a bit rattled at wasting my time, but also a bit merry having sunk two pints on an empty stomach."

"Did you see anyone you knew on the bus?"

Kevin shook his head. "The bus was busy but to be honest, I dozed off and only came too just in time, when we were approaching the park. I had to shake myself awake so I didn't miss my stop."

"And what time was this?"

"I guess it must have been after half six, maybe going on seven."

"Okay, let's go back in time a little bit; you said that Billy called to arrange the meeting but didn't show up. How did he call you, was it to your work or mobile?"

"No, I'm not allowed to take private calls and I'm not meant to use the mobile in the office either, but I usually leave it on, switched to silent. I got a text from Billy and that's how I replied to confirm the arrangement. Here, see for yourself."

Alex checked the phone records and noted Kevin's message to Keiran and his dialogue with Billy. "This shows a mobile number which sent and received the texts from Billy, but it's different from your phone book listing for Billy Marshall."

"Yes, now you come to mention it, I didn't see his name when it came in. I assumed he must have changed his phone and thought no more about it. I haven't had a chance to update his number yet."

"You didn't try both numbers when he didn't show up?"

"No, it didn't occur to me."

"Do you mind if we hang onto this for a while to check a few things out?"

"No, take it, not a problem."

"Thanks. Now, picking up where we left off, you said you got off the bus at Queens Park."

"Yes, that's right. It's only a few minutes walk."

"Keep going."

"I came up to the flat and let myself in."

"Was everything the same as normal? Was the door locked?"

Kevin paused to think before answering. "It was closed on the Yale, as I'd expect when someone's home. Sometimes when Keiran was working, I'd be the first one home and I'd have to unlock the mortise as well."

"You didn't use the security intercom before going up."

"No, we both have keys so there wouldn't be any point."

"Okay, you let yourself in. What next?"

"I called out to Keiran as I went to the kitchen to put the wine in and get water for the flowers. I thought it odd when she didn't answer. I hung up my jacket and then realised there was no sign of any cooking going on. I checked the fridge and saw all the ingredients were prepared but she hadn't started making the meal."

Alex nodded.

"I thought maybe she'd gone out, but the door hadn't been locked. Then I thought perhaps she was unwell. I went to check the bedroom and found her lying on the bed." Kevin shook his head, trying to dislodge the image. "She looked bruised, her eyes were wide, staring blankly at the ceiling and her mouth was open. I could tell she was dead. I didn't know what to do. I just sank to the floor. I couldn't stop looking at her."

"Did you touch her, take her pulse or move anything?"

"No, I don't think so. I was in a bit of a daze. I don't know how long I sat there before I came to my senses. I phoned emergency services and then I came here to Mrs. Gallacher."

"Can you tell me if there was anyone who you or Keiran had fallen out with? Was there anyone you know who may have had a grievance with either of you?"

"There was no-one; she was a lovely person. Everyone she met liked her. She made friends really easily."

"Okay, if she was that popular then how about people who might have been jealous? Do you know of anyone who may have resented her popularity?"

"Really, there's no-one that I can think of."

"What about family? How did they take to her shacking up with you? Did you get on?"

Kevin paused for a moment, before looking back at Alex. "Other than her sister, I haven't met any of her family. They didn't approve of her living with me out of wedlock and I doubt they'd have been any happier with her marrying someone who wasn't a Moslem. Although Keiran had no religion, to my knowledge her family were still devoted to Islam."

"And what about your own family how did they react to you and Keiran being a couple?"

"Once they got to know her, they accepted her. As I said before, everyone loved her."

"Thank you for being so helpful. I don't think we need to ask you anything else just now. You won't be allowed back in the flat tonight, not that you're likely to want to be there. Is there anyone else you can stay with for the time being?"

"I guess I can go back to stay with Mum and Dad. They're not far away. They live in Giffnock."

"Okay, we can take you there. Once we get clearance from our forensic people, you'll be able to gather a few belongings, then one of our officers can drive you there. Would you like us to call them for you or would you prefer to let them know yourself? We'll need to interview them too at some stage."

"Thanks, but I think it would be better if I spoke to Mum myself."

Chapter 3

Sanjay was waiting for Alex outside Mrs Gallacher's flat.

"What did you think, Boss?"

"It's going to take a lot more probing, establishing the exact time of death may prove crucial. It doesn't ring true that McGowan was eager to come home for a cosy anniversary meal yet went off on a failed mission to have a drink with one of his buddies. He's hardly helped himself. He's given us nothing to confirm his claimed timeline. What's more, we have the extra hour where his movements can't be unaccounted for. Even if we accept his story, he's come home later than planned and been bevied up."

"That was my concern, too," Sanjay replied. "I'd better update you on other developments. Duffie's finished up for now and away. He's arranging for the body to be transferred and will do the P.M. in the morning. Before he left, he told me there were definite signs of recent sexual activity. In his words, 'she's taken quite a pounding'. One possibility is very rough sex, but it's far more likely to be rape. Some kinky sex involving strangulation, going wrong, can't be ruled out either."

"Damn it! We could have done without that complication."

"There's more, and you're not going to like it. Scene of crime technicians have still to run tests and give their full report, but Connor has given me some provisional findings. The door hadn't been forced so whoever did this either had a key or was let in. The place is untidy but there are no signs of any scuffle or resistance, other than on the body itself. It's pretty battered, with what appears to be some defensive bruising on the arms. She is clothed, sort of. No underwear and whoever attacked her must have rearranged her dress before they left. Either that or McGowan did it after he found the body. What may be of greater interest is what they found in the trash. The cleansing uplift only took place this morning but nevertheless there was a bag at the bottom of this flat's bin. Possibly, it had been missed but more likely it went out at some point today. In any event, amongst the garbage, it contained two used condoms. Perhaps of even greater significance, inside the kitchen bin, they found a pregnancy test kit and the blue line indicated a positive result. No doubt, Duffie will be able to tell us more when he does the P.M."

"This just keeps getting better and better," Alex said with undisguised sarcasm. "I think I'd better have another word with young Mr McGowan before we send him on his way."

"The door-to-door hasn't yielded much of value. An upstairs neighbour thought he may have heard shouting about six o'clock. They didn't regard it as unusual because it's happened often before and when they'd checked, the source had been old Mrs Gallacher's choice of TV viewing."

"Not a lot of help."

"I did go down and speak to Fulton," Sanjay continued.

"And?"

"The guys a bit of an arse, but I don't believe he had anything to do with it. I asked him about the argument and he tried to explain. His story: He'd had a crappy day. He'd been overlooked for a promotion at work that he'd earned. He had all the training and experience but instead it had been given to an Asian woman who didn't have a clue. She only got it, so the company could meet its quota of recruiting and promoting women and racial minorities, so he says."

Alex chuckled.

"Yeah, that's what I thought too. The bastard stared at my stripes and it wasn't too difficult to see what he was thinking."

"Don't take it to heart," Alex said, and gave Sanjay a friendly pat on the shoulder.

"To add insult to injury, his next comment was, 'I'm not a racist; really I'm not'. He went on to explain that after getting the bad news, he'd gone out and got drunk, Then, on his way home, he'd seen Keiran coming in from the back court and she got the sharp end of his tongue as a result. He hadn't meant what he'd said. Anyhow, he and his wife have been home all afternoon and evening and she's given him a solid alibi."

* * *

"Kevin, something else has come to light that we need to talk about."

"I thought I'd told you everything."

"It appears that Kieran may have been pregnant. Did you know about it?"

"What? Is this some sort of sick joke?" Kevin turned away.

"I want you to look at me. This is serious Kevin. What can you tell me?"

"It's not possible; you're trying to trick me. I've read about weird mind games the police use to try to confuse suspects or witnesses. Surely you don't consider me to be a suspect?"

"Let me assure you Kevin that this is no game. Our people found a pregnancy tester in your flat showing a positive result. If it wasn't Keiran's, then whose could it be?"

"But it's not possible."

"I'm afraid it's very possible. You've already confirmed you had a sexual relationship and I'm sure you know that condoms are not a foolproof method of birth control."

"No, you don't understand. She couldn't be pregnant. I couldn't make her pregnant." There was a long pause before Kevin continued. "I had a tumour some years back. It was successfully treated but the radiation resulted in me having a zero sperm count."

"If that's the case then why did you use condoms? You've been in an established relationship for two years. If it wasn't for protection against pregnancy, what were you protecting against?"

Kevin's head slumped. "I didn't tell her. When we first got together and had sex, it was common sense to wear protection. At the start, we were both students with no thoughts of having kids. Once we became a couple, I didn't want to say that I was infertile. As the relationship developed I realised she loved children. I knew she'd want her own at some stage, but we didn't ever discuss having kids and I was afraid if she knew then she may not want me. I wanted to tell her, but the longer it went on, the more difficult it was to say anything."

"Well Kevin, this creates a new problem. If Keiran was pregnant and you're not the father; that means that somebody else must be."

Kevin looked as if he might be sick. Mary passed him a glass of water.

"This can't be happening. It has to be some big mistake, or a hoax. Please tell me it's not real."

A full two minutes passed in silence, with Alex giving Kevin time to digest the information.

"Can you give me any clues? Have you had any suspicions that Keiran may have been playing around?"

"No, absolutely not!" Kevin spat back. "We loved each other. There was no-one else for either of us. We spent all our time together when we weren't working."

"Maybe there was someone at her work she was close to. Besides, you didn't always take time off together; today, for instance."

Kevin shook his head. "Never, I don't believe it,"

"We'll have to talk to her colleagues. Where was it she worked? Oh, and just so you know, we also need to speak to your employers. It's standard procedure."

"She worked at the new Queen Elizabeth hospital. She's a pharmacist and was offered the job straight from university."

"Right, we'll get onto it, but for now, we'll take you over to your parent's house. I know this has all come as a shock to you, but you need to get some rest and we can talk again in a day or two."

"You don't seriously expect me to get any rest after what's happened and what you've told me."

Chapter 4

"I need to have a chat with Connor. Mary, I'd like you to go with Sanjay to break the news to Keiran's family; Phil can you find Donny and take Kevin to his parent's house. Let's meet up first thing tomorrow to compare notes."

"Will do, Sir," Phil replied. "The old bugger's been a bit illusive today, not quite himself."

Alex looked up and grinned. "Do you mean more, or less, grouchy than usual?"

"Definitely more, Sir. He's been a bit touchy, but that's not all. It's normal for him to be a bit untidy, but today he seems … I don't know, looking a bit uncared for. He's showing a bit more grey, his face as well as his hair, but maybe he's just run out of tint." Phil grinned.

"Perhaps, he's just having an off day; but laughing aside, let's keep an eye on him."

Alex left them to it and went through to find the scene of crime specialist. Even dressed in his coveralls, the little man exuded the impression of precision and efficiency. Although the hood of his protective suit had been lowered, not one of his lacquered sandy-coloured hairs was out of place. Alex found him crouched over a table, feeding data into his laptop.

Connor looked up. "Evening, Sir. I knew you were here and I was wondering when I'd see you. Would you like the guided tour?"

"Yes, please. Phil's already described the layout and my own flat's not dissimilar, so just tell me your findings so far."

"Right-o, the body's now on it's way to the mortuary. The place is untidy and hasn't had a thorough clean for some time, so there ought to be no shortage of prints. The difficulty will be sifting out what's relevant. As the killer must have let himself out, we're hoping to pick up something from the door handle either inside or out."

"He didn't wear gloves or wipe the handles?"

"It doesn't look like it, as there's no smear marks. She and the boyfriend were the last ones we know who went in and left so theirs ought to be there. It's down to luck what else we get."

"I know it's not very scientific, but we'll keep our fingers crossed."

"In the kitchen, we found the wine on the table, flowers propped up in a vase and his jacket on the rack all of which supports the boyfriend's story."

Alex frowned.

"Sanjay talked it through with me. There's nothing else of note here other than what we found in the bin. I guess he told you about that."

"The pregnancy kit, yes he told me."

"For completeness, we found a till receipt from ASDA. It's timed at half past twelve this afternoon which shows when it was purchased. I reckon that suggests it can't have been anything pre-planned. Also, on the receipt are most of the contents of the fridge; a veritable feast by all accounts, for the celebratory dinner.

"There's nothing to report on the small bedroom or the bathroom either. We're running the usual tests and checking wastes but no results yet."

"Tomorrow, do you think?"

"I expect so; the lab's not too busy at the moment and I know you'll want this prioritised."

"Thanks."

"Now to the bedroom," Connor pushed the door open. A couple of his assistants were scurrying around collecting and logging the last of their samples and sealing them in evidence bags.

Alex's gaze quickly scanned the layout and contents. Large for a bedroom, the floor area looked to be about five metres by four. The ceiling was high and decorated by ornate cornicing. Decor was fresh with surfaces coloured the standard magnolia and white favoured by landlords, complemented by beech effect laminate flooring. The large bay overlooking the front of the building had white uPVC double glazing with heavy dralon-velvet drapes. A scattering of wardrobes and drawer units sat against the walls, but the most prominent features were a solid, wood-framed, king-sized bed, facing a wall-mounted, fifty-inch, SMART television. Surfaces were dusty and there was discarded laundry lying in a heap. Alex's gaze was drawn to a framed photograph depicting a scantily clad couple posing on a sun-drenched beach. Alex recognised the pale skinned Kevin McGowan. The attractive young Asian beauty he had his arm around must have been Keiran; this was the first time Alex had seen her. It could have been the photo of a model, tall, long dark hair, shapely and with a flawless complexion. Involuntarily, he gasped in air and exhaled slowly.

"That wasn't how she looked when we got here," Connor advised.

"No, I don't suppose so. What a waste of a young life."

With a shudder, Alex turned toward the bed.

"We haven't lifted and bagged the bedclothes yet; thought you might want to see what it looked like first. Obviously, we have photos as well, before and after the body was moved."

"Thanks, I'll need to see them."

Alex shook his head as he looked at the assemblage of crumpled and soiled bedding.

In his usual matter of fact manner, Conner started to list findings. "Female, aged twenty-three, height, one metre seventy; Asian; likely death by suffocation - presumed strangulation. Bruising to throat, arms, upper legs and internally - indications of violent sexual activity. No sperm evident. We're running tests for condom use. We've found pubic hairs on the bed too, not the victim's. The body was clothed in a long dress, an expensive looking silky chiffon number, not one for doing the housework in. However, she wasn't wearing any underwear, and none were discarded nearby."

"Interesting there was no underwear on the body. How do you read that?"

"There are various possibilities, but it's more your area to find out why," Connor replied. "What I can tell you is that she wasn't wearing any and we didn't find anything recently discarded in the trash or the clothes heap and the washing machine was empty."

"Could her attacker have undressed her and taken them as souvenirs or perhaps to dump elsewhere?"

"It can't be ruled out, but I think it unlikely as there were no marks on the body to suggest she was forcibly stripped. While on that subject, there were scratches and abrasions on her legs likely to have been caused by a zip rubbing and some shoe marks on the bedclothes." Connor pointed in turn to various scuff marks. "My reading is whoever had sex with her was dressed, with his trousers pulled down below his knees."

"Any indication of type or size of shoes?"

"Aw come on Alex, have you been watching C.S.I. again? At best I can give you a colour - black."

"Okay, so if she had no undies, why would that be? She already had the classy dress on and she hadn't prepared the dinner yet. Maybe she was getting ready when she was disturbed. Did she have her war pain on?"

"No, hardly wearing any make-up, but don't read too much into that, she didn't need it."

"Well, the evening was planned as a special celebration. Maybe she was intending to play the seductress and of course the act might not even have been intended for McGowan."

"Another possibility is the attacker threatened or frightened her into undressing herself."

"Good point, I hadn't considered that," Alex said.

"I'm glad I've been of some help. Now, if you're done with me, I'll finish getting cleared up in here and away."

"Good idea, and I'll get back to Sandra. She'll be wondering whether I've got lost."

Chapter 5

Sanjay was driving with Mary. He pulled up outside the Sharma residence, a spacious detached villa in Burnside. The clock on their car's dashboard showed ten-twenty. Feet crunching on the gravel path, they approached the front door.

"Who's there?" a cautious voice enquired in response to the doorbell, a man's outline was barely discernible through the opaque glass door.

"Mr Sharma, it's the police, Detective Sergeant Guptar and Detective Constable McKenzie. Can we please come in and talk to you?" The door opened a fraction, while still secured on a chain.

Sanjay presented his warrant card for inspection.

"What's this all about? What are you doing calling at this time? Is it the shop?" the man asked, his voice hesitant.

"Please can we come in so we can talk to you?" Sanjay asked.

"What is it, Papa? Who's there?" A young female voice called out. A television was blaring in the background.

The metallic clinks of the chain being pulled aside were audible and the door was opened by a small dapper-looking man, dressed in trousers and a shirt. "Come in, come in, what's wrong, has there been a break-in?"

"We need to speak to you and your family," Sanjay requested.

Mr Sharma looked perplexed. Pointing towards the first doorway off the hall, he walked forward leading Sanjay and Mary to the room. He stood at the entrance and beckoned them to pass.

An attractive lady jumped to her feet. She looked to be aged in her forties and was dressed in a plain-coloured suit of loose fitting trousers and top. "Please sit down; can I offer you some tea?" Her hand reached for the remote control enabling her to mute the ITV news showing on a large screen.

The source of the voice they'd heard earlier became evident. An alert looking younger version of the girl in the photo sat on the opposite sofa. Although, on first impression, she appeared too old to be a pupil, a Holyrood school tie was draped loosely around her neck, complemented by a tight-fitting, open- necked white blouse and a skimpy plain skirt.

"No thank you. I'm sorry to say that we're here to give you some bad news," Sanjay said. "Will you please sit down."

With apprehension, Mrs Sharma sank back into her seat, her husband remained standing near the door.

"It's about your daughter, Keiran."

"I have no daughter, Keiran," Mr Sharma replied. "She…"

"No, tell me what's happened. Has she been arrested? Has she had an accident? What is it?" Mrs Sharma interrupted.

"Quiet woman!" he yelled. "She is not our daughter. We gave her every chance. We gave her everything and she threw it back in our face. She shamed us. Ibrahim was right. We should have kept her under our control and found her a husband. Instead, …instead…" In frustration he slapped his hand down on the sideboard. "And as for this one, Jamilla," he pointed at his younger daughter, "just look at her. You allow her to dress like this and she'll turn out the same." He turned to Sanjay, "I want you to leave."

"Tarik, stop it!" Mrs Sharma shrieked. "You don't know what you're saying. Keiran's a good girl, we've never had a moment's bother with her. We've never been religious, so why follow customs. Why should it matter, what those fools at the mosque, think? It's only your foolish pride that's driven her away."

The pantomime was playing out in front of their eyes. From past experience, Sanjay and Mary were all too familiar; the argument was a sham, the Sharma's way of avoiding an inevitable truth. They instinctively knew something awful was going to be said and for as long as they didn't hear the news, then it hadn't happened."

"Enough; both of you, be quiet." The girl cried, showing more maturity than her parents. She faced the police officers. "Tell us what's happened." All eyes turned to Sanjay.

He inhaled deeply, "I'm sorry to have to tell you that Keiran is dead."

"No, it can't be," the mother shrieked, her hand flying up to cover her face. "I only spoke to her this morning. She was well then." Tears ran down her cheeks as she slid to kneel on the floor. "Tell me it's not true."

"I'm afraid it is true," Sanjay said.

"No, no, it can't be," Tarik added, his complexion visibly paling.

"What happened?" the girl asked.

"She was found this evening, in her flat." Sanjay said.

"How could that be? Did her heart fail? Was it an accident? How did she die?" Tarik asked.

"We don't yet know all the details but suffice to say, she'd been attacked." Sanjay replied.

"Was it a robbery? Did somebody break in and she got in the way?" Mrs Sharma asked.

"We don't believe so," Sanjay answered.

"What are you telling us? She was murdered? Was it that bastard boyfriend? I always knew he was no good. I'll kill him," Tarik said.

"Please don't go jumping to conclusions," Sanjay replied. "From what we know, Kevin McGowan came home from work and found her dead and then reported it. It's too soon for us to know anything for sure. But let me assure you that no effort will be spared to find out what really happened."

"Pah," Tarik spat.

Mrs Sharma remained on the floor with her head in her hands, wailing uncontrollably. Her husband, in shock, was pacing the floor. The girl, with tears streaming down her face, moved to comfort her mother. In desperation, they clung to each other.

"Can we bring in some help for you? Would you like us to call a relative, or friend, or perhaps your doctor?"

"I am a doctor," Mrs Sharma replied. "No, just go."

"We'll need to get a formal statement from each of you, but we realise that perhaps this is not the best time. How about we come back to talk to you tomorrow?"

Chapter 6

"Take a left here," McGowan instructed, "we're almost there. You can drop me here if you like."

"That's alright, Kevin. We'll come in with you and speak to your parents if you don't mind," Donny replied.

McGowan's brow furrowed. "Pull up there; it's number seventeen. I've got a key but I'd better ring first, before going in, so I don't give them too much of a shock."

Donny and Phil followed him along the driveway, Phil carrying the boy's holdall.

A petite, middle-aged, woman was already approaching the door as McGowan walked through, followed by the detectives.

"Kevin? What are you doing here? Is everything okay?"

"Oh Mum, It's awful. Keiran's dead. These men are policemen." He reached his arms around his mother, stooping to bury his head in her shoulder. |Hearing the news, a plump, bald-headed man came though to the hall. His eyes were wide and his jaw slack.

"What happened? Was there an accident? Why are the police here?" he asked.

"She's been murdered," Kevin blurted, between sobs. "I came home from work tonight and found her dead. I can't stay in the flat, so I came here. Is it okay?"

Mr McGowan threw his arms out engulfing his wife and son. "Of course, it's okay. This is your home, you can stay for as long as you like. You know that we revamped your room as a guest room after you moved out, but it's still your room,"

"Oh my God, my poor boy," Mrs McGowan cried, "and poor Keiran. Why would anyone want to kill her? Who could have done it? What am I thinking? Come in and sit down." She led them all into the lounge.

The room was compact and very clinical with all decor, furnishings and accessories perfectly matching and looking as though they'd been exactly positioned using a micrometer. Everything was clean and tidy with nothing out of place. Phil was reluctant to sit, fearful he might create an international incident if he accidentally displaced a cushion. Donny, while aware of the precision, showed no such concern.

"I'd better call your brother and ask him to come home. Robbie should be here. The family need to stick together at a time like this," Mr McGowan said. "I'll be back in a moment."

"I'll go and put my bag up in my bedroom," Kevin said.

Donny waited until he had left before starting. "We'd like to take a statement from you while we're here."

"Yes, of course," Kevin's mother replied. "I don't see how we can help, but we'll do anything we can. What would you like to know?"

"To start with; how well did you know Keiran?" Donny asked.

"Very well indeed; ever since Kevin first brought her home, she's been part of our family. She was like the daughter I never had. Sometimes, we would chat for ages or go shopping together."

"I see," said Donny, taking notes.

"Of course, with the way her parents treated her, she didn't have her own family to talk to. We were happy to make her part of ours. It was the Christian thing to do."

"It didn't bother you that she wasn't a Christian?" Donny asked.

"Och no. Well if I'm honest, I'd have preferred Kevin to have had a girlfriend who'd join our church, but I hadn't ruled out that may eventually happen with Keiran."

"Wanted what to happen?" Kevin asked, only hearing the last part of the conversation.

"I was just saying I'd have liked it if you and Keiran had joined our church." she replied.

"What on earth are you talking about?" There was anger in Kevin's tone. "That would never have happened in a million years. Keiran didn't have any religious belief and neither do I. It was one of the first things we found we had in common. It brought us together, wanting to escape the limitations and restrictions put on us by our families' faiths."

Tears filled Mrs McGowan's eyes. "Don't talk to me like that, and certainly not in front of strangers," she eyed the two policemen. "Besides, I've had chats with Keiran before, and she seemed quite open to the idea."

"For God's sake, Mum. She was just being polite. That would have been the last thing she'd ever have wanted," then seeing the irony in his statement, he couldn't suppress a maniacal. laugh. |The spell was broken when his father entered the room.

"What's all this about?" McGowan senior asked. "Are you going crazy?"

"I'm sorry, Mum, Dad. I can't deal with this anymore. I think I need to be alone for a bit. I want to lie down and get a rest."

"That's probably a good idea," his mother answered. "Can I get you a hot drink, maybe an aspirin or something?"

"You might be better with a good stiff whisky," his father suggested.

"No, thanks, I just want some peace and quiet away from it all."

"Okay, Son. Tell me if you want anything?" his voice lost to the boy who had already exited the room.

"Did you get hold of Robbie?" Mrs McGowan asked.

"Yes, he's out with some friends in the West End. He said he'll come home but he may be a while yet. They've had some drinks and don't have a car with them."

"You should have told him to take a taxi," his wife replied.

"Yes, probably, but too late now. It's not as if there's anything he can do."

"We'll be away now," Donny said, standing to leave. "We'll be back across when we have some more information, might be tomorrow. We'll need to have a chat with Robbie at some point, too."

Chapter 7

Having cautiously slipped his key in the lock and gently pushed the door open, Alex winced when the creaky hinge reminded him that, yet again, he'd forgotten his promise to oil it. *Why do I only ever remember when I hear that noise?* he wondered.

"Alex is that you?"

"Were you expecting anyone else? Sorry luv, I didn't mean to wake you?"

"I wasn't sleeping. I'm only lying in bed because it's more comfortable. C'mon in."

Alex opened the door. The bedroom dimensions and layout weren't too dissimilar to the one he'd just left. As his eyes absorbed the scene, Alex was acutely aware of the differences. The decor and furnishings of his flat were warm, cosy and personal, they were his. They were chosen with love and most important to him, they were shared with Sandra.

"You look exhausted. Come and sit here and I'll give your shoulders a rub," Sandra offered.

Alex removed his jacket and sat as instructed. Relaxing at last, he luxuriated in their closeness as she gently kneaded his muscles before he yelped, feeling a solid thump near the base of his spine.

"Did you feel that too?" Sandra squealed.

"Too bloody right I felt it," Alex moaned, "nearly broke my back."

Her voice full of joy, Sandra replied, "That was *your* child, wanting in on the act. You'd better get used to it."

Alex turned to face Sandra and, albeit a stretch, enveloped her in his arms.

"What's the story? Tell me what you've found out." Sandra asked.

"You're on leave, Sandra. You don't want to be hearing about all that."

"Too bloody right I do. It seems I've been sitting here for weeks, not allowed to do anything interesting. I'm getting stir crazy. The telly's boring, never anything new. Tell me about your case. I may not be able to do anything tangible but it least I can feel like I'm part of it."

Alex relented. "Okay. let me get washed and changed first." A few minutes later, they were both sitting up in bed while he gave Sandra a full account.

"It's early days. You've barely started and there are so many lines of enquiry to follow," Sandra said.

"That's the problem. As usual, we've limited resources and a near infinite number of questions to be answered."

"Why don't we talk it through," Sandra suggested. "Let's list possible motives."

"Okay, first there's the racial angle. There are still a lot of people who object to interracial relationships. Although we need to consider the various random nutters, the ones most likely to take exception are the families affected."

"Yes, particularly if there's any fundamentalists amongst them," Sandra added. "There could be the possibility of an honour killing."

"God forbid," Alex said. "Sorry, pun not intended. The last thing we need is the press making a story out of an honour killing in Glasgow by Islamic fundamentalists. Christ, can you just picture the front page of the Mail or the Record? We have to be very careful with what, if any, information gets released and how it's handled."

"Yeah, you'll need to keep a tight rein on Donny for a start." Sandra smirked at the thought. "Better you than me," she added.

"I suppose he can be a bit of a bull in a china shop, but he's still a good detective. Back when he joined the force, nobody gave a stuff about political correctness. He's almost at retirement so it's understandable if he's a bit primitive."

"Primitive? His views on racial and sexual equality are positively prehistoric," Sandra said, laughing. Anyway, what are the other possibilities?"

"Next, it could be a straightforward sex attack." Alex suggested.

"Straightforward?" Sandra asked, her tone was accusing.

"You know what I meant. An attack or rape, leading to death. By saying *straightforward*, I wasn't playing it down, I meant unaffected by race issues or existing relationships."

"Okay, fair enough," Sandra conceded. You did say she was a very attractive girl, so it's not unlikely she could have drawn unwanted attention."

"Then we've got the complication of the pregnancy. If McGowan's to be believed, then we've another potential partner who may not have been happy about becoming a father."

"But how would he have known?" Sandra replied. "If McGowan hadn't told Keiran about being infertile, wouldn't she automatically assume he'd be the father, or at least be the main contender. She'd only just taken the test, so would she really expect it to have been someone else."

"True, unless that sex had been unprotected," Alex countered.

"Okay, there's a possibility, but what about McGowan himself? Hasn't he got the prime motive? Try this scenario. He comes home. She tells him she's pregnant. He realises it can't be him; ergo, she's had it off with someone else. He flies of the handle and kills her."

"Yeah, that works, always assuming it's true that he really is infertile," Alex replied.

"Or at least, *he* believes it's true."

"There's the timing issue," Alex continued. "I don't like the story about going for a drink before coming home. We need some corroboration and he hasn't offered any. If he'd come straight home from work, then there'd have been plenty of time for him to do the deed and think through his story before calling us in."

"If so he's taken quite a risk. He'd be praying no-one had seen him," Sandra said.

"We need to check for sightings of him. Anything that might corroborate or refute his version; phone records, timed purchase receipts or bus tickets, anything."

"You said he'd appeared very credible," Sandra said.

"Yes, all the signs of shock and grief appeared genuine, but it proves nothing. It can be faked. Anyhow, I'm knackered; I'll need to get some shut-eye before the morning. It's likely to be a heavy day."

* * *

Alex's slumber was brought to an abrupt end by Sandra. She was standing over him poking at his ribs.

"Wake up, Alex. The big day's arrived."

Eyelids flickering, Alex strained to lift his head, turning towards his clock-radio. "What was that? What time is it?"

"It's three-thirty in the morning and my water's broken. Rise and shine."

Instantly alert, Alex threw back the quilt. "It's too soon; you're not due yet."

"You know that, and I know that, but no-one seems to have told junior and he or she is the one calling the shots."

"I guess it's not an exact science. Helen was late with both of our boys. Sorry, I shouldn't be talking about them. This is your time. What do you want me to do?"

"For a start, maybe get some clothes on so we're ready to go."

"What about your bag, what do you need me to pack?"

"Relax, it's all done. I prepared it ages ago, just in case. I listened to what they taught me at the anti-natal classes, so I'm quite confident. I want us to be ready to go then we can sit around until the contractions start getting a bit closer."

"Shouldn't we go to the hospital now, so you can be checked over?"

"Don't panic, Alex. I know what I'm doing. We need to be patient."

For the next three hours, a gaunt and pale-faced Alex paced the floor, frustrated at everything being out of his control. In his one concession to thinking about work, he texted Sanjay to explain Sandra was in labour and he wouldn't be available for some time.

Eventually, with the rate of contractions starting to increase and unable to stand Alex's tension any longer, Sandra conceded it was time to go.

The high step to get Sandra into Alex's Hyundai Santa Fe proved a struggle, but once aboard she sat comfortably. The car roared forward and, with hazard warning lights flashing throughout the journey, Alex covered the distance to the maternity unit of the Queen Elizabeth University Hospital in record time. He stopped immediately in front of the maternity unit entrance and helped Sandra out and through to the building's reception, before dashing back to move his vehicle into the car park. Afraid he'd be too late, Alex sprinted back to find the labour ward.

"You'll have to wait here for a few minutes," a nurse advised him. "Sandra's getting settled into her room and we're setting up the monitors. You need to put on a gown before going in."

Once admitted, Alex pulled up a chair next to the bed. He held Sandra's hand, "Not long now, Luv. How are you feeling?"

"I'm a bit uncomfortable but otherwise okay, so far at least. But you look pale as a ghost. Are *you* okay? I don't want you passing out on me."

For several hours, forced conversation continued as they tried to take their minds off any fears and apprehensions. This was interspersed by the comings and goings of Siobhan, a trainee midwife who'd been assigned to keep an eye on Sandra. Siobhan was jolly and cheerful. She'd grown up in Cork and entertained Sandra and Alex with stories from her childhood.

Shortly after midday, Sandra's contractions became far more frequent and intense. Alex called Siobhan for help.

"Don't worry, it's too soon." she replied. However, after quickly examining Sandra, she needlessly announced, "The baby's coming," and then rushed away, trying to find a more qualified medic who wasn't already engaged with another patient. Some ten minutes passed with Alex fearing he may have to deliver his own child before Siobhan returned along with an experienced midwife.

Only minutes later, following the delivery of a healthy baby girl, Alex and Sandra were left in privacy to marvel over their daughter.

'Congratulations, you have a baby sister. She and Sandra are both well; three-point-five kilos (that's seven pounds, twelve ounces in my language). You'll get to see her tomorrow. I'll pick you up at six for visiting, if you like. Talk later. Love Dad.' Using longhand script, Alex laboriously texted to both of his boys, having never really got the hang of text-speak. He realised that, while both Craig and Andrew were at school, they'd be unable to take a call. Sending a message was the fastest and most efficient way of passing on the news.

Immediately afterwards, he called Sandra's parents. "She'll be too tired for visitors tonight, but you can see her tomorrow afternoon. If she's not already home, I'm planning to take the boys up in the evening."

Having passed on the good news to all immediate family, his adrenaline waned and Alex realised how tired he was. Checking his watch, he saw it was nearly three o'clock in the afternoon. He called Sanjay to let him know. "I'll be in by four. Can you get the team together, so I can catch up? I won't stay long but it'll bring us all up to date with developments."

Chapter 8

Alex wearily climbed the stairs to his office, scanned over new correspondence then made his way into the meeting area of the general office.

To his delight, he was greeted with enthusiasm. His team stood to give him a round of applause accompanied by hearty backslaps and handshakes.

"Congratulations, Boss," Phil announced, being first to welcome him in. Two, large pink, celebratory balloons, each stating *baby girl*, inflated with helium, were hovering below the ceiling. Taking pride of place, a furry Bugs Bunny soft toy sat atop several wrapped packages and envelopes on the table.

"What's Up Doc?" his team all called out together.

"Thank you all very much," he replied, breaking into a broad grin. "I didn't expect this. I know Sandra will appreciate it too. I'll take the gifts to open with her when I visit tonight."

"Have you decided on a name, yet?" Mary asked.

"We've still to make a final decision. We'd been down to a shortlist of Fiona and Catriona, but now we're also considering Siobhan, after one of the midwives."

"Can she have visitors yet?" Phil asked.

"Sort of, but not today," Alex replied. "Only me, and I'm going back tonight after I finish here. There's open visiting for partners, but only specific times in the afternoon and evening where anyone else is concerned, and then no more than two at a time. Sandra's mum and dad will be going up tomorrow afternoon and I'll take the boys up in the evening. Ricky, her brother and his wife, will be dying to see her too. Her sister's down in London. No doubt, she'll be coming up but not straight away. I expect Sandra, along with the baby, will be home in a day or two, so there's really no chance for anyone to visit other than immediate family."

"I'm dying to see her, and the bairn, of course, but I guess we'll have to wait," Mary said.

"I've a photo of her holding the wee one. Here, have a look." Alex passed around his phone and was met with a gushing of ooh's and aah's.

"Okay, much as I appreciate all your kind wishes and comments. We've got a case to solve. More to the point, I'm planning to take time off as paternity leave as soon as Sandra gets out. I'd like everything cleared up double quick. I don't want to leave any loose ends; so let's get down to business."

Everyone took a seat around the table. Sanjay and Mary, followed by Phil and Donny, provided Alex with a summary of their meetings with Keiran and Kevin's families.

"I've checked out the landlord," Donny said. "His name's Radford. He confirmed the tenancy details and said there hadn't ever been any problems with them as tenants and no issues had even been reported. Rent had been paid on time and the flat was kept in an acceptable condition."

"Model tenants then," Alex said.

"His only grouse was that McGowan had fitted a wall bracket for the TV in the bedroom without asking permission, but that was resolved when the boy confirmed the bracket would be left, if and when the tenancy came to an end. Radford had refurb'd the flat before the tenancy and didn't want to be left needing to re-plaster and decorate at the end because of a bloody great hole in the wall."

"Understandable; but more to the point, who all had keys?" Alex asked.

"He confirmed that he kept a set, in case of emergencies. He said that although he managed his own properties, he used an agent to tenant-find and for viewings and they had a set, too. He told me he had a mandate authorising him to keep them."

"What's that about?" Mary asked.

"Apparently, under private letting legislation, landlords aren't allowed to keep keys for their own properties unless they have the tenant's permission," Donny advised. "He said it's rare for permission not to be granted because the tenants like to have a back up in case they accidentally lock themselves out."

"Yeah, but that means he or anyone from the agency could have let themselves into the flat without Keiran knowing," Phil said.

"And what about previous tenants, wouldn't they have keys, too?" Alex asked.

"I already asked him about that," Donny replied proudly. "Radford had a system. The door on his flat had two mortise locks and one Yale. Whenever he has a change of tenancy, he changes the Yale and gave the new tenant the key along with the key for one of the mortises. Then at the next change, he'd use the other mortise."

"That would mean the tenant could feel secure that a previous tenant couldn't let themselves in," Alex surmised.

"Yep, and because Radford had a number of flats, he could even recycle the Yales so he had no waste," Donny added.

"Clever," Alex said. "But it still leaves the possibility of Radford or someone from the agency. What about Keiran and Kevin. Did they each have their own keys?"

"Yes, Sir. They each had a set with the Yale and mortise along with a fob for the security entry system and a key to the back court. McGowan told us he'd also had a spare set cut which he left with his parents. He couldn't copy the entry fob though. So, to get in, the outer door would have to be left open or they'd have needed someone in one of the flats to buzz them in."

"Moving on. Anything from the door-to door?" Alex asked.

"Not a lot. It's the same old story; no-one saw anything; no-one heard anything," Sanjay replied. "A few of the neighbours had met one or other of the couple, mainly Keiran, but not yesterday. We tried to check out Kevin's story, but he wasn't spotted in the pub or on the bus."

"Mmm, not unexpected," Alex said.

"We were able to check with his work though and it's not as we first thought," Phil said. "Based on what he'd said, we assumed he'd left the office at five, as that would have been the normal close of business."

"That's what I'd understood," Alex replied.

"In actual fact, he left at three-thirty. He was meant to be working until five, but he had a document which needed to be hand delivered in Motherwell. We've confirmed that it was received but can't be certain who took it. If it was him then the timing doesn't change much, but if he'd arranged for someone else to take it then we've the best part of another hour and a half when his whereabouts are unknown."

"And…"

"And he didn't mention it to us yesterday."

"Have you spoken to him about it?"

"No, Sir, not yet."

"Any other checks?"

"We're having any relevant CCTV analysed. If he went to Motherwell, we're almost certain to be able to pick him up. It's almost as likely if he didn't go. We'll find out one way or the other and it would be better to know before we start to quiz him."

"Good thinking. Did you get anywhere tracing his friend: Billy Marshall wasn't it?"

"Yes," Sanjay replied, "but it doesn't help. We called the number listed on his phone and got him. He said he was in Aberdeen and knew nothing about any exchange of texts and the other number meant nothing to him, either."

"Have you traced the number that texted him?"

"Yes, Sir. It's a pay as you go SIM card, bought from a newsagent. It's less than a month old and no easy way to trace the owner."

"I don't care about easy," Alex snapped. Surely you can find out what other calls or texts were made from the phone, or what websites he visited, and that could lead us back to whoever used it."

"We're trying, Sir. So far, the provider's refused to give us any information. They're claiming it's confidential and we'll need a court order to access it."

"I'm sorry, Sanjay. I shouldn't have spoken like that. You've done very well. I've had very little sleep and my nerves a bit frayed."

"No problem, Boss. I understand."

"If the pal didn't send the text, then who did and why?" Donny asked.

"Someone must have set him up. Maybe it was to get him out of the way, so he could meet up with Keiran." Mary suggested.

"That's possible, but perhaps it was a planned murder and he wanted to cast suspicion onto Kevin," Phil added.

"I doubt it," Sanjay replied."There'd be too much chance it wouldn't work. If anyone saw Kevin or he was picked up on video, then the set-up would be blown."

"Perhaps it was Kevin, himself. He could have set it up to fake himself an alibi," Phil said.

"If so, he must have planned what was going to happen, so he'd send the texts early enough to seem genuine. It would need to be really convoluted." Sanjay replied.

"It might all be a red herring as far as the murder's concerned. He could have set it up to give himself an excuse to come home late, for whatever reason," Alex said. "Anyhow, we're not going to be able to do much on that just now. So, let's move on. We ought to have heard from Duffie by now."

"Yes Sir. I spoke to him today," Sanjay replied. "The formal report is some way off, but I've had some useful feedback."

"Go on."

"First of all, time of death. It's not precise but reckoned to be close to six o'clock. The cause has been confirmed as strangulation. No ligature was used. She was throttled, and the hyoid bone was fractured."

Sanjay paused for a moment before continuing. "The marks on her arms are consistent with her being held firmly; maybe she was held down during sex, which accords with the internal bruising."

"For the marks to show, she must have been held down before she was strangled."

"I guess so, Sir. He didn't actually say, although I'd expect it will be in the report. Should I call him to ask him to clarify?"

"Leave it for just now," Alex replied.

"So, rape's been confirmed," Phil stated.

"That's not absolutely certain but it's the most likely explanation - Duffie's words, not mine. She'd had sexual relations within a short time of death and a condom was used. Also, there was some skin tissue under her nails. It's too early for DNA results but the blood group is 'A positive', the same as the boyfriend."

"It's also close to a third of the population" Alex said.

"Yes, Sir. Even if it is him then it doesn't prove anything as he told us they had sex that morning."

"Have the medics carried out a physical examination of McGowan?"

"No, Sir, not yet. I'll get one organised. One last thing; he told me he was able to confirm the pregnancy kit result. The foetus was about four weeks. As her blood group was O, we can determine that the father's blood group must have been 'A positive'."

Alex briefly closed his eyes and shook his head.

"I've spoken to Connor, too," Sanjay added, "only about half an hour ago."

"Do I want to hear this?" Alex asked, a wry smile playing at the edges of his mouth.

"I think you do," Sanjay replied, defying any trace of humour. "Again, it's only interim findings, but he said there was a fair bit to report."

"Don't keep us in suspense." Alex said.

"He said I should call him when you arrived and he'd come along to tell us himself."

Chapter 9

Connor gave Alex a warm, congratulatory hug and then took his seat at the table.

"What have you got for us?" Alex asked.

"Prints, as expected, loads of them everywhere. Nearly all of them are Keiran or Kevin, but there's a number of others too, mostly partials. Unfortunately, the door handles only had theirs on it and smudges."

"That's not much to go on," Alex said.

"No, but this is more interesting. The two used condoms found in the trash were both the same type and were a match to those in a bulk-buy box found in the bedside cabinet."

"Kevin's a randy little bastard," Donny interrupted.

Dismissing the comment with a frown, Connor continued. "The semen was the same in both. And here's what's really interesting, the sperm count was unusually low, less than five percent of normal, but it was present."

"You're telling me that Kevin may have been the father," Alex said.

"It's looking that way. The chances of him impregnating her must have been exceptionally small, what between the low count and him using a condom, but it's a distinct possibility."

"Right, we have a possible scenario where Kevin gets her pregnant, she tells him and because he believes he's sterile, he's convinced she's been screwing around," Alex suggested.

"Then he goes ballistic and kills her," Donny finished off.

"How does that fit in with our timeline?" Alex asked.

"It works," Phil replied, "provided he got home not much later than six. He could have carried out the deed and then reported it at seven, claiming he'd just arrived home. Then he makes up the story about going for a drink to fill in the missing time."

"Okay, we have to check every aspect of his story really thoroughly and find evidence to prove where he was and when."

"We're working on it, Sir. I've drafted in Fitzpatrick, to study the CCTV," Sanjay replied. "He's the best man for the job."

" Go on," Alex said, looking at Connor.

"The condom used immediately before death hasn't been found nor has its foil wrapper."

"How do you know it wasn't one of the ones in the trash?" Alex asked.

"From testing the body, the lubricant was different; it's not even the same brand. And just to complicate matters further, McGowan did have a packet from matching ones. We found them in the inside pocket of his leather jacket, hanging on the hallstand. The packaging was worn. I couldn't decipher the *best before* date, but it looked as if it may have been there for a while. It was a pack of three with one left in the pack."

"So, why's he been carrying around condoms with him? Is he the one who's been screwing around?" Phil asked.

"That's one for another day," Alex replied. "Have you any more information about the missing underwear?"

"There were various laundry items scattered about the flat, but no undies," Connor replied. We've discovered that the washing machine was used during the morning. The wet washing was hung on the pulley. Lot's of undies there, both his and hers. The odd thing is that she wasn't wearing any and there weren't any used ones in the flat. Either she's been walking about *commando* since she put the machine on, or someone's taken them away."

"But that wouldn't really be consistent with the McGowan scenario we discussed a moment ago," Alex said.

"It doesn't rule it out, but you're right, it doesn't make a lot of sense." Connor agreed.

"Did you find anything from the bedclothes?" Alex asked.

"DNA results are pending. The lab hasn't supplied any results yet. We did get various samples of fluids, hairs and skin fragments. It may take a while, but hopefully it will be worth it."

"Bloody marvellous, the cop shows on telly have DNA results coming back within minutes, but we normally have to wait the best part of a week," Donny moaned.

"We have technology which can get answers within hours, but not the resources to use it," Alex said. "The budgets are so tight, even a priority case can take days."

"Let me brighten up your day with something else," Connor said. "Are you ready for the kinky stuff?"

All heads turned, enthusiastically to face him.

"I've already told you about the condoms found in Kevin's top drawer. Well, the bottom drawers of Keiran's bedside cabinet had a number of, what shall I call it, *sex toys*."

Donny was almost drooling, "Tell us more."

"Okay, for starters some risqué clothing: basques, french knickers, crotch-less pants and the likes. There were also a couple of different vibrators and other stimulators and some soft porn DVDs. But now it starts to get interesting, at least from the point of view of the case."

"What do you mean?" Donny asked.

"There were restraints and chains with velvet and leather handcuffs and ankle cuffs. Some whips as well."

Alex exhaled in a low whistle.

"What's so exciting there? We've seen it all before," Donny said.

"Don't you see?" Sanjay said. "If Keiran was into experimenting and liked a bit of S&M then maybe her death was an accident, a bit of game playing that went wrong. Whether it was Kevin or anyone else, perhaps things just got a bit out of hand."

"I know a lot of folk who buy these things as a joke," Phil said. "Was there any reason to believe they'd been used?"

"That's a very good point," Connor replied. "In fact, the whips and some of the other items were brand new and still in their packets. However, scratches on the bedposts indicate restraints had been attached. Some of the clothing had definitely been worn and we're waiting for the results of tests to see if they or the cuffs show anything."

"Okay, it looks like the victim wasn't so lily-white, if you'll pardon the expression." Alex said. "That doesn't explain or justify why she should be attacked and choked to death."

"Always assuming it wasn't an accident," Phil replied.

"We've also found some photos," Connor said.

"This just keeps getting better and better," Donny said, smiling.

Mary thumped him on the shoulder, "Behave yourself."

"You can't grudge me some small pleasures; when you get to my age you have to take what opportunities you can,"

"No, please, Donny, too much information," Phil said.

Donny's face turned crimson. "No, that's not what I meant." Donny sighed. "All I was saying was…"

"Let's cut the banter or we'll be here all night, and I, for one, have better things to do." Alex broke into a grin, remembering why he wanted to get away.

"The photos," Connor continued. "It appears the young couple were quite dab hands with a camera. In fact, they used the camera on their tablet and then used its memory card to have them printed. They used the self-service facility at Tesco to produce the prints if that's at all relevant."

"Why should it be relevant?" Phil asked.

"When you see them, you'll realise why they might not have wanted their local Boots sales assistant handling them," Connor replied with a chuckle.

He opened his satchel and lifted out a folder, spreading twenty prints across the table for inspection, each had an identification number. Most were nude shots of one or other of the young couple in various alluring poses with some of Keiran wearing exotic lingerie or showing her chained to their bed.

"Now we know the cuffs were used," Sanjay said.

"It may only have been for the photos. The tests should be able to tell if there are skin fragments, which would indicate *actual* use. Irrespective, these are copies and we've printed them straight off the memory card," Connor advised.

"She's quite stunningly beautiful," Phil remarked.

"He's not so bad looking either," Mary said. Then with a wicked smile she added, "He's a big boy. Do you think you could measure up, Donny? I've got a tape measure in my desk if you're up for the challenge."

He couldn't meet her gaze, instead mumbling, "I preferred the old days, when women kept their mouths shut and their legs open. Lie back and think of England."

"You really are a Presbyterian old bastard, aren't you?" Phil replied.

"And not very sexually adventurous," Mary added, smirking from ear to ear.

Donny's face was crimson. He turned away at the sound of their guffaws, unsuccessfully seeking to hide his embarrassment.

"Are you setting up a sideline selling pornography?" Sanjay asked, breaking the tension.

Connor winced before replying. "This isn't only for your entertainment. I've printed them for a reason," he paused before continuing. "They were produced out of the pictures file on the tablet, but prints were in the drawer of all these photos except numbers fourteen and fifteen."

Sanjay leafed through the photos to reveal and pull out the identified numbers. The first showed Keiran naked, standing partially crouched with her hands on her knees in a Marilyn Munroe style pose, blowing a kiss. The second had her lying on her back, her arms and legs pulled towards the corners of the bed, restrained, with her hips raised in anticipation.

"So why were these not included in the prints?" Donny asked.

"I believe, in all likelihood, they were printed," Connor replied, "but something has happened to them. Perhaps McGowan has kept them somewhere special as a keepsake." Another pause. "Then, maybe again, someone else has them."

"But who? I don't reckon that our Islamic Extremist friends would be too impressed," Donny said.

"More to the point, they'd want her punished; they'd want her stoned in the street," Sanjay added.

"Or maybe strangled to death," Phil replied.

"You made mention of someone when you interviewed Keiran's parents, Alex said."Wasn't it a relative who wanted Keiran married off? Who was it, Ibrahim or something like that?"

"I didn't follow it up, Sir. I'll look into it now." Sanjay said.

Chapter 10

Knowing Sandra's love of red roses, Alex detoured past the Ibrox ASDA superstore to collect every one they had left on their shelves. After parking at the hospital, he gathered the flowers and laboured with multiple bags before arriving on the ward to visit Sandra and their child.

As Sandra and the baby were both sound asleep on his arrival, he took his time to fill vases and arrange the envelopes for her inspection, placing the gift bags on the floor. He then sank into the visitor's chair to rest his weary bones. Almost immediately, his eyes closed, and he drifted into oblivion.

"Alex, are you okay?" He felt his shoulder being shaken and the sting of penetrating, bright light as he fought his way back to consciousness.

"I must have dropped off for a moment."

She smiled. "A bit more than a moment; I came to, more than forty minutes ago. I don't know how long you were dozing before that. Oh, and thank you for the flowers. They're amazing."

Alex pulled himself to his feet and stretched over the bed to embrace her. When Sandra yelped, reacting to the sudden movement, a concerned look crossed Alex's face." I didn't mean to..."

"No, it's okay, I'm really alright, only a little bit fragile."

"You look great and you did it. You've produced a beautiful daughter for me." Alex's face melted at the sight of his child gurgling away in her crib.

"You can lift her. I think she needs to get to know her daddy a bit better."

Alex reached over and lifted his daughter. He swaddled her in blankets and carefully cradled her in his arms, gently swaying back and forth.

"I must get the birth registered, I could pop into Martha Street tomorrow" Alex said.

"To do that, we'll need to agree on a name. Have you thought any more about it?"

"Like we were saying this, morning, Siobhan's a definite contender. Siobhan Warren's got a nice ring to it. Although I really like Catriona, it's bound to get shortened to Cat and I'm not so keen. Similarly, Fiona might become Fee and either one with Warren can be made into annoying nicknames."

"Of course, we don't need to use the surname Warren," Sandra said.

When she saw Alex's face collapse, she quickly added, "I was only joking. Of course, her name will be Warren; Siobhan McKinnon Warren to be precise."

"There's a decision then," Alex said, enthusiastically. "Now we've got that decided, there's still one big outstanding question."

"Not now, Alex, please."

"When then?"

"I don't know, but I don't want to think about it now," Sandra said.

"You know it would make your folks really happy if you married me. I'm sure your dad thinks it's me who's not prepared to commit and it's really not true."

"I've already put him straight on that. In any event, what my parent's think is not a good enough reason for us to wed. I know you love me and you want to marry me and yes, I am flattered, but quite frankly I don't see what difference it makes."

"It means Siobhan will have parents who are husband and wife."

"But it's irrelevant, I don't see how it changes anything. It doesn't mean I love you any the less, but I just don't see the point. Why is it so important to you?"

"I don't know. I guess I'm just old fashioned."

"You weren't so old fashioned when you asked me to move in with you," Sandra argued.

"But that's different. I don't know. I just feel it would be better for the wee one."

"Okay, I know your thoughts on the matter, just as I know what Mum and Dad think. But I'm not ready. I need to feel it's something I need to do if I'm going to get married. Convince me, give me one really good reason and I'll say yes."

Alex pondered the question. "It would make a big saving on Inheritance Tax, if we ever become wealthy enough to have to pay it."

"Fine, that's decided then. When we become rich enough to worry about Inheritance Tax, then we'll get married."

Alex shook his head in exasperation. "Okay, you win. We'll put off the discussion for another time."

"How about we put it off indefinitely, until I bring it up again?"

"Okay, it's your decision. Just so you know that I'm willing."

"Yes, you've made that perfectly clear. Now, what's in all the packages you've brought?"

"I'd forgotten all about them," Alex said. "There are cards and gifts from all the team in the office. Let's have a look."

As Siobhan had fallen asleep, Alex carefully laid her back in the crib, placing the plush toy rabbit alongside. One by one, he emptied the bags onto Sandra's bed and they each took turns opening and reading the cards and then the packages, revealing a range of stretch-suits, hats and booties along with teething rings, and an assortment of toys. He lifted all the cards to display on the window ledge.

"Everyone's been so kind and generous," Sandra said.

"You're a very lucky girl," Alex whispered to his daughter. "All these people love you already and this is only the start."

"Alex, you look really exhausted and you're working again tomorrow. Have you eaten anything?"

Until that point, Alex hadn't realised he'd gone the whole day without food, having only the odd cup of coffee to keep him going. His stomach involuntarily growled in response to the question. "I don't think there's anything in the fridge. I'll maybe grab a chippie on the way home."

"You ought to get some food and some sleep. Off you go home. I'm being looked after well enough here."

Alex started to protest, but realised she was correct. Following a night with very little sleep, he'd been on the go for a straight eighteen hours, including events of great emotion and intensity. "You're right. I'll get off home and I'll be back to see you in the morning. Is there anything you need?"

"No, I'm fine. I have everything."

Alex kissed his two girls, lifted the bags of gifts and made his way out of the ward.

Chapter 11

Being a proficient cook and liking home-produced meals, Alex couldn't remember the last time he'd bought a fish supper, carry out. He was aware his previously favoured chip shop had changed ownership so knew he'd need to try somewhere untested.

On his way home, Alex pulled his car to a halt outside a shop near to Eglington Toll. He entered and paid for a can of Irn Bru and a standard fish supper, with the usual lashings of salt and vinegar. Marked by a frown, he noted the steep escalation in price since he'd last bought one. Armed with his meal, supplied in a polystyrene container and wrapped in brown paper, he left the shop. Realising he didn't want his car contaminated by the smell of his meal, he chose instead to sit at a bus shelter and unwrapped the package.

Inside were two, large, deep fried fillets of haddock, covered in batter and sitting atop a mountain of oily chips. Being late in the evening, Alex surmised the food had been prepared much earlier and now lacked the crispness he'd remembered and preferred. Nevertheless, feeling ravenous from his day of fasting, he popped the can and munched into his feast with enthusiasm.

Memories flooded back of previous times he'd sat in a bus shelter eating chips. His mind filled with pictures of himself with Helen, his now ex-wife. It was back when they were courting, while living at home with their respective parents and had little privacy. At that time, as they had very little money, a good night out's entertainment was going for a walk and sharing a bag of chips. His lips creased into a nostalgic smile at the thought. So much time had passed. A more euphoric grin took over thinking of today's events and the birth of his daughter.

"Hey, mister, gonna gie me a chip?" the spell was broken. Two waif-like, youngsters, probably only aged about twelve were standing a couple of yards away, staring at him. Alex looked down at his meal. He'd already devoured one of the fish fillets and he'd made a sizable impression on the chips but already they lay heavily on his stomach and he no longer felt hungry.

"Here lads, help yourselves," Alex passed them the pack and made his way back to his car.

* * *

Although pleased to find a parking space only a short walk from the front door, an inexplicable foreboding enveloped Alex as he parked. He felt dog-tired and he was returning to sleep alone in his empty flat. Although they had lived together for less than two years, Sandra wouldn't be there to warm his heart and his bed, and it didn't feel right.

Keys in hand, he collected the bags of presents then activated the car alarm. He swiped the building's door entry scanner and lumbered along the close and up the stairs.

No, it wasn't because Sandra was away, something was wrong. The door of his flat wasn't properly closed.

Muscles wound tight as a drum, he deposited the bags on the landing, inhaled deeply then pushed the door open. The familiar creak of the hinge did nothing to settle his nerves. With caution, he stepped into the hallway, listening intently hoping to detect any foreign presence. On first glance, nothing appeared out of place. There was no indication of the door being forced.

Alex wracked his brains trying to remember the events of the early morning when they'd departed. Could they possibly have been so distracted that they'd failed to lock or even properly close the flat before leaving? It couldn't be possible, but how confident was he? There was no other rational explanation.

With apprehension, he checked each room in turn. Although no damage or violation was apparent, someone had undoubtedly been in and removed any accessible valuables. The small but beloved collection of art and antiques lay undisturbed, leaving Alex to conclude it had been an opportunist who only wanted items which were easy to dispose of and hard to detect. Alex called his local constabulary to report the theft and while waiting for a response he carried out a meticulous check to list missing items. Most obvious was his television set and laptop computer, but there was also a tablet, the PlayStation, he'd purchased for his sons' visits, a wallet containing euros and his prized bottle of Benlochy, twenty-five year old, single malt scotch. Alex was relieved, when he checked, to find the hidden external storage disk he used for the computer. He was always very careful not to retain any sensitive information on the machine's hard disk, instead using an encrypted, removable drive as a security precaution. After checking, to assure himself that the contents hadn't been tampered with, he poured himself a healthy measure of whisky from an open bottle of Grouse which the robbers hadn't touched.

No sooner had the first sip warmed his throat than he heard his entry phone announcing the arrival of police. He was impressed as he knew non-urgent crime did not normally receive such rapid attention. He suspected his rank had earned him special treatment and he wasn't complaining.

He buzzed them up and wasn't sure whether to be pleased or disappointed to recognise PC Stuart Black, from the previous evening at McGowan's flat. Accompanying the youngster WPC Janice Shilton appeared every bit as green.

Alex made a statement and provided a handwritten schedule of the missing items, together with their serial numbers. "I know the stats and I don't suppose there's much chance of recovery, but I can always hope. All the electronic items have my identification details printed on them using a UV pen and there's a tracker inside the laptop."

"You've clearly done everything right from a crime prevention point of view, Sir. It's just a pity the door hadn't been secure," Black said, without any hint of sarcasm. Nevertheless, Shilton had to turn away to hide her mirth.

"I know it's a bit late, but I'll check round your neighbours in the close to see if any of them saw or heard anything suspicious," Black offered.

Shilton examined the front door. "This closes on a latch which can be pushed open if it's not locked. But anyone coming in would have had to get through the security entry first. Who all had keys?"

"I've got a set and so does my partner, that's DI Sandra McKinnon and my sons each have a set too. I've not had time to check if they're all accounted for," Alex replied.

"What about the close? Who all have keys for the entry system?" Shilton asked.

"Each of the neighbours will have their own and as a couple of the flats are rented, there could be landlords or agents." Alex drew breath before continuing. "There's a local housing association which factor the building and obviously they'll have access. Besides, any of the neighbours can buzz up visitors. Of course, there's also the service button for deliveries. Anyone can get in by pressing it between seven and nine in the morning."

"Doesn't sound very secure," Shilton said.

"No different to about ninety percent of the flats in Glasgow. It keeps out general riff-raff and stops drunks from stumbling in, particularly at night. More to the point, it means anyone in the close who's not meant to be there are that much more obvious."

"Okay, Sir. We'll make the rounds before it gets too late," Black said.

Alex sat back on the couch to nurse his whisky. Pondering the events of the day, and with adrenaline wearing off, he was fatigued. He wanted to lie down to rest but suspected he'd hear back from Black and Shilton before they left. He automatically reached for the remote before remembering the telly was gone. Realising his frugal music collection was undisturbed, he selected a Coldplay album, *A Rush of Blood to the Head* and put it to continuous run on his portable CD player. The music started, and he rested his eyes.

The track *In My Place* was on it's second round of play when Alex heard his doorbell. He invited Black and Shilton into his lounge and muted the sound.

"Any joy?"

"I'm not sure, Sir," Black answered. "We got an answer at every door. Most tried to be helpful but didn't have a lot of information. Nobody saw anyone in the close, although the old woman upstairs said she thought she saw a white van parked outside."

"If anyone knows what's going on around here, it's her," Alex remarked.

"I'm afraid we got some *doctor, heal thyself* sort of comments, too," Shilton said.

"Sorry?"

"You know what I mean; with a policeman's house being broken into, isn't it up to him to sort the problem?"

Alex raised an eyebrow.

"There was no malice, only good-humoured banter," Shilton said.

"Yeah, I suppose. So not much to go on, hardly surprising."

"There was one thing I thought might be worth checking," Black said. "I noticed in a number of the flats, they'd received a flyer from a company offering electrical repairs. When I asked, I was told they had come in today. As it wasn't with the mail, it must have been hand delivered. I have one here." He handed Alex a pink-coloured, printed A5 sheet.

"Let me check." Alex looked in his mail basket. "I didn't get one. You said everyone else had one. Now that really is strange. You may be onto something. It definitely sounds worth following up."

"I've already looked them up online, Sir. They have their own webpage. They run a repair service and they also offer to buy old and broken appliance and sell refurbished ones. I thought it a coincidence with most of the items you lost being electrical appliances. One problem if it is them is, they'll know to remove the tracker."

"That's good work, Son. I think you might have a future in this job."

Black's face was glowing with pride as he left.

Chapter 12

It took very little time for Sanjay to identify that Ibrahim Sharma was Tarik's brother and therefore Keiran's uncle. Further investigation showed he had no criminal record, but there had been a file opened on him because he was known to fraternise with Islamic extremists. No suspicion was ever shown of him engaging in criminal activity, which is more than could be said for many of his friends.

Sanjay checked with colleagues in Special Branch to ensure he wasn't crossing any lines, then called Phil to join him, as he planned to carry out an interview.

They drove to Govanhill then parked in a brightly lit section of Calder Street, having hope more than expectation for the car to be in one piece when they returned. A short walk took them to the outer entrance of Sharma's flat. The panel for the entry system was hanging from the wall suspended by wires, the security door was missing. They kicked their way through piles of rubbish in the close before climbing two flights of stairs. Between two dingy looking entrances each having flaking paint, a polished hardwood door had a plaque stating,

Sharma.

Sanjay gave the door a sharp series of knocks.

They detected a presence on the far side and from the change in light knew someone was surveying them through the peep hole.

"Whose there?" a gruff male voice enquired.

"I'm DS Guptar and this is DC McKenzie." They both held out their identification.

The door cracked open a fraction. "What do you want?"

"We'd like to come in and speak to you."

"Why would I want to talk to you? Is this more racial persecution?" He looked at Sanjay and sneered. "Ah, I see they've sent the token brown skinned man thinking I'll feel empathy. Don't waste my time."

"It's not like that..." Sanjay started.

"You should be ashamed of yourself," Sharma interrupted. "You disgust me. You sell out your own people and make friends with the enemy. Ttss, I spit on you."

Phil could see Sanjay's mounting anger. He placed a reassuring hand on his shoulder, simultaneously drawing him backwards, and pushed the door gently forward, providing himself a better view of Sharma. The man's mouth was pursed shut, he was slight of stature with angular face and sharp features. He was dressed in a white two-piece suit of loose fitting trousers and jacket buttoned up to his neck.

"We are not the enemy, Sir. As police officers, we maintain the rule of law and keep order. We are here to help the public and honest, law-abiding citizens have no reason to fear our presence."

"Nonsense, this country has no order. There are no values and no morality. Our mullah teaches us order. The police only protect the rights of the ruling classes."

Sanjay considered asking the obvious question of why Sharma should choose to live in a country he appeared to despise so much, but his better judgement quelled his outrage.

Two teenage girls, both dressed all in black approached Sharma, "What is it, Papa? Who's there?" one of them asked speaking in Urdu,

"Be quiet. Get back to your room and don't come out unless I say," Sharma scolded, also in Urdu. It was clear he'd been unsettled by the interruption.

"We're not here to discuss politics. We want to talk with you about your niece, Keiran Sharma," Phil said.

"I know of her death, there's nothing to discuss. Go away. I don't need to talk to you," Sharma said.

"It's up to you, Sir. We can do this here and now or we can ask you to accompany us for a discussion at the station. Either way we *will* be talking to you," Phil added.

Sharma looked uncertain. After a short pause, he stepped back allowing the officers into his hall but invited them no further.

"You knew your niece had left home?" Phil asked.

"I warned Tarik years ago, not to give his girls so much freedom. He wouldn't listen. No, worse, he let his stupid wife have a say." He spat the words. "Because Nadia had an education, he thought she knew how to raise a family. She let the girls act as badly as Scottish children. The fool, he wasn't in control of his own house."

"You don't think that should have been allowed?" Phil asked.

"My children know who rules. They've studied their religion and they show respect."

"Is it respect or fear?" Sanjay couldn't stop himself from asking.

"You have to ask. You don't get respect unless they fear the consequences. Keiran had no fear. She didn't follow Allah and you see what happened."

"You can't be saying that what happened was a result of her lack of faith," Sanjay stated.

"Of course I can. If Tarik wasn't weak, it would never have happened. Even when she started to stray, I told him we could save her. Her reputation was ruined here but we might still have found her a match with an older man. We have family in Wolverhampton and in Islamabad who could have seen to it."

Phil was stunned.

"Instead, he did nothing. He stood by while she humiliated us. At least now she can bring no more shame on the family."

"Are you actually telling us that you thought she deserved to die?" Phil asked.

"That wasn't what I said," Sharma replied. "She gave up her right to be part of our family. Whatever happened afterwards is of no concern to us."

Sanjay and Phil exchanged glances, neither one convinced they'd heard correctly.

"Can you tell me where you were yesterday afternoon, between the hours of four and seven?" Sanjay asked.

Sharma laughed, "You don't honestly consider me a suspect. Anyhow, I was in a meeting of the council at the mosque all of yesterday afternoon. You can ask the others if you don't believe me. You remember where the mosque is?" he asked, looking directly at Sanjay.

Chapter 13

Albeit a restless night, Alex rose early, revived. Although, disappointed at his losses from the robbery, nothing could wipe the smile from his face thinking about his daughter. He quickly showered and prepared breakfast. Only when munching through his second slice of toast did he remember; he'd forgotten to fulfil his promise to call his boys.

Hoping he'd be able to make up for lost time, he phoned the landline.

"I believe congratulations are in order," Helen said. Despite her words, her tone was caustic. "I guess you were out celebrating most of the night because you didn't call. Craig and Andrew stayed in all evening expecting to hear from you. They were very disappointed. You shouldn't let them down like that."

Over the years, Alex thought he'd become immune to Helen's barbs and was usually able to ignore them. Not this time, he was riled. "It was nothing like that, as you must well know. Will you let me talk to the boys, please?"

"They're running late for school. You can't expect…"

"Hello, is that you, Dad?" Craig's voice broke in, having picked up an extension. "Congratulations! great news."

"I'm sorry, Son. I meant to call you last night. But I had an important new case just kick off, and then I went to see Sandra at the hospital. It was late when I got home, and then I walked into a crisis. I'll tell you about it later."

"No problem, Dad. Don't fret. Is everyone okay?"

"Yes, fine, and we've picked a name. Your new young sister is being called Siobhan. I'm planning to pick you up at six tonight. Can you be ready?"

"Yeah, sure. Siobhan, I like that. When will they be getting home?"

"From what we've been told, I expect they'll be released tomorrow morning."

"Released? You make it sound like a prison sentence."

Alex laughed. "From what Sandra told me about the regime, it's not a bad comparison. But seriously, they're being very well taken care of. I'd better let you go and get ready. Can I have a quick word with Andrew?"

"He's not out of the shower yet. But don't worry, I'll fill him in."

"Thanks; see you at six."

* * *

Alex pulled out a chair and sat down at Sanjay's desk. "What's new?"

"I hear you had a bit of bother last night," Sanjay said. "Is there anything I can do?"

"Word gets around quick. It was nothing too serious and the uniform boys have it in hand. Besides, I need all of your skills on this case.

Sanjay reported on his meeting with Ibrahim Sharma and advised that afterwards Phil had checked at the mosque and had Sharma's alibi corroborated.

"He gave you quite a hard time by all accounts?" Alex said.

"Too bloody true. I could have swung for him. I was seething but knew I daren't open my mouth as it would only make matters worse. I can't praise Phil highly enough; he handled it brilliantly."

"Yes," Alex replied, "he can be a real pain in the ass at times, particularly with his bad jokes, but when push comes to shove, he's a damned good copper."

"I agree, but for god's sake don't let him hear you say it. He's insufferable enough as it is."

Alex laughed at the thought. "Getting back to our friend, Ibrahim, do you believe his story, or do you think the alibi's a fix?"

"It's hard to tell. The mosque he's part of has a hard core of militants. I've checked and their mullah's under surveillance by our security boys. They suspect he might be grooming an extremist cell. We can't go too close without their okay."

"That's all we need." Alex replied.

"Sharma's alibi probably means nothing, but there's little we can do about it. Not now, anyway. In any event, even if he wasn't personally involved, it wouldn't mean he hadn't set something up."

"We can't just leave them alone," Alex said.

"I'm the last one to want to make excuses for him, but I very much doubt Sharma's involved," Sanjay said.

"Why's that?"

"Well, if it was an honour crime, Keiran would have been punished because of her rejecting her religion, more to the point, because she was shacking up with an infidel."

"So?"

"Why wait until now? Also, our first indications suggest she was sexually assaulted, if not raped, before she was murdered. That would be inconsistent with an honour killing."

"Okay, I bow to your better judgement," Alex replied. After pondering for a few moments, he added, "Let's not be too hasty though."

"What do you mean?"

"We know Keiran engaged in rough sexual activity before her death."

"Yes."

"We don't yet know who with. It could have been McGowan; it could have been someone else."

"Right," Sanjay said.

"Irrespective, it doesn't automatically follow that the one who shagged her is the same one who killed her."

"Okay, I follow what you're saying, but wouldn't that be stretching credibility a bit for her to be attacked twice in the same day? I thought you didn't believe in coincidence."

"Take a step back. You're assuming the sex wasn't consensual. You saw the photos. It's clear that Keiran wasn't a shy and reserved sort of girl. Maybe she liked a bit of rough."

"I see where you're coming from," Sanjay replied. "That would mean that Sharma and his Jihadi band of friends are still in the frame."

"For the time being, at least."

"But where do we go from here?"

"Same as normal. We explore every avenue and we test out every theory until we come to an inevitable conclusion."

"Yeah, yeah, 'when you eliminate the impossible, then what's left, no matter how improbable, must be the explanation. Classic Sherlock Holmes, right?"

"The quote's not quite there, but you've got the right idea," Alex replied. "What else?"

"I've arranged an appointment for Donny and Phil to speak to McGowan's parents and his brother. Once done, they'll bring our boy in for a little chat."

"Good, let's see what that brings out."

"Mary's at the Queen Elizabeth, speaking to Keiran's work colleagues. Steve's back off leave and I sent him with her."

"Missed opportunity, they'll be in the next building along from the maternity unit where Sandra is."

Sanjay smirked. "You're not seriously suggesting Sandra could summon Keiran's workmates to her hospital bed, so she can interview them. I know we're short staffed, but…"

"Very funny! You know what I meant. I'm already up and down to see her at least a couple of times today. I could have fitted in some interviews while I was there."

"Yes, Sir. Mind you, I think you've got enough to think about when you're visiting. It's best this way."

"You're probably right; have you anything else?"

"A little. Donny went to McPhail and Morgan, spoke to some of McGowan's workmates."

"And?"

"By all accounts, he seems to be pretty solid. His bosses said he was a good employee and not afraid to put in the hours. The other trainees found him pleasant enough, but it was noted he wasn't too social. It was rare for him to attend nights out. He'd claimed it wasn't his scene."

"There's nothing wrong with that." Alex said. "Not everyone wants to spend their spare time with the same people they work with. And from what we've learned, we know he may have had good reason to want to get home quickly."

"Yeah, there's that. But we had one or two comments suggesting they suspected he may have been a bit fond of the grape juice."

Alex frowned. "What's that all about?"

"Apparently, on the only two occasions he did socialise, he was guilty of overindulging and had to be sent home in a taxi."

"Was that it, or was there more to it?"

"No, that was it; no obnoxious behaviour. I think he just drank until he was out of it and then fell asleep. There was some suspicion that he may have had a problem and that's why he often kept to himself."

"Mmm," Alex pondered. "One interpretation of the evening Keiran dies, he's out allegedly to meet a friend and he has a few drinks. His workmates seem to suggest once he starts drinking, he doesn't know when to stop."

Sanjay glanced at his notes. "By his own admission, he'd sunk a couple of pints and fell asleep on the bus home. We don't know just how much he may have drunk, but there's a consistency with what his workmates said. If we'd taken a blood sample at the time, then we'd have had a better idea."

"Too late now," Alex replied.

"Does that help or hinder his alibi?" Sanjay asked.

Alex shook his head. "At this stage, your guess is as good as mine." After a moment's thought, he added. "Even if it supports the story of having a drink before he went home, it doesn't put him in the clear.

He comes home, a bit tanked up, then perhaps Keiran has a go about the state he's in when they're meant to be celebrating together. Then again, maybe there's the scenario, as before, when she tells him she's pregnant. Who knows? We need to find out more."

"I'll go and check if there are any more reports. We should have heard something from Connor by now."

"Fine, I'll be in my office. I've a number of other things to catch up on."

Chapter 14

As their arrival was expected, McGowan senior was waiting. He showed Phil and Donny into his front room.

"We'd like to speak to each of you separately, if that would be okay," Donny asked.

Mr McGowan nodded and closed the door to afford some privacy, then ushered them to sit.

"How's Kevin?" Phil asked."

McGowan shook his head. "We don't know what to do for him. He's hardly spoken a word. He doesn't want to leave his room and he's hardly eaten a thing."

"It's a very difficult time," Phil acknowledged. "It could be worth speaking to your G.P. about grief counselling."

McGowan nodded. Donny allowed a short period of silence to pass before commencing. "Your wife told us, the other day, about how well Keiran fitted into your family,"

"Yes, that's true."

"And they'd been together for what, about two years?"

"That'll be right, because they talked about it being their anniversary since they'd started seeing each other. For most of that time they were dating. It's only in these last six months, they moved in together, after Kevin rented the flat."

"It couldn't have been very long after he started his job," Donny said.

"Yes, you're right. Kevin was lined up to start with M&M as soon as he'd graduated." McGowan's voice was filled with pride. "Keiran too. She was offered a job by the health board, working at the new hospital." Donny nodded. "What with the two of them in good jobs, that's how they could afford to rent the flat. We helped out, of course."

"How did you help?"

"His mum and I, we lent them the money for their deposit. The agent also wanted a guarantee because neither of them had a track record renting and they were both new to the jobs market as well."

"I see," said Donny, "and you didn't mind?"

"You do whatever you can to make your kids happy. Particularly with Kevin, after his health problems, we'd do anything."

Donny was pleased; McGowan had raised the subject uninvited, making it easy for him to pursue. "Tell me more about it. What was wrong with him?"

"It's a while back now, but it still feels as raw as if it had been yesterday; we were scared we were going to lose him," McGowan started. "Kevin was only twelve and he'd been suffering from terrible headaches. It went on for months before he was properly diagnosed." McGowan's eyes welled up at the memory. "As soon as they realised it was a tumour, he was rushed into Yorkhill. You remember, where the Sick Kids Hospital used to be? They operated straight away. It was touch and go for a bit but thank God they were successful; they got it all." McGowan swiped at each eye in turn with the back of his hands. "We lay awake for days, hoping and praying. All of the congregation said special prayers too."

Donny and Phil both nodded.

"Our prayers were answered, and he came through."

"Was that the end of it?" Phil asked.

"No, he had to go through radiotherapy as well and he still has regular check-ups, just in case. But he's been okay since."

"Has it affected him at all?" Phil asked.

"We were warned there could be a chance of brain damage, but thankfully no. Not only was Kevin okay, but we discovered he was very smart. He did well in all his school exams, four A's and a B in his Highers. Then he studied law at university and now he's doing his training."

Donny, anticipating Phil's typical humour might relate brain damage to anyone wanting to be a lawyer, gave his friend a savage look as a warning to stay silent. Phil made the briefest of smirks as an acknowledgement.

Unaware of the silent exchange, McGowan continued, "We spoiled him rotten of course, but he's a good boy; he never gave us a moment's grief." The expression was out of his mouth before he realised, and he hung his head.

"It's good it hasn't affected his life or had any side effects," Phil said."

"Well, that's not strictly true," McGowan replied. "The cancer itself hadn't affected anything, but one result of the radiation treatment is that he's unlikely ever to be able to have children of his own."

"How unfortunate," Phil replied. "Why is that?"

"His doctor explained it to us. After the treatment, he was left infertile. It was a small price to pay for saving his life."

"Was it a permanent impairment or could it be reversible?"

McGowan looked perplexed. "The doctor said he didn't expect it to change and it's never been an issue, but why are you so interested? What's it got to do with why you're here?"

"It probably won't have any bearing at all so let's move on. Tell us about how you first met Keiran?" Donny asked.

"They'd already been seeing each other for about a month before Kevin said anything. He told us he'd met a girl. He said he really liked her and he wanted us to meet."

"And you were happy for him," Donny surmised.

"Well, yes. We thought him a bit young for a serious relationship but then the missus and I met when we were only eighteen, so we could hardly criticise. We said he should bring her home for dinner."

"Did you all get along from the start?" Donny asked.

McGowan took a moment to respond. "It was a bit of a shock at first. Kevin hadn't said she was Moslem. The first we knew was when he introduced us. We're not prejudiced, you understand. It was just that we didn't expect it and of course we've always wanted the best for our son. We were worried about all the problems he might face being in a mixed-race relationship."

"At first, you weren't in favour." Donny probed.

"It wasn't that. It was only that we were taken by surprise. If he'd prepared us it would have been different. Anyhow, once he'd explained that she didn't really have any religion and we got more used to the idea, then it all worked out fine. As Lizzie said, we get on like a house on fire." Remembering that Keiran was dead, he looked downward and added, "Well we did, you know what I mean."

"Would you have felt differently if she'd been a practicing Moslem?" Donny asked.

"Lizzie and I are Protestant and we're regular churchgoers. We brought up our boys to love God and Jesus. I don't truly believe Kevin could have fallen for a girl who actively practiced a different religion." McGowan thought deeply for a moment before continuing. "As I said before, we love our son and we'd do anything for him. If he met somebody who made him happy, irrespective of their beliefs, we'd have been able to accept them."

"It could have been worse," Donny quipped, "at least she wasn't a Catholic."

Rising to the bait, McGowan chuckled. "Even if he'd picked a Catholic girl, we'd have tried. We wouldn't have stopped loving him. I'm only joking, of course; I've got nothing against Catholics except when there's an Old Firm game on."

With the mood lightened a little, Phil brought the discussion back on course. "Although you may have welcomed Keiran into your family, we understand that Kevin wasn't accepted by the Sharma household."

"Their loss," McGowan replied. "They weren't prepared to meet him. I don't think they wanted to know anything about Keiran and Kevin being a couple. Keiran was afraid to let them know throughout the time she was studying in case they took her out of university. It wasn't until she'd graduated, and they were planning to move in together when she told them."

"What was their reaction?" Donny asked.

"Her father went ballistic. He gave her an ultimatum; it was them or Kevin. She thought he was bluffing at first. Her mother tried to intervene and may even have succeeded but there was other family who put pressure on him."

"I know what you mean; I've met the uncle," Phil said offering encouragement.

"Keiran was distraught and Kevin was terrified; he thought she might leave him. In the end, she chose Kevin and her father threw her out of the house. We told her that she could live here with us until they found a place of their own. The father said she'd never be allowed to return. He didn't even allow her to take her belongings with her."

"How awful," Phil said.

"The mother and sister packed her things and met her outside the house to pick them up. As a matter of fact, it was from the street, around the corner, because he didn't want Keiran even coming near the house. I drove her across to collect the bags."

"Did you meet Mrs Sharma?"

"No, we didn't want to risk making matters worse - as if that was possible. Kevin stayed home while I drove her across and parked. I left her my car keys and went for a walk. While I was away, she met her mum and got her stuff."

"You said she lived here with your family," Donny asked, while glancing around the room.

Reading the unstated question McGowan replied, "Yes, it's a three-bedroom house; the boys each have their own rooms. Although we were happy enough taking Keiran in, we couldn't let her and Kevin sleep together, so we had the two boys share the bigger bedroom and let Keiran use the small one."

Donny's raised his eyebrows.

"I'm not naive, detective; I'm a man of the world. I know what the young-uns get up to; it doesn't mean I have to approve or facilitate it. The way Lizzie and I were brought up, we kept our pants on until after we were married. Kids may think that's fuddy-duddy thinking now, but we can at least set the rules in our own home. Until they found their own place, we were happy to let Kevin and Keiran sleep under our roof but sleeping in the same bed was something else."

"You think that will have stopped them?" Donny asked.

"Of course not, I wasn't going to give it my blessing though."

"Do you believe they kept to your rules while in the house?" Donny asked.

"I suspect not. They knew our feelings on the matter, so they weren't going to embarrass themselves or us. They knew it wouldn't be for long either, as they were looking to find their own place."

"And how they behaved in their own home didn't bother you?" Donny asked.

"Yes, it bothered us. We believe in the sanctity of marriage. We would have preferred them not to be living in sin, but we are realists. Unlike the Sharma's, we weren't ready to lose our child because of our own pride."

"I have some more news for you, which you may find disturbing," Donny said.

McGowan looked alarmed.

"I assume Kevin can't have told you, but Keiran was pregnant."

McGowan's jaw dropped. When he regained his composure, his voice was little more than a whisper. "No, it can't be. There must be a mistake."

"There's no mistake, Mr McGowan, the medical examiner's report states the foetus was about four weeks old," Phil replied.

McGowan's eyes filled up, " But that means…"

"At this stage it means nothing conclusive," Phil interrupted, anticipating McGowan's next words. "We've nothing further to ask you at the moment. If it's okay could you ask your wife to some through to speak to us now."

Chapter 15

Mary and Steve located the pharmacy and were shown into the head of department's office.

"Hello Officers, what's all this about?" Fraser Sinclair stood; he slicked thin wisps of grey hair off of his face, extended his hand in greeting, then pointed to the utilitarian plastic chairs facing his desk.

Watching the pharmacist, Steve was all too aware of his own bald pate, although unlike Sinclair, his baldness was compensated by a recently grown full beard. Almost subconsciously, he ran his fingers through the hairs covering his chin as he nodded to Mary to commence the questioning.

"Mr Sinclair, thank you for seeing us at such short notice," Mary said as she sat down.

"It's Doctor Sinclair." Seeing the quizzical look, he added, "I'm not a medical practitioner, I have a scientific doctorate." He perched on the edge of his chair.

Mary nodded, "We believe you have an employee, Keiran Sharma?"

"Yes, that's correct. She's only worked here for a few months now."

Mary nodded.

"However, you can't see her. She's been on holiday for the last couple of days and was due back this morning. She didn't turn up, so I'm sorry if it's wasted your time." Defying interruption, Sinclair rambled on, "For me too, I can't be having this sort of unreliability, particularly since my deputy is off on long term sick. It's caused me all sorts of problems. Why do you want to see her, anyway? Is there something wrong?"

"Your problems might continue for a while. She won't be back," Mary replied.

"Why? Has she had an accident?" Sinclair asked.

"It wasn't exactly an accident," Mary replied. "I'm sorry to tell you, but she was found dead in her apartment two nights ago."

"Oh my God! What happened?" Sinclair sank back into his chair.

"It's early in our investigations. Suffice to say, we're treating her death as suspicious." Mary said.

"Oh my, she was such a nice girl, and from a good family. Her mother's a doctor, I understand."

"Yes, we believe so," Mary replied, while failing to comprehend why Sinclair thought it made any difference.

"How can I help you? You must have a reason for coming here."

"We're trying to get a better picture of her life, her friends and her colleagues. It's a standard procedure in any investigation."

"I'd be happy to help but I doubt I can tell you very much. She was diligent with her work, but I really didn't know her very well."

"Perhaps you can tell us if there was anyone who did know her better, someone she may have been close to?" Mary asked.

"As I said, I didn't know her at all well. But I believe she worked quite closely with Shirley. You might want to speak to her."

"Thank you, that helps. Is she working today and is there an office we can use to speak to her privately?"

"Yes, of course. The only thing I'd ask is please don't keep her any longer than absolutely necessary. It's only because we're short staffed and patients are dependant on us providing the prescriptions they need."

* * *

Shirley was the embodiment of an absent-minded scientist. Multiple biros protruded from the breast pocket of her lab coat and she wore thick, dark rimmed spectacles which made her eyes appear enormous.

She was small, rotund and greeted them with a cheery smile, her rosy cheeks shining.

Any indication of welcome disappeared once she was informed about Keiran's death. She sank into a chair, her head in her hands, weeping inconsolably.

Only once she'd controlled her breathing enough to speak, Shirley asked "But why? She was so young and beautiful and talented ... and happy. What on earth could have happened to her?"

"We're treating the death as suspicious. We're still trying to work everything out," Mary answered.

"Surely you're not suggesting that she might have been murdered?"

"There's no certainty, but we haven't ruled it out," Steve replied.

"No, it can't be. She was so nice. Nobody could ever have wanted to hurt her."

"We're looking into everything; that's why we wanted to speak to you. We understand that you were quite close," Steve said.

"I like to think we were best friends. We often spent our meal breaks together, but we hardly ever spoke outside of work." Shirley drew in a deep breath. "She was kind to me, though. You may find it hard to believe, but lots of people in this place are cruel and nasty. They say things behind your back; some even say horrible things to your face." Another deep breath. "Keiran wasn't like that. She was kind and open. There were even times she defended me when other people were horrible."

"How did she get on with everyone else?" Mary asked.

"Really well. Everyone loved her. Even Dr Cartwright, the gorgeous registrar over at A&E had a thing for her." Shirley bit her lip. "I shouldn't have said anything, sorry, it just slipped out."

"Who is this Dr Cartwright?" Mary asked.

"No please forget I said anything; it's the shock, it makes you say stupid things."

"Let us be the judge of that," Steve said. "Tell us about him."

Shirley couldn't meet their gaze. "He's a young doctor, very arrogant and condescending. He thinks he's god's gift to women. He's very handsome and he knows it. Being smart and wealthy doesn't hurt either. Most of the young nurses would kill for the chance to ensnare him … No, no, I'm getting my words confused. I didn't mean it like that."

"Please go on," Steve said.

"What I meant was, so many of the girls wanted have to a fling with him and from the stories going around, he put himself about a bit." Shirley stared at the floor.

"Did you have any involvement with him?" Steve questioned.

"Of course not, he wouldn't have given me a second glance."

"What about Keiran? Did she like him?" Mary asked.

"At first no. She said he was annoying. Maybe he thought she was playing hard to get, but he seemed really interested in her. He made all sorts of excuses to talk to her. Over time, she warmed to him and they built up this risqué banter."

"Was that all there was to it, or did they meet outside work?" Mary asked.

"No, not to my knowledge." After a long pause, Mary added. "I promised I wouldn't say; I gave her my oath. But, now she's dead, I suppose it doesn't count."

"More than that," Steve said. "Now she's dead, you owe it to her to tell us anything which could be of any help."

"Yes, I suppose. There was one time; I think about a month ago."

"Go on," Mary coaxed.

"Keiran told me she couldn't come to lunch with me. She seemed quite agitated too. Anyhow, I went to the canteen myself, but on the way back, I came through the car park and saw her climbing out of Dr Cartwright's car. She looked a bit dishevelled and was tucking in her blouse."

"You asked her about it," Mary said.

"Yes, I tried making a joke about her bedding Dr Perfect. She didn't find it at all funny. She really seemed mad. She made me promise not to say."

"You said there was *one time*. Did they not meet up again?" Steve asked.

"Not as far as I know. In fact, I thought it strange that there wasn't any contact between them afterwards. I interpreted it as Cartwright living up to his reputation. Once he'd got what he wanted, he lost any further interest."

Once Shirley had left the room, Mary and Steve compared notes.

"Much as she may have seemed upset, she really couldn't wait to dish the dirt," Steve said.

"Yeah, I detected more than a hint of jealousy too, not of being killed of course," Mary added, giving a wry smile.

"Mind you, if what she's told us is correct, we may have just found, our father. The timing matches well enough. It's going to be interesting to find out what the DNA shows us."

Chapter 16

Donny and Phil realised their mistake the moment Lizzie McGowan entered the room. They should have known better. Obviously, one of them should have escorted Mr McGowan out after his interview and brought in his wife before he had a chance to speak to her.

Her face was crimson, her arms flailing, out of her control. "I can't believe the little hussy. How could she have betrayed us in that way? After everything we'd done for her. My poor, poor boy; now I understand why he's hidden away and couldn't speak to us."

"Please calm down, Mrs McGowan. It's too soon for you to make any assumptions," Phil said.

"What do you mean? You told Frank that Keiran was pregnant. That can only mean one thing."

"The girl's dead…" Phil started with total dispassion.

"And maybe that's a good thing. Perhaps it's God's judgement. If I'd got my hands on her…" Mrs McGowan turned her face, sank into a chair and burst into tears.

"You're jumping to conclusions," Phil said. "The post mortem showed she was pregnant but at this point we can't know that Kevin wasn't the father."

"You're talking nonsense. The doctors told us that Kevin would never be able to father his own child."

"We've now learned different. It's true Kevin has a low sperm count which considerably lowered the chances of Keiran conceiving from him, but it's still a definite possibility. In fact, unless a DNA test shows something different, it's the most likely explanation," Phil said.

Mrs McGowan gasped for breath, before he continued. "Did you understand what I said? Do you realise this means that the child she was carrying might well have been your Kevin's child?"

Mrs McGowan's eyes opened wide. Her face was bewildered. "I can't get my head round this. I've got the choice of believing that my first grandchild is dead before he or she even had a chance to be born, or else the girl my cherished son loved and adored had been cheating on him. What sort of alternatives are they?"

Phil's stomach churned with distaste at the woman's insensitivity. He knew he could be held to account for anything he said, so he fought back his urge to tell her what he really thought of her outburst. A silence filled the room, then, appreciating she must be hurting, he gave a tempered response, "Your son will be grieving, and he'll need all the support you can give him."

"Yes, my son. Whatever happens, I must look after Kevin," she whispered.

"We suspect that Keiran didn't know she was pregnant until the day she died," Donny said.

"Why do you say that?"

"We found a pregnancy test kit in the flat showing positive. We have reason to believe it was only purchased on Monday," Donny explained.

"What difference does that make?" Mrs McGowan frowned, not understanding.

"If she didn't know then she couldn't have told anyone else, could she?" Phil said.

"I still don't see your point."

"Assuming it's murder, we haven't yet established a concrete motive," Donny said.

"I don't understand. If it wasn't murder, what else could have happened?" Mrs McGowan asked.

Seeing her reaction, Donny realised he'd already said too much. "In a case like this, we have to consider every possibility."

"But what other possibilities are there?" Mrs McGowan asked.

Donny flushed. He didn't want to say more and certainly not to discuss the possibilities of auto-erotic sex going wrong. "I'm sorry, until we know more, I'm not at liberty to say."

Phil, realising that Mrs McGowan was too self obsessed to provide any useful information brought the interview to an end. He accompanied her out of the room and brought Robbie back with him.

* * *

Robbie appeared to be a younger, fitter and more muscular version of his brother. He was dressed in the conventional jeans and tee-shirt favoured by his generation, but his pupils looked constricted, indicating he may have been under the influence of chemical stimulants.

"We understand that you were out with friends when your father tried to call you with the news on Monday," Donny started.

"Yes, that's right. Some of my pals are in their first year at Glasgow Uni and they're staying in the *Halls*. We met up at a pub in the West End for a couple of jars. As soon as I heard, I left and came home. I was back within the hour."

"It must have been quite a shock," Phil said.

"It certainly was. Keiran was always so full of life." He frowned as his own inappropriate choice of words.

"You'd got to know her fairly well then,," Phil surmised.

"Well, yes, I suppose."

"Tell us about it?" Phil continued. "How did you first find out about her?"

Robbie was silent for some time, his eyes glazed, reminiscing. "Kevin told me about her. The first I knew was when he said he'd met this gorgeous *burd* at his drama club. I thought he was just winding me up, because he did that a lot."

Both Donny and Phil detected more than a hint of antagonism.

"I don't know if they'd even got to the stage of dating at the time. It was long afterwards before he said anything to Mum or Dad."

"You didn't believe him then?"

"Not at first. He showed me a picture he had of her on his phone. I couldn't argue she was a doll, but I still didn't believe she was his girlfriend and I told him so."

"How did he convince you?" Donny asked.

"When he made a selfie of them together, kissing and he texted it to me. Even then, I thought it was a fake, a photoshop job. But afterwards, he made a videocall to me when they were together, I couldn't argue with that. Well I did, actually, but it was just to give him a hard time."

"Did it make any difference to you that she was Asian?" Donny asked.

Robbie drew in a deep breath, composing his thoughts. "Hell no; why should it? As for Mum and Dad, that was another matter. They're really into their church and can be quite narrow when it comes to matters of religion. Anyhow, Kevin told them about him having a girlfriend, and one time he arranged to bring her home. I think it was just to make sure that I couldn't say anything first. Even then, it gave them a surprise."

"It sounds like you had a bit of sibling rivalry going on," Phil said.

"If only. I don't think I qualified as a rival," Robbie replied. "Mum and Dad idolised Kevin. I never had a look in." He stopped to inhale before blurting. "After his operation, they couldn't do enough for him. It was as if they thought they'd caused his problems and had to make amends. They treated me as if I was there only to fetch and carry for him, and I didn't matter as far as they were concerned. I'm nearly five years younger, but I was expected to make his tea and clean up after him."

Donny and Phil looked at each other, surprised first by the outburst and secondly that he was so much younger than they'd thought. On first impressions, they'd imagined he could even have been the elder of the two.

"I'm sorry; you don't want to hear about my problems."

"I guess you think that your parents were overprotective of your brother, and that left you out in the cold," Phil said.

"I don't think, I know."

"Okay, we understand," Phil said. "Now, getting back to what you were saying, how did your parents react when Kevin brought Keiran home?"

"You mean on the first visit. While she was here, they were nice, sickly sweet in fact. After she left, Mum went apeshit." Robbie laughed before continuing. "She tore a strip of Kevin, asking what on earth he could be thinking of bringing home a 'Paki'."

Donny rolled his hand in a circle, indicating Robbie should continue.

"As usual, Kevin talked them round. Well he could do no wrong, could he? He convinced them he had no interest in religion and neither did she. He said he loved her and if they wouldn't accept her then they'd lose him as well. They gave in and promised to give her a chance. Actually, once they got to know her, I believe that they did genuinely quite like her."

"And what did you think of her?" Donny asked.

"Are you serious? You want to know what I thought?" His surprise was as if no-one had ever asked his opinion before.

"Completely serious," Donny replied.

"She was divine." Robbie closed his eyes before continuing. "Not only was she beautiful; she was thoughtful and caring. She listened when I spoke to her."

"And what did you talk to her about?" Phil asked.

"Oh, I don't know, anything and everything, I suppose. She always seemed interested."

"She sounds perfect," Phil said.

"She was; well almost."

"How do you mean?" Donny asked.

Robbie looked away. "Nobody can be absolutely perfect," he mumbled.

Believing he'd get no further, Phil thought he'd try another tack. "You must have been really jealous."

Robbie stared at his feet. "I guess. It wouldn't have been so bad if Kevin hadn't taunted me. He used to goad me that I'd never be able to get a girlfriend like her, or any girlfriend, he'd say." He paused. "It wasn't so bad at first, but for the time when Keiran moved into our house, it became torture."

"How so?" Phil asked.

"I was made to share a room with Kevin because Mum gave my room to Keiran. He'd tell me about what they did together. There were a couple of times, I saw her coming out the bathroom wearing only her wrap." Robbie stopped talking, his eyes glazed. "She was truly beautiful."

"I guess you really fancied her," Phil said.

Robbie's mouth felt dry; he swallowed to create some saliva to enable him to continue. "There were times, he sneaked to her room. I knew what they were up to. Mum and Dad would have been furious."

"And you knew this for sure?" Donny asked.

"There was one time; it was afternoon. Dad was working, and Mum was at a church group. Kevin went to Keiran's room."

"That doesn't mean much," Donny said.

"I've not finished. Mum had asked me to do some weeding in the garden. When I was there, I could see her curtain wasn't properly shut." Robbie swallowed. "There was no doubt about what they were doing. They were going at it like rabbits."

"But you didn't say anything." Donny said.

"No, I didn't want to risk being made out as being the bad one for telling. It was a relief though when they moved into their own flat."

"Did you see much of her after that?" Phil asked.

Again, Robbie looked away. "Not as much, of course. But I did visit them a few times. We'd sometimes go out for a meal or a drink."

"Is there anything else you can tell us?" Donny asked.

"No, I don't think so. I'm just so sad."

Chapter 17

"Excuse me, Boss, Can I disturb you?"

"Yes Sanjay. Come right in. What have you got?"

"Don't worry, Sir, it's not contagious."

"Bloody hell, Sanjay; you must be spending too much time with Phil. His terrible humour's rubbing off. Come on, out with it. What have you got to tell me?"

"I've had some more results through from Connor's people and I thought you ought to know."

"Fire away. I've got a few minutes before I step out. I'm going to drop in on Sandra again and I want to get the birth registered first."

"Didn't you say you saw her on the way in this morning?"

"Yeah, but partners are permitted to visit as often and for as long as they like. It's a far cry from how it was with the boys. Do you think it's overkill, with her likely to be out tomorrow?"

"It's not for me to say. It was the same when my kids were born. No restrictions, I was allowed in to see them at any time of day."

Alex smiled. "What is it you have to tell me?"

"The DNA results are in for the foetus. It looks like Kevin was the father."

"You said *looks like*. Can you not be more certain?"

"As you know, Sir, it's not an exact science. Matching is mathematically calculated. The technology with paternity tests may be able to give us an absolute negative, when someone can't be the father. But, when it's positive, it can only tell us that someone can be, and then give a statistical probability. In Kevin's case, it's highly likely."

Alex stood, shook his head while pacing around his room. "Poor lad; thinks he'll never be a father and then, when he gets his one big chance, this happens." Alex's thoughts turned to his own situation, newly becoming a father. "I don't know if I could have coped if it had been me."

"It's a tragedy, always assuming he's not the one who killed her."

Alex blinked, forcing back any emotion. "Anything else?"

"The cuffs and ankle restraints had seen some action. They weren't only used for the photos, judging by the wear. The trace particles were almost certainly caused by friction. Another thing, Fitzpatrick's been working flat out on the CCTV. No positive results so far. There's been a few possible sightings of McGowan, in and around Glasgow, but the clarity is suspect so we can't be certain.

"Very strange. There are so many cameras about these days. What's the chances of him not appearing clearly in any?"

"Very slim indeed, Sir. Perhaps, he was in disguise, or maybe he was being particularly careful to avoid being seen."

"But why?"

"So far, there's nothing to corroborate his story, which works against him. However, equally there's nothing to prove he was lying."

"Again, I have to ask, why would that be?" Alex said.

"If he's the killer and it was premeditated, then he'd have had good reason not to want to be spotted. Then again, it could be much more innocent. He could have been covering his tracks to hide evidence of a drinking problem."

"Neither one works for me. If it was only his drinking, he may have taken steps to give himself an alibi, but he'd be hardly likely to worry about anyone checking CCTV." Alex considered options. "Then, if it was premeditated murder, what's the motive? I can imagine one after he found out Keiran was pregnant and he suspected she'd been sleeping around. But if she only realised on Monday, Kevin wouldn't have known until he'd gone home. Motive - maybe yes, but not premeditated, and no real opportunity to set anything up."

"Perhaps she phoned to tell him earlier in the day," Sanjay suggested.

"It's not impossible, but it's not the sort of news she'd be likely to give over the phone, whether she thought it good or bad. To be more precise, whether she thought he'd take it well or not. Even if she did phone him, he'd have had little chance to plan anything," Alex said.

"I suppose not."

"Better check all the phone records, anyway; just to be sure."

"That's already in hand, Sir. I made the request yesterday. I'd better check to see if anything's come back."

"Be quick, I'd like to hear before I leave."

Almost ten minutes elapsed before Sanjay returned, carrying a wad of computer paper. "Sorry, I was a little bit longer than planned. Both Mary and Phil left messages about their interviews. They'll be back soon to give us a full report."

Alex nodded, looking at what Sanjay was carrying.

"I've got prints of Keiran's mobile use and of the landline for the last month. It could take a while to have them properly analysed but already it's raised a number of interesting questions."

"What?"

"First of all, it appears Keiran did call Kevin around about lunch time on Monday. The call lasted only a couple of minutes."

"At what time was it, precisely?" Alex asked.

"Thirteen ten, ten past one. Why?"

"And what time was the ASDA receipt?"

"Half twelve, if I remember right."

"That doesn't help a lot. It's unlikely, but it is theoretically possible, she bought and used the kit before she phoned him. You said it was a short call too; it doesn't ring true as being the big reveal. More likely she was calling to find out when he'd be home."

We can check it out with him after Phil and Donny bring him in," Sanjay said.

"Yes, but I always prefer to know the answers to questions before I ask them."

"Yes, Sir. For the record, we can confirm Kevin's story; he did text to say he was running late. He didn't explain why, though," Sanjay added.

"Not surprising. What else was so interesting?"

"There's a mobile number which appears frequently on Keiran's iPhone log and there were calls to and from the landline on Monday."

Alex raised an eyebrow, "One of her friends, maybe."

"It's the same number that Kevin gave us. The one arranging the rendezvous he didn't have with Billie Marshall."

Alex drew in a deep breath. "It looks like someone wanted Kevin out of the way for a while and whoever it was wanted to see Keiran without him knowing."

"So, Keiran was having a relationship with someone else." Sanjay surmised.

"It's looking more likely, but there could be other explanations. Equally, Kevin's not out the frame for the killing. This might even magnify his motive."

Sanjay stared at the ceiling, musing. "I suppose it could also be a very elaborate hoax by Kevin creating the phone record to use as an alibi."

"If so, he'd been working on it for some time or he'd had another reason to have the second phone. If we can just trace the phone, we'll have the answers to a lot of our questions."

Chapter 18

With a parcel wrapped in baby paper, carried under his arm, Alex bounded up the steps to Sandra's ward before charging in. His eyes were immediately drawn in the direction of his baby, fast asleep in her cot.

"Hello stranger," Sandra welcomed. "I didn't expect you back so soon. Much as I'm pleased you want to spend time with us, I suspect I'm not the main attraction."

"Again, you're proving your amazing detective skills. It's not hard to see why you won your promotion to Inspector," he said, a big grin covering his face. Alex leaned across to hug and kiss Sandra.

"What have you got there, who's the present from?"

"First I've got this to show you." Alex produced the birth certificate. "I called in at the registry office on the way over. Surprisingly, it wasn't queued out. Now, Siobhan McKinnon Warren is official and legal."

"Even though you're concerned about her not being legitimate," Sandra added with a smirk.

Alex's face fell, but only for a second seeing the mirth in Sandra's eyes.

"What about the package?"

"Oh yes. This is from Siobhan's daddy." Alex ripped off the paper to reveal a small, pink, teddy bear.

Sandra laughed. "I thought we agreed not to buy any toys until we'd seen what we were given. We've already received so much; we're going to run out of space."

"I know but this is so tiny and cute; I couldn't resist it. I didn't plan to buy it. I parked at the St Enoch Centre and when I was leaving, I saw it through the window in Boots. You can't deny me the right to spoil my girl."

"It's okay Alex, I think it's gorgeous. Mind you, it might get you into trouble with the P.C. brigade."

Alex looked confused. "What are you talking about?"

Sandra gave Alex a stern look. "Isn't it obvious? You've picked a pink toy for a baby girl. She's only a day old and already you're guilty of gender stereotyping. It's not politically correct. You're meant to let your children grow up without any kind of influence and let them make their own decision about what sex they want to be." Open mouthed, Alex's face was a picture of dismay, until Sandra couldn't continue the act and burst into peals of laughter, quickly joined by Alex.

"Okay, I fell for it. My brain's not as sharp as it should be; I must have sleep deprivation."

"I'm sorry. I wasn't thinking about your trauma last night. Have you heard any more about the break in?"

"No, nothing yet. I'd meant to call to ask if the investigation of the electrical company got anywhere, but I haven't had a chance yet. I still find it difficult to believe we left the flat and didn't lock up properly."

"Don't beat yourself up over it, Alex. It's happened, and we can't turn the clock back. I think I may have been the last one out anyway and, if so, it was my mistake."

"Well, you did have other things on you mind. It was my responsibility. But you're right, it's in the past. I should give myself a break."

"We must get a new telly. If it's any consolation, the old one was looking a bit beyond its sell by date," Sandra said.

"I've not had a chance yet, but I can borrow a small portable until I get it sorted out. Sanjay offered it to me; he said he kept it as a spare for his guest room and it was rarely needed."

"Have you made an insurance claim yet?"

"I phoned it in this morning. The cheeky bugger I spoke to said I'd need a police report," Alex said. "He failed to see the funny side when I told him that what I was making was a police report. I had to explain to him that I'm a DCI. You'd have thought they'd have realised, because our policy was taken out through the police federation block discount scheme."

"What did you expect? You were probably speaking to call centre ten thousand miles away," Sandra said.

"Yeah, anyway the good news is the cover provides new for old, so all I need to do is get receipts for the items we replace."

"I wonder if the new for old will apply to your special bottle of whisky. What was it, a twenty-five-year old?"

"You're not very funny," Alex replied.

"I don't see it that way," Sandra said, chuckling. "Changing the subject, Mum phoned this morning. She and Dad are coming to see me this afternoon."

"Yes, I know and it's almost visiting hour. I'll get away to leave you some time with them. I spoke to your Dad; he's coming across to the flat later to bring the cot. He's also bringing the baby seat and pushchair we stored at their house. He said he'd give me a hand building the cot. Everything should be set for you coming out tomorrow."

"That's great. I can't wait to get home. But for now, give me some mental stimulation," Sandra asked. "Tell me how your investigation is going."

Sandra remained silent while Alex updated her with the latest information.

"I know what Sanjay meant when he was talking about the DNA matching. Don't you remember, I did an update on my forensic training a short while back." Sandra considered the possibilities. "If Kevin was a good match, then the chances of anyone else, taken at random, being the father would be infinitesimally small. However, the probability would rise steeply for members of Kevin's family. A twin might have an equal chance, but any brother, father, uncle or even cousin could be a realistic possibility. Even more so if the family came from a close community, like the islands, where there might be lots of inbreeding. Maybe Kevin had a long, lost sibling who might have turned up unexpectedly?" Sandra joked.

"Thanks, You're right. I'll arrange to get samples from all the family," Alex said.

"You can cut your cost in half, if you only test the men." Sandra playfully punched his arm.

"Now look who's gender stereotyping? You're quite the joker today."

"It's because I'm happy, Alex, very happy."

Alex kissed Sandra again. "I'd better get going." He stood transfixed staring at his daughter for a few minutes and then waved as he left the ward.

Chapter 19

"I'm sorry, Sir, we screwed up," Sanjay greeted Alex's return.

"Kindly explain, what's gone wrong?" Alex asked.

"It was a new boy in Connor's team, Derek Francis is his name. One of the lads given the job to bag and tag, but he was the one who also compiled the inventory. He was diligent enough with what he did. The only problem was he didn't tell anyone about the important items."

"That can't be right. We were told about the photos and condoms and about the other items in the bedside drawer," Alex said.

"Yeah, for obvious reasons, they were immediately selected as being relevant. He was meant to talk through the whole list with a supervisor to identify what needed to be highlighted. Instead, he filed the report and didn't talk to anyone, or recognise the significance of anything else. From what I've heard, Connor given his arse a good kicking," Sanjay said.

"What was missed?"

"There were two identical sets of car keys in the bureau drawer, as well as a file in the cabinet which held all the papers. The car was registered under Keiran's name, but Kevin had been added to the insurance cover. Until now, we didn't know that Keiran owned a car. Connor is on to it now. They found it parked near to the flat and his people are giving it top priority. They're checking for prints and anything else. It's damnable, we've lost the best part of two days on it."

"How did you realise?"

"After you left this morning; I was compiling what we had ready for the meeting. I happened to scan the inventory. I'm sorry, I didn't look sooner."

"Better late than never. It was well spotted by you, Sanjay."

"Not good enough, though."

"I guess we had no reason to expect it - a young couple renting an expensive flat *and* owning a car."

"Yes, Sir. For the record, it's a five-year-old Fiat Punto. Judging from the purchase invoice, it seems Keiran's folks bought her it as an eighteenth birthday gift. We hadn't suspected," Sanjay said.

"We weren't to know."

"That's the thing," Sanjay confessed. "We should have suspected. The till receipt for the purchase of the pregnancy test was from ASDA, Toryglen. She's hardly likely to have travelled all the way there if she wasn't driving?"

Alex frowned. "You're right, one of us should have picked up on that. Okay, let's get the team together so we can discuss reports and then we'll all be singing from the same hymn sheet."

"An unfortunate turn of phrase, given the varying religious convictions of the McGowan and Sharma families."

"I've a couple of calls to make. Get everyone together and I'll join you in a few minutes."

* * *

Looking around the room, Alex was immediately conscious of an air of tension.

"What's going on?" he asked.

Nobody said a word.

"Sanjay, you've been in charge. What's wrong?"

"It's really nothing, Sir, just a little bit of aggro. It's over"

Alex looked in turn at each of their faces. Donny was scowling, and Mary had her fists tightly clenched.

"Okay out with it. Mary, what's your problem?"

"I'm sorry, Sir. I should have kept my mouth shut. It's just that he's been like a bear with a sore head for days."

"I want to make a complaint, Sir. It's blatant ageism. Her words were, *You're a grumpy old bastard. Isn't it time you retired?* She shouldn't be allowed to get away with it."

"I wasn't questioning his ability to work because of his age, Sir," Mary said. "It was because of his bloody-mindedness and his outdated attitudes and values."

"And what about you, Donny. Did you say anything to provoke her attack?"

"I may have, Sir. I might have said she was a *stupid wee lassie.*"

"This gives me a problem. We have the potential of two complaints, one for sexism and another for ageism. Unless we can resolve this, here and now, I might have to suspend the two of you while I get an independent officer to investigate. It could take weeks and we'd be up to our arses, no make that up to our elbows in paperwork. I can't see anyone coming out of it smelling of roses. In the meantime, we still have a case to investigate, or at least whichever of us are still in a job. Am I making myself clear?"

"Yes, Sir," both Mary and Donny answered.

"If I'm to run this department and get results, I need a team that can work together and respect each other's abilities. We don't always have to be best friends, but we do need to get on. Understood?"

"Yes, Sir."

"Are you both prepared to put this behind you, make up, shake hands and agree to work properly?"

"Yes, Sir." They shook hands, and each said, "Sorry."

"Okay, that's better. All of you, go and get some work done. We'll resume the meeting in about an hour; I've a few things to do first. Donny, give me five minutes, then come to my office." Alex disappeared to check his emails and correspondence.

Donny knocked his door. "Are you ready now?"

"Yes, come in, shut the door and sit down."

Donny looked apprehensive.

"Out with it."

"It's nothing, Sir."

"It's not nothing, Donny. I've known you for what, near enough twenty years now. You've always been a cantankerous old sod. But you're our cantankerous old sod, so we put up with you."

Donny gave a nervous laugh.

"It's true you can be awkward and opinionated, but basically you're a good cop with a sense of fairness. You've not ever turned on your workmates like that, before. So there has to be something."

"With respect, Sir. It's got nothing to do with you or anyone else. I'll deal with it."

"On the contrary. You haven't been dealing with it. If you had then we wouldn't be having this conversation. As it's affecting your work and your work relationships then it's everyone's business."

Donny hung his head. "I guess you're right. Can we keep this between us, for now at least? I don't want the others laughing at me."

"I'm certain no one would be laughing, but I agree, I won't say anything if you don't want me to."

Donny's breathing came in deep gasps as he considered how to begin. Alex sat patiently.

"My home's in turmoil. Cath and I had been getting ready for my retirement. We thought, now all the kids are grown and independent, everything would be great. We'd been planning to buy a cottage in the Highlands as a holiday house."

Alex nodded; Donny had often told him about his plans.

"We'd have been able to spoil the grandkids when we chose, and we could come and go as we pleased. Now it's all turned to shit."

Alex dreaded what was coming next, suspecting a health problem or a betrayal. He counted the seconds, waiting for Donny to continue.

"It's Ben, our eldest, he's back home."

Alex tried to remember what Donny had told him about Ben in previous conversations. From recollection, he was his pride and joy, married, two kids, two dogs, a cat and a high-flying, banking job in London.

"He found out his wife had been cheating. In fact, she told him, admitted it to him. She said she couldn't go on living a lie."

"What about the kids?"

"She said she wants to keep them and she needs the house so as not to unsettle them."

"He doesn't need to accept that."

"No, he doesn't. But it's not that unusual. Look at your own situation."

It jarred Alex to be reminded. After Helen's affair, he'd allowed her to keep the house to raise their boys. Alex had been working all hours while Helen stayed at home, so it had seemed the right thing to do. The situation appeared similar.

"Is there no hope of a reconciliation?"

"It doesn't look like it. She's moved her partner into the family home. Apparently, it has been going on for three years, behind his back and he didn't have a clue. She'd even been using the kids as a screen. She'd claimed to be taking them to their activities and then meeting her partner in secret."

"I'm sorry to say, it's all too common these days. Why are you so concerned about anyone else knowing?"

"That's the awful part. Her partner's another woman. She's kicked him out to move in her lesbian lover."

"It doesn't make any difference, Donny. A betrayal's a betrayal. Whether she's gone to a man or a woman, the issue hasn't changed. What about the kids; how are they handling it?"

"I can't honestly say. We haven't seen them since it happened. Ben's not taken it well though. He can't cope. It's as if he's lost the will to go on. He packed in his job and moved home. He just mopes around the house and hardly speaks."

"I guess all you can do is try to be supportive."

"I'd do anything I could to help him, but it doesn't make any difference. He needs to stand on his own two feet if he's to get a life back and I keep telling him. Cath, on the other hand, wants to mother him. She's trying to wrap him in cotton wool, thinking it'll stop him from hurting. I think that's the worst thing because he'll never get his life back if he doesn't face it."

"I see," Alex said.

"It's been causing rows. Cath thinks I'm being too hard, whereas I think she's not helping him. In the meantime, we're not seeing the other kids or grandkids and I feel our life is on hold. Cath won't even consider a weekend break to get away from it."

"Maybe, you need to take some time off, so you can try to sort things out at home."

"Christ no! The only respite I get is coming in to work. If I didn't have that, I might have a breakdown."

"That's only a help if you can leave it behind. It won't work for you or anyone else if you come in here like, as Mary put it, *a bear with a sore head.* I know you said you didn't want anyone else to know, but quite frankly I don't understand what you think you have to feel embarrassed about. A member of your family has a problem and you're trying to help, end of story."

Donny stood and shook Alex's hand. "Thank you for being so understanding, Sir. I think it's helped me to talk. I've been bottling this up for the last two weeks and felt there was no-one I could say anything to. I couldn't talk to Cath, and our other kids know nothing about it. She wants no-one to know because she thinks everything will go back to the way it was."

"I reckon you're right that she needs to face reality. Digging your head in the sand isn't going to do any good. Maybe talking to your doctor or a councillor would help."

"It may be worth a try. We're both due a routine check-up. Perhaps I'll say something to our G.P. It can't do any harm.

* * *

Sanjay, a word please, before the meeting starts."

"Yes, Sir."

"I'm concerned about this incident with Donny and Mary. There was a developing problem and I walked into the middle of it."

"I know; it just seemed to spark off from nothing. It took me by surprise."

"That's my point. These things do happen from time to time, fortunately not too often. You need to know how to handle them and nip it in the bud. If you're going to have any chance of progression in this job, you need to work on your leadership skills."

"Yes, Sir. As it happens, there's a training course next month on staff management. I wanted to ask you if I can attend."

"I don't see why not. But bear in mind, there's more to management than what you read in a textbook or learn on a course. An awful lot of it comes down to basic common sense."

Chapter 20

The meeting resumed and Phil and Donny, followed by Mary and Steve, provided details of their interviews and Sanjay advised of the latest technical reports.

"We wasted half an hour looking for this Doctor Cartwright fellow, only to find he wasn't on duty this morning," Steve said. "No point in following up, now, since the DNA report puts him in the clear."

Alex frowned. "Whoa, hold on there, you're jumping the gun a bit. Because the DNA result indicates a likely match to Kevin, it doesn't disqualify anyone else until we've checked that their result is negative." Alex remembered Sandra's quip about the possibility of a long-lost sibling. "Besides, the only thing being matched was the likelihood of fathering Keiran's baby. If Cartwright did have a relationship, then there's potential for a motive, either from him of from Kevin finding out. Did you get his home address?"

"Yes, Sir," Mary said. "He might be asleep just now. I found out he's working nights."

"Good. When this meeting's finished, your first task is to get over there and see if he's got a good story to tell us."

"Talking about stories," Sanjay said. "We need to examine Kevin's a lot closer. We'd all considered his grief appeared genuine. With his brother telling us that Kevin and Keiran met at a drama group, we know he's at least had some practice in acting. We can't take anything for granted."

"It was good he agreed to a medical examination," Donny said.

"It suggests he's either got nothing to hide or he's confident it's too well hidden for us to find," Phil replied.

"Once he's finished with the doc, we'll be able to go through everything with him again. We can take his story apart to see if anything doesn't fit," Sanjay said.

"Has anyone spoken to the sister yet? Jamilla, wasn't it?" Alex asked. "I mean without the parents present. It's not unlikely Keiran may have confided in her, things she didn't tell anyone else. She's probably the best one to tell us what other friends Keiran had, too. We need to speak to everyone she was close to," Alex said.

Nobody responded.

"Mary, I'd like you to lead on that as well. At risk of sounding sexist, I think she'll more likely open-up to another woman. Once you've finished with Cartwright, drop Steve back here. We'll arrange for a W.P.C. to go with you."

"Still no joy from Fitzpatrick but we've traced most of the phone numbers on Keiran's log," Sanjay announced. "Most of the calls and texts were to her sister or her mates from university and one or two old school chums. There's nothing remarkable except for one."

All eyes turned in anticipation.

"One number which appeared quite regularly," Sanjay started but his flow was interrupted by the ringtone of Alex's mobile.

"Hold on a second, I need to take this." Checking the screen, Alex had spotted Sandra's name. He walked to the door to afford himself some privacy.

"Alex, I know you're in a meeting. I didn't mean to disturb you. I'd planned to leave a message."

"You've got me now. What is it, Love?"

"It was only to say, don't panic getting everything ready for us coming home. There's going to be a slight delay."

Alex's face paled. "What's wrong? Is Siobhan okay?"

"Calm down, your golden girl is fine. It's me who's not. Don't worry, it's nothing serious. I've got a mild urinary infection and it's given me a temperature. The doc saw me just after Mum and Dad left. He's probably being overcautious, but he wants to keep me in for an extra day or two to be on the safe side."

It was only when Alex loudly exhaled, he realised he'd been holding his breath. "I'm sorry, Pet. I know how keen you were to get home. But I guess he's right; we want to be sure that you're fit and well. Are you still okay for the boys to visit you tonight?"

"Yeah, yeah, no problem. I'm looking forward to seeing them and showing off our little bundle. Anyway, you'd better get back to your meeting. I'll see you soon."

Returning to his chair, Alex slipped his mobile back into his pocket. "Where were we?"

"Is everything okay, Boss?" Phil asked, noting the change in Alex's demeanour.

"Nothing to worry about," Alex's response was dismissive. "Now let's get back on stream."

"I was just saying, one number appeared quite regularly -it's been traced to the uncle, Ibrahim."

"What's all that about?" Donny questioned. "I thought He was the radical who wanted Keiran banished from the family. What was she doing talking to him?"

"I think it's time we brought him in for a chat. First get clearance from Special Branch, then pick him up," Alex instructed.

Chapter 21

With everyone assigned their respective tasks before the meeting broke up, Alex picked up his phone to call P.C. Black. "Hi Stuart, Alex Warren, here. I'm calling to ask if you've made any progress."

With Alex not quoting his rank, yet speaking in familiar terms, it took Black a moment to recognise who he was talking to and the meaning of the question. "Sorry, Sir. I should have got back to you, but we've been run off our feet."

"Same story everywhere. Is it a yes or a no?"

"Well, Sir, there is some progress, but we haven't got too far yet. I told my Sergeant about our suspicions with the flyer from the electrical repair company. He said he'd let me run with it, in between my other duties. He said not to approach the company yet, but instead make some more background enquiries."

"Makes sense," Alex replied.

"Anyhow, I think it may have paid off. I've listed other break-ins and the like within a couple of miles radius in the last two months. I've concentrated on ones where electrical goods were taken and I've asked a few questions of victims and neighbours. So far, I've only been able to check six, but in three of the cases, someone has a recollection of receiving a flyer around the time of the theft."

"Too much of a coincidence."

"Yes, Sir. That's what I thought. My Sergeant agreed and he's arranging a search warrant, so we can check out the store. Would you like me to tell you when we're going in?"

"Yeah, I'd kind of like to be there, but chances are I won't be available. I'd appreciate if you could keep me informed."

"Will do, Sir."

Alex wore a broad smile as he hung up the phone. "The daft boy might actually come good," he muttered under his breath.

"Did you say something, Sir?" Sanjay asked, while gathering up his papers.

"No, it's okay. I'm just thinking aloud. Thanks again for lending me the telly. I'm heading off now to meet Sandra's Dad."

* * *

Alex drew to a halt outside his flat only moments before the Volvo S80.

"Hello Mr McKinnon. Good timing. Let me give you a hand unloading. Thanks for offering to help me put the cot together. I'm not very skilled when it comes to that sort of thing."

"Let's get a few things straight, Alex. First, I think it's beyond the point you need to call me Mr McKinnon. *Dad* might be a bit too familiar, so how about Jimmy and of course the Missus is Angie."

"Right-o, Jimmy it is."

"Next, even if you were a DIY specialist, I'd still want to be the one putting this cot together. It's a family heirloom so it means a lot to me."

"I didn't realise."

"Yes, Angie and I bought it new for our Alice. It served her well and for Ricky too, before Sandra was born. With Alice going down south after she married, her little-uns never got the chance, but Ricky's did. I know Sandra wanted to buy everything new, but this is special. Right, grab an end and we'll get it upstairs."

"Yes, Sir, I understand, sorry, I mean Jimmy."

Within ten minutes, the cot had been assembled and the new pushchair unwrapped.

"All ready for use tomorrow, when they get home."

"What, did Sandra not call you? she won't be out for another day or so."

Jimmy was aghast. "Why didn't you tell me?"

"I assumed you already knew. You were up seeing her this afternoon. Now that I think about it, she didn't call me until after you'd left. I'm sorry."

"Never mind all that; what's wrong? Why aren't they coming home as planned?"

"Relax, it's nothing serious. Sandra's temperature is a little bit raised and the hospital are being extra careful. They want to keep an eye on her for a bit longer. I'm taking my boys to see her in a couple of hours, so you can rest assured I'll make certain she's okay."

"You speaking about your boys, reminds me there's something I need to talk to you about. I know Sandra didn't want me interfering, but all the same, she is my daughter."

"Alex tensed, "What is it, Jimmy?"

Although Jimmy stood erect, being eight inches shorter in height, he had to lean his head backwards to directly look at Alex. "I'm not happy about my granddaughter not having a father."

"What are you talking about? I'm her father."

"You know what I mean. It's not right; she doesn't have her father married to her mother."

"Now just a minute, Jimmy. She's no less my daughter. It's my name on her birth certificate. She's Siobhan McKinnon Warren." Alex gasped in a breath, ready to make further protestations. Then realising the ridiculousness of the situation, he broke into a laugh.

"What's so funny?" Jimmy's tone was angry.

"Nothing's funny, nothing at all. I realised I was about to start giving you all the arguments that Sandra's been giving me. The strange thing is I was doing it to support her when I don't believe any of it myself."

Jimmy looked confused, "What are you on about?"

"I want to marry Sandra; she's the one who won't have me. Well, maybe that's not fair. We do live together like husband and wife. I've asked her to marry me - not once, many times. She says she can't see it makes any difference and I've been unable to convince her otherwise."

"She said the same to me, but I didn't believe her. I thought she was only trying to protect you because you wouldn't commit."

"I can assure you that isn't true, Jimmy. We're both fighting on the same side. That is, if you'd accept me as your son-in-law."

Jimmy's expression was rueful. "I guess I wouldn't have a choice. All we need to do is convince Sandra to change her mind."

* * *

As usual, Alex received the warmest welcome from the dog. Jake's tale rotated with enthusiasm and he yelped intermittently until Alex had knelt, cradled his head and rubbed behind his ears. Although he'd arrived a full fifteen minutes early, Craig and Andrew were ready and waiting, each with their coats on and carrying a gift bag. He wasn't unhappy to discover Helen was nowhere to be seen, but he was surprised to find Jenny accompanying them. Jenny had been Craig's steady girlfriend for over two years.

"You don't mind if I come too, do you Alex?"

Alex cringed a little. Much as he liked the girl and knew she and Craig were good for each other, he felt uncomfortable with her use of his forename. He knew no disrespect had been intended but marvelled how the younger generation were so much more at ease addressing their elders in familiar terms. Even as an adult, and a high-ranking police officer, he found it difficult to call Sandra's father by his first name, and that was even after Jimmy had invited him.

"It's not that I mind, but the ward rules state only two visitors are permitted per patient, at a time. You might go all the way there and not get to see them."

"I'll take the chance if you don't mind. I've never seen a wee baby so young. I want to study nursing and train as a midwife so it's really important for me. And I've brought a pressie for the wee one."

"Please, Dad," Craig added. "I could stand outside for a little while, just so she gets a chance."

"Okay, okay, we'll give it a try, but I'm not making any promises. We've a while yet before visiting starts, so I thought we could pop into my flat, so I could show you my artistic talents – I redecorated the second bedroom as a nursery. I only finished it at the weekend."

"Yes, great, let's have a look," Craig replied. Jenny, too sounded keen, but Andrew's silence was ominous.

Some minutes later, they parked. Alex led the way; only a short walk and a brisk climb to the first floor. He unlocked then held the door wide, ushering the youngsters in and pointing towards the second bedroom.

"Aw, that's really cute. Was Peppa Pig your idea?" Jenny enthused.

"No, it was Sandra's choice. I did the papering though. Sandra helped of course; she pasted, and I hung the paper." Alex chuckled remembering the experience. "She hardly needed to use a pasting table. With the size of bump she was carrying, she could barely reach the table and I reckon she got more paste on herself than on the paper."

"I guess that means Siobhan contributed to the job as well," Craig said.

"What a great cot," Jenny said, "and you've got it all made up and ready. I love the balloon mobile."

"We've got Sandra's dad to thank for it. He brought it over this afternoon and put it together."

"What happened to the telly and the games console," Andrew asked, deep concern showing in his voice.

"Did I not tell you about it? We were robbed. It happened yesterday after I'd taken Sandra to the hospital."

"Do you know who did it?" Craig asked.

"Nothing certain, but we have our suspicions. I've got someone working on it. In any event, we're unlikely to see any of our stuff again."

"Was much taken?" Jenny asked.

"Just the usual, easy to resell stuff: telly, tablets, cash, PlayStation, some games and my prize bottle of whisky."

"What, they got my games." Andrew sounded shocked.

"Yes, amongst the other things."

"But they were important to me. My special edition of Destinty2 was there. I left it here the last time I stayed over. I remember buying it the day it came out. I'd queued up for hours." Andrew's eyes were filling.

"Don't worry son, we're insured. We'll be able to replace everything that was lost. You make a list of anything you had that's not still here."

"It's not the same," Andrew turned away, clearly upset.

Alex wrapped an arm around Andrew's shoulder and led him into the kitchen and sat him at the table. "What's all this about? You've not been yourself all day."

Andrew's shoulders heaved, and he sniffed to contain a sob, before starting, "You don't want us anymore. You've got your new family and we don't matter."

"Don't be ridiculous. Of course you matter. You're just being plain silly. How could you possibly think that?"

"It's obvious. You've got Sandra and now there's the baby. You've turned my room into a nursery and got rid of my stuff. I know you don't want me. It's not so bad for Craig; at least he has Jenny and Mum's got a new boyfriend. But I'm all alone."

Alex's reflex reaction was to laugh thinking it a joke, but within a second, he choked back any sound. He was overcome by sadness at his son's plight. He wrapped his arms around him and hugged him in close. "I'm so sorry, Andrew. The last thing in the world I wanted was to upset you. I love you dearly and no less now than ever before. You're always welcome here and I know Sandra feels the same way."

Andrew pulled back. You're just saying that."

"No, I'm not. You are welcome here, and you're welcome to stay anytime. I didn't think. I should have spoken to you before I redecorated your room. Yes, it is still your room, for you and Craig to stay over anytime you like. But it will be Siobhan's room too, once she's old enough. To start with, her cot will be in the same room as Sandra and me. Please believe me."

Andrew sniffed deeply. Alex handed him a tissue and he smacked tears away from his cheeks and then blew his nose.

Alex knew he'd badly miscalculated. Nearly sixteen, his son was now in his late teens. He hadn't anticipated that he would feel threatened and insecure by the new arrival and he hadn't prepared him. Worse still by turning the bedroom into a nursery, he'd manifested the boy's worst fears. "As for your stuff. It wasn't my fault. Someone broke in and robbed us. But I promise you that everything will be replaced by the same or better."

Andrew nodded, his face bleak.

"As for the wallpaper, I can change it back. I don't suppose Peppa Pig is good for the street cred of a young man."

Andrew smiled weakly. "It's okay, Dad. It's done now. It's not very often I stay over, only once or twice a month, and Siobhan will be here all the time. I can live with it, I suppose."

Alex could feel his own eyes a bit watery. He felt heart sorry for the upset he'd caused. "It won't be for long, anyway. Sandra and I are planning to look for a bigger place, somewhere with an extra bedroom. When we do get it, I promise, I'll let you choose the décor of your room." Then after thinking for a second, he added, "Well within reason. Listen, why didn't you say anything to me before? I could have reassured you. Did you not discuss it with Craig or anyone?"

"I talked to Mum."

"And what did she say?"

"Not a lot. She did say you still loved me and Craig, but she said you had so much more to think about, what with work and Sandra and a new baby."

"Bitch!" Alex swallowed the outburst, not wanting to upset his son further. He realised Helen was playing games, feeding their son's apprehension rather than reassuring him.

Chapter 22

"This is how the other half live." With undisguised envy, Steve eyed the ornate decoration inside the building's lobby.

"I don't know about half, I reckon it must be down as low as the top one or two percent who can afford this sort of luxury," Mary replied.

They showed their warrant cards to the concierge and stated their business. "I'll call up for you and let Dr Cartwright know you're here," he offered.

"No, please don't. We'd rather introduce ourselves," Steve replied.

They found the entrance to Cartwright's apartment immediately facing the lift and Steve gave a sharp knock. Only after a third attempt did they hear the noise of scuffling and a voice called to ask who it was.

"Dr Cartwright, it's the police, DC Fleming and WDC McKenzie. We've some questions we'd like to ask you."

They could hear a bolt being jerked aside and a key turning. Cartwright looked them over, then invited them in. He appeared sleepy with heavy eyelids and ruffled hair. He was wearing a fleece dressing gown, it's belt tightly tied round his waste. His chest and legs were bare and, other than slippers, appeared to be wearing nothing else. Besides his attire, or lack of it, and apparent tiredness, Cartwright looked as if he'd walked off a film set. Blonde, blue-eyed, handsome, muscular and bronzed. Mary wondered how someone could look so attractive having freshly woken.

"You'd better come in; take a seat," he showed them towards a spacious open plan lounge/kitchen.

"We're sorry to have disturbed you, Sir, but we're carrying out a very important inquiry, and we believe you may have some useful information," Steve apologised. "Can we please ask you some questions?"

"Oh, you weren't really disturbing me, I was working all night and hadn't intended to sleep for more than another three hours." Cartwright's manner was offhand and arrogant. He looked towards Mary. "I'm back on duty at my ward this evening. But it's always a pleasure to help our local constabulary, particularly when they come in the form of attractive young ladies."

Mary felt unhappy knowing she was coming under scrutiny and aware Cartwright's gaze was lingering over her figure. Perhaps her earlier opinion of Shirley had been unjust. The assessment she'd given of Cartwright may have been more accurate than she'd imagined possible.

"Anyhow, what's this all about? There can't have been a complaint, can there? It's becoming a real problem when patients self-diagnose before seeing a doctor. Then, when they don't get the treatment they've read about on the net, they try to cause problems."

"No, Sir, nothing like that. We understand that you know Keiran Sharma, she works in the hospital pharmacy," Steve said.

"I sure do. She's one good looking girl. What's she done?"

Mary was uncomfortable with his glib attitude and she had no wish to protect any sensitivity he may have. "If you must know, she's gone and got herself killed."

"What?"

"I said, she's dead. You must understand dead. You're a doctor." Steve tapped Mary's arm to get her attention and shook his head in a message for her to back off."

"My God, what happened? Was it suicide or maybe drugs?" Cartwright collapsed back in a chair, his previous composure lost, completely stunned.

"Why would you think that?" Steve asked.

"I've no reason to think it of her." Cartwright's voice was unsteady. "It's only when someone so young and healthy dies, there has to be a cause. It's a matter of statistics. I see it all the time in A&E."

"At this point, there's no reason to suggest suicide or drugs were involved," Mary said. "However, the circumstances are suspicious. We're investigating…"

"You can't mean…" Cartwright was unable to complete his sentence.

"She was found dead in her flat on Monday evening," Steve continued.

"Do you know what happened?"

"We're still investigating. Now, if you'll please let us ask the questions, we'll get through this a lot quicker," Steve said.

"Yes, of course, officer." The colour had drained from Cartwright's face.

"We understand that you knew her quite well," Steve started.

"Not really. I saw her in work quite often, but that was about it."

"We've been led to believe you may have had a relationship."

"That's simply not true," Cartwright spluttered. "Yes, I liked the girl. She was pretty and very sexy, but nothing ever happened between us."

"Perhaps you wanted it to," Mary interrupted.

"What? No, well yes. Oh, I don't know. I was certainly attracted to her. She was intelligent and fun. We had this sort of rapport."

"You're telling us, it was only ever talk?" Mary asked.

"Yes, yes. We used to joke about a bit, but that was all."

"Joking as in fooling about?" Mary pursued.

"Fooling about with words, yes. There was nothing else."

"Now what if we told you, we have a witness statement telling us she was seen getting out of your car, in the middle of the day, in, how shall I say, not her normal state of dress."

"How do you know about that?" Cartwright's paled even further. "I promised not to say."

"So, you've been lying to us," Mary accused.

"No, not at all. I promised Keiran that I'd keep her secret."

"Keiran's dead. Any promise you made is null and void. What happened between you?" Mary asked.

"No, it's not what you think. I never touched her. Well, not the way you mean."

"In that case, how?" Mary demanded.

"She asked me to examine her. Medically, I mean."

"Why would she do that?"

"She knew that I was planning to specialise in plastics and she wanted my advice. She had a problem she wanted to know what I thought."

"What sort of problem?" Mary asked.

"She had a birth mark. It had been bothering her for a long time."

"I don't understand. Why would she come to you?" Mary pursued.

"Her mother is a doctor and told her to ignore it. She said it wouldn't do her any harm and would fade over time. Keiran wasn't happy with that." Cartwright paused, thinking how best to express himself. "She felt she wasn't able to speak about it to her own G.P. because she's a friend of her mother's. She wanted independent advice that wouldn't go on record. She wanted it from someone who wouldn't tell her mother and even more importantly, someone her mother couldn't influence."

"I see," Mary replied, now with marginally less antagonism.

"Her mark was rather large. It's what we call a Mongolian blue spot. In Keiran's case it was more than eight centimetres in diameter and it was located on her right buttock, her inner buttock to be more precise. She said it was very embarrassing for her."

"It's a rather intimate area," Steve said.

"Yes, you could say that. The sort of mark and the position isn't unusual, particularly for Asian people. I didn't want to get involved. I told her that I could give general advice without examining her. Keiran insisted it would be meaningless without me having a proper look so I could, at least, advise her what to do."

"You said earlier that you thought of her as beautiful and sexy," Mary said, "You'd hardly be likely to turn down the opportunity to give her an intimate examination in private."

"It wasn't like that. She insisted. But you're right, I'd be a liar if I claimed I protested too much."

"So, what happened?" Steve asked.

We met one lunchtime and I drove her to a secluded area I knew so I could examine her."

"And this took place inside your car," Mary said.

"Yes, it was really awkward. I drive an MX5 so there wasn't a lot of space for her to strip, so I could examine her properly."

"It doesn't sound too proper to me," Mary said. "You claim all you did was look."

"Yes, absolutely. Well I did touch the affected skin but only to confirm the earlier diagnosis. There was nothing unprofessional about it."

"What was your advice?" Mary asked.

"That's what upset her. Very often the marks disappear by themselves as a child gets older, but this hadn't happened in Keiran's case. I told her that I thought her mother had been correct. It was harmless, and she should try to ignore it." Cartwright let out a sob, "She wasn't happy and claimed she wanted it to be removed. She wanted me to do surgery or laser treatment. I told her it was wrong to undergo unnecessary treatment, and in any event, I wasn't trained to do it. After I drove her back, she stormed off and I hardly saw her again."

Can you tell us where you were on Monday afternoon?" Mary asked.

"Yes, I was working. I started at 2pm and was there half the night. You can check the A&E records of you like."

"And would you mind giving us a DNA sample?" Mary asked.

"Why on earth would you want that? I've got nothing to do with this. What are you trying to show?"

"If you've got nothing to hide then why should you object?" Mary said.

Cartwright relented. "You're wasting your time and your resources, but okay, I'll do it. I don't see how it's going to help you solve what's happened."

Chapter 23

"We've had Ibrahim brought in; he's been sitting alone, stewing in an interview room for the last forty minutes. Do you want to carry it out yourself?" Phil asked.

"No, I think I'll sit this one out. You did well last time and I don't want to give him any distractions. I'll observe from the outside and I'll pass you a message, if need be," Sanjay replied.

"Donny can come in with me then. He's been warned to be on his best behaviour."

"Have you covered all the formalities. Ibrahim's just the one to claim procedure wasn't followed if we leave him any loophole," Sanjay warned.

"It's okay. Everything's been done by the book. He's on record as turning down the opportunity to have a lawyer present."

"Don't let that lure you into a false sense of security. I'm certain he'll know his rights down to the last detail. Before you start, there's one other thing you may find of interest. The forensic examination of Keiran's car found Ibrahim's prints on the dashboard at the passenger side. See how you can use that. Right, if you're ready, let's go."

Phil and Donny stepped into the room and sat opposite Ibrahim. Donny started the recorder and stated the preliminaries.

"Ah, you've found time in your busy day to talk to me," Ibrahim's sickly-sweet tone was laced with sarcasm. "I've no pressing engagements, so your mind games won't work on me."

Despite his words, Ibrahim looked tense and Phil regarded his show of bravado was more to calm his own nerves than to convince anyone else. Intending to utilise any weakness, Phil sat appraising him in an uncomfortable silence for a bit longer, before commencing.

Using the same low tone, and speaking slowly in the manner he'd seen Alex use to great effect, Phil started, "You haven't been very forthcoming, have you?"

"What are you talking about?"

"You weren't honest with us the last time we spoke."

"Completely untrue. You asked me questions and I gave you answers."

"You withheld information."

Ibrahim gave a nervous shrug. "How should I know what you want to find out, if you don't ask me. I didn't lie, and I didn't withhold information."

"You gave us the impression that you hadn't spoken to your niece for some time."

"I didn't say that. You can't hold me responsible for wrong assumptions that you've made. You profess to be doing an important job. Take responsibility for your own failings." Ibrahim's lips spread, revealing a mouthful of misshaped and decaying teeth, formed into a hideous smile. "And where's the brown man, today? The one who's meant to be your boss and says he's a Moslem. Is he in hiding; could he not face me again. Did he not want to hear more about how things really are?"

Fearing Donny might be goaded into losing his temper and saying something unacceptable, or even hitting the man, Phil placed a restraining hand on his arm. To his surprise, instead, Donny broke into a broad grin and said, "You're free to think what you want." Phil waited, expecting him to complete the statement with something awful, but was relieved when he didn't. "We're not here to discuss your misguided views on our systems. We brought you in to tell us more about your niece."

"What makes you think I have anything to say, you want to hear?"

"It's not for you to make assumptions about what we want to hear. For starters, we'd like you to tell us about all communication you had with her. We want to know when you spoke to her, or met her, and we want to know what you discussed."

"Why do you think I spoke to her or met her?"

"If you don't mind, we'll ask the questions. Even if you do mind, we'll still be the ones asking the questions. We don't have to tell you about our source of information. Now, please answer what we asked."

"I don't know that I need to tell you anything. Maybe, I should speak to a lawyer."

Phil nodded to Donny, indicating he wanted to take over. "We have on record that you turned down your right to have a lawyer present. If you're saying you've changed your mind and you want one now, then it can be arranged. But, with or without a lawyer, you will answer our questions. If not, we can have you charged with obstructing the police in the course of their enquiries."

Ibrahim smiled again. "That shall not be necessary. I spoke to my niece once every week; either she'd phone me, or I'd phone her."

"What did you talk about?"

"This and that, family matters."

"What in particular?"

"I would talk to her about our family and its history; she wanted to know about where she came from. I would also tell her how she could be saved."

"Did she want to be saved, as you put it?"

"No, she would tell me she was happy as she was."

"But this wasn't a single occasion. There were many calls."

"Yes, and each time it would be the same. We would chat, and I would offer to help her, and she would decline. Sometimes she would call me. I believed in time she would come to her senses. I'm sure she would have. I wanted her to know there was a way back, if only she returned to her faith."

"Her father gave us the impression you would not accept her into the family."

"You're not wrong, but you don't understand. For as long as she lived with that, … that infidel, she could not be part of our family and she couldn't be welcomed into any of our homes."

"You thought her parents were wrong in how they brought her up."

"Of course. If they'd taught her proper values, there would not have been a problem. But I knew she was a smart girl and she could change. And when she did, I would have been there to help her."

"Tell us about Monday?"

"I told you before; I was at a meeting in the mosque."

"What about the morning?"

Ibrahim was hesitant. "I went shopping. Why does it matter?"

"And where did you shop?"

His eyebrows furrowed. "It was ASDA."

"And who might you have happened to see?"

"How do you know?"

"As we said before, we'll ask the questions. Now tell us what happened."

"It seems you know already," Ibrahim said, hoping it would suffice. Instead, Phil and Donny remained silent, awaiting a proper response.

"It wasn't planned. I didn't expect her to be there. On a Monday, at that time, she'd normally be at work. … We bumped into each other in one of the aisles. I didn't want anyone to see us talking. Although I had hope for her, for as long as she was living with *him,* she was not part of our family."

"But you did talk."

"Yes. I asked her to drive me home, so we could speak without being seen."

"You saw what she was buying?"

"She had her shopping," Ibrahim was nervous,

"It wasn't only groceries."

"How can you possibly know?"

"We have our ways," Phil answered. "You were angry." Phil played his hunch.

"Of course, I was angry. How could she be so stupid. I needed to speak to her and not where we could be overheard. I told her she would drive me home."

"Told her? And she agreed?"

"She wasn't happy, having been caught, with me seeing what she had. But yes, she agreed."

"You fought in the car."

"I wouldn't call it a fight. I told her I'd seen the pregnancy test and she was ruining her life."

"I don't understand. You knew she was living with Kevin. You must have realised they were in a relationship. There would always be the chance of her becoming pregnant."

"It was bad, really bad, she was living with *that* boy. But she could have been saved if she'd come to her senses. We could have sent her away. We could have found her a good man, who would marry her." Ibrahim stopped and wiped his brow. "But for her to have a child with the boy. That would be the end. There could be no turning back."

"You told her this."

Ibrahim looked at the floor; he could not answer.

"Did you tell her to have an abortion?"

"No, no. The Qur'an tells us to believe in the sanctity of life. An abortion would have been unacceptable."

"Aren't we getting ahead of ourselves?" Donny questioned. "You know she had purchased the test, but that, in itself, didn't mean she was pregnant."

Ibrahim gave him a withering look. "I knew. I knew the girl. I could tell from looking at her."

"When we last spoke, you said," Phil checked his notes, '*She gave up her right to be part of our family. Whatever happened afterwards is of no concern to us*'. I don't see that as being consistent with you wanting to save her."

"You're playing with words. Yesterday, I was angry. I didn't mean what I said."

"And were you not angry on Monday, too?"

"I have nothing further to say. I want to leave. Are you going to charge me or am I free to go?"

Chapter 24

"I'm glad you're back, I think we're ready to talk to McGowan now," Sanjay said.

"Have you heard how his medical exam went?" Steve asked.

"The tests results will take some time, but we know his back and arms have scratches. Some are quite deep and ragged. They might well be from fingernails."

"Did he get them from being fought off, or was it the result of frenzied passion?"

"Your guess is as good as mine," Sanjay replied. "We need to handle this carefully. Although we don't want to be considered callous in our treatment of him, we can't lose sight that he could be a practiced actor. We need to view any emotional reactions with some scepticism."

Okay, I'm ready to go," Steve said.

"One more thing. Fitzpatrick's given us a sighting. It's not too clear, but it might be McGowan walking along Minard Road in the direction of his flat. It's timed at half past five on Monday afternoon, which is an hour earlier than he claimed and would put him right in the frame."

"This could be the break we've been looking for. Why aren't you more enthusiastic?"

"I don't know if it helps. It may not be him. If it was McGowan returning from work, he'd have been dressed in his grey suit. The guy in the picture is different. The jacket's too dark."

"Could it be his leather jacket? Maybe, he had it on over his suit or perhaps he changed."

"I don't know. Fitzpatrick's trying to marry up any other sightings to see where he came from. Hopefully he'll get a better image and then we can either rule it out or confirm his whereabouts. Now, let's get started."

Although less than two days had elapsed since they'd last seen him, Kevin had aged. His complexion was sallow, and he had dark rings surrounding his eyes. Dressed casually, his clothes hung limply to his frame. They doubted he'd eaten anything nutritious since they'd last spoken.

"Please sit down. Can we get you something? A tea or a coffee?" Sanjay asked, while Steve handled the formalities.

A tray of teas was produced together with a plate of digestive biscuits.

"Before we start with questions, I'd like to ask you for the names of Keiran's friends, people she was close to, or those she spoke with on a regular basis."

"I'll try. She didn't socialise a lot, but I know some of her friends from Uni. I'd only be guessing as to when they last met or even spoke. There are other names I've heard her mention whom I've haven't met. There was an Alysha something or other, but, other than her sister, and a woman, Shirley something, I think, she talked about at work I'm not aware of anyone she saw."

Steve took careful note of everyone Kevin could think of.

"You haven't listed any boys, or men?" Sanjay queried.

"There weren't any that I'm aware of, other than friends we both had at Uni."

"Right. Let's press ahead. We'd like to go through everything from the start."

Kevin sat forward at the interview table, his elbows positioned at right angles to the surface and he lifted the tea mug and clutched it in both hands. He wasn't drinking, instead trying to draw warmth and sustenance from sense of touch. His face was pointed downwards, unable or unwilling to meet their inspection.

"Let's start with how you met Keiran," Sanjay said.

Kevin raised his head, uplifted by the memory. "We were both in the university drama club. I think I was in second year when I first saw her. I thought she was adorable, but she didn't know I existed." Kevin's lips formed an ironic smile. "For months, I'd admire her from afar, but we hardly spoke. I desperately wanted to ask her out, but I didn't know what to say. I was frightened she'd reject me."

"But that changed," Sanjay encouraged.

"Not at first. It wasn't until the following year. We were rehearsing a new show, and, to my amazement, I was given one of the leading roles. It wasn't a big production or anything. It was a new play, written by the company's director. There were some scenes, near the end, where I played opposite Keiran and, because we had to rehearse together, we got to know each other a lot better."

"You asked her out then?" Sanjay asked.

"No, I didn't dare. I was happy being able to spend some time with her and I didn't want to spoil anything."

"So how did it change?" Steve asked.

"It was Keiran. She took the initiative."

"She asked you out." Sanjay said.

"No, not exactly. It happened during the final performance of the play."

"What happened?" Steve asked, now quite intrigued.

"There was a scene, very near to the end. Keiran's character was meant to be leaving to catch a train. Before going away, she had to say goodbye and kiss me on the cheek. For the weeks we'd been rehearsing I'd loved that scene, because it brought us close."

"This time was different." Steve said.

"It certainly was. She didn't kiss my cheek. Instead, at the last moment, she turned and kissed me on the lips. No ordinary kiss either. Her tongue explored my mouth. It must only have lasted a couple of seconds, but I was frozen in time. I couldn't believe it was real."

"And"

"She turned away and left the stage as was scripted, and I stood there like an idiot, transfixed. Hardly anyone realised what had happened; all they saw was me standing, as if I'd forgotten my lines. Well, at that point, I had, I suppose."

"What did you do next?" Steve asked."

"I was fed my final lines and the show finished quickly. It must have come across as very awkward and amateurish. The director was livid. You won't be surprised to hear that my acting career didn't go anywhere." Kevin chuckled.

"That's not what I meant. What happened with Keiran?" Steve asked.

"After the show was finished, I went looking for her. I needed to know what it was all about. I thought, maybe I'd imagined the whole episode or at least had an exaggerated recollection. |I needed to know; I had to find her, to ask her why it had happened. Eventually, I caught up with her; it was hours later, in the bar of the student union."

"And?"

"She tried to avoid me at first, but I cornered her and asked why she had done it. She laughed and said it had been a dare. When she laughed, I thought she was making fun of me. I was so riled, I thought I might have slapped her. Then I saw that beautiful smiling face. I had to kiss her. I returned the kiss she'd given me."

"What did she do?"

"She responded to my kiss and, as they say, the rest is history. We went for a drink together; we became a couple, we became inseparable."

"Did you ever discover who made the dare?" Sanjay asked.

"I'm not sure. She said it was one of her friends from the drama group. But it was irrelevant, Keiran could be quite daring on her own."

"What do you mean by that?" Sanjay asked.

"She could be quite adventurous, always challenging us to try new things."

"What sort of things?" Sanjay asked.

"Anything and everything. We did a parachute jump, for instance. We tried all sorts of unusual foods."

"What about sexually? You should know that we've seen the photos from your bottom drawer."

Kevin's face flushed. "But that's private, you've no right."

"We've every right," Sanjay replied. "This is a murder investigation, so nothing is private. The photos show that you were, let's say, sexually liberated. Whose idea was it?"

Kevin hung his head. "We both agreed and we'd both make suggestions, but it was Keiran who started it. Sometimes we'd watch videos and see things we'd want to try."

"And did this involve other people?" Sanjay probed.

"I don't see what you're getting at."

"Was she sexually promiscuous. Did she or you have other partners?"

"No! Absolutely not. We were loyal and faithful to each other." Kevin paused for a moment. "You're asking about the pregnancy. I still can't believe it. Mum keeps going on about it all the time and I can't take much more. I can't believe that I would have been a father if only …" The cup now abandoned, Kevin held his head in his hands, his eyes welling with tears.

"Can we go back in time again please?" Sanjay asked. "You said that Monday would have been your second anniversary. Was that from the time you started going out together?"

"Yes, that was the date of the theatre performance."

"And you've been a couple since then."

"Yes."

"With no breaks or splits."

"No, never. I won't pretend we agreed on everything, but we were very close. We understood each other."

"To prepare you, I need to ask you some very personal questions. It's necessary, so that we can understand the evidence we've accumulated." Sanjay commenced his new line of questioning.

Kevin looked perturbed but nodded accepting the caution.

"I want you to cast your mind back. After you came home on Monday and found Keiran, did you move her at all or alter her clothing."

Kevin pondered the question. "No, I don't think so. I'm sure I didn't. I could see she was definitely dead; her eyes were open and staring, so there was no point trying CPR."

"She was wearing a dress, but she wasn't wearing underclothes. Are you certain, you didn't adjust her dress, so she didn't appear naked when the police arrived?"

"It's all a little bit hazy. I was really shocked to find her like that, but I don't think so. I'm sure I'd have remembered. Why is it so important?"

"You aren't showing surprise about her not having on any underwear. Was she in the habit of not wearing underclothes?"

"It would be wrong to say it was a habit, but there were other times, special occasions or times when she had an intimate evening planned, if you know what I mean."

"It wasn't that unusual, then," Sanjay said.

"I remember the first time as if it was yesterday; it really gave me a surprise." There was a smile on Kevin's face and his eyes looked distant. "We'd been going out for several weeks, but we hadn't had sex together, not properly. We decided to take a trip to Loch Lomond, because it was a lovely sunny day and neither of us had lectures. Keiran's suggestion. It was a Wednesday afternoon and we'd taken the train."

Kevin paused but Sanjay urged him to continue.

"We were going to Balloch and we'd almost reached there; I think we'd already left Alexandria. The carriage was nearly empty. Keiran asked me if I'd brought protection. I didn't realise what she meant; I thought she was talking about being prepared for a change in the weather."

Steve laughed.

"She had this odd smile. She stood up in front of me and took my hand, guiding it to stroke up the back of her leg and over her thigh and buttocks. She wasn't wearing knickers." Kevin's eyes closed, and his face took on a contented look, lost in the memory. "At first, I thought she may have been wearing a thong, until I realised she had nothing on under her skirt."

"Were you shocked?" Sanjay asked.

"I suppose I was stunned. I'd been sitting next to her for the last hour without realising. Then, I understood what her question meant. I asked her if she was serious. She nodded and said she wanted it to be really special."

"It was certainly a different way to get started," Steve said.

"As soon as we got off the train, I found a shop with a vending machine which sold condoms and I bought a packet. We strolled along the side of the Loch. We must have walked for half an hour or more until we found a suitable, secluded spot. The scenery's beautiful around there, but I didn't notice a thing. My mind was on other things."

"That was your first time together. Was she a virgin?" Sanjay asked.

"I don't know. She said she was, and I believed her. I guess I wanted to believe her. Until now, I've not really questioned it, but, looking back, she seemed confident and knowledgeable. That said, she was confident with most things."

"Now if that was not long after you started going out, it must have been the best part of two years ago. How many other times has Keiran surprised you with her *no underwear act*?"

"It must be four or five. No, it was definitely four. I can remember every one of them."

"Was each to celebrate a special occasion?"

"Each became a special occasion. Yes, I know what you mean. Every time it happened, it was different but there was always an event, a birthday or holiday or something."

"And were there any other *al fresco* occasions?"

"No, that was the only one, unfortunately. There was one time, we made love in the back seat of her car, but it didn't go well. There was no space and I twisted my back. Never again."

"Uh huh, moving on. Let's get more up to date. you told us that you had sexual relations on Monday morning."

"Yes."

"We found two used condoms in the trash and we know it had been emptied on Sunday."

Kevin's face was grim. "We had sex on Sunday night, too. If that's what you're asking."

"Thank you. Can you tell me if either, or both of these occasions, was forceful or rough intercourse?"

Kevin's eyes widened. "What on earth are suggesting? This is unacceptable."

"We have good reason for asking," Sanjay replied. "You've already confirmed that sometimes you weren't averse to trying new things. Please answer the question."

Kevin's head dropped again, unable to maintain eye contact. "Our lovemaking could be adventurous at times. We weren't always particularly gentle, but I wouldn't say it was forceful or rough. Now, what's this all about?"

"When Kieran's body was medically examined, there was bruising to her arms, legs, thighs and internally. We're trying to establish if that may have been caused by vigorous loveplay or whether she'd been attacked."

"Oh My God, you think she was raped."

"We haven't ruled out the possibility."

"But surely your forensic people would have been able to tell."

"Not necessarily. That's why we're asking you these questions."

"Oh Christ! This keeps getting worse and worse. It's a nightmare I can't wake up from."

"We haven't finished yet. Do you need some time to compose yourself before we go on? Would you like some water?" Sanjay offered.

Kevin shook his head, not as an answer, more trying to clear his brain. "No, thank you. Go on. Let's get this over."

"Have you had intimate relations with anyone else?" Sanjay asked.

"Hell no! I told you before, we were loyal; we were faithful to each other, if that's how you'd describe it."

"In that case can you explain why we found an open packet of condoms in your jacket pocket." Sanjay asked.

Kevin looked stunned. "You found what? Wait a minute; it must be my leather jacket you're taking about."

"Yes, I believe so."

"They've been there for ages. In fact, I can tell you exactly when. I bought them in Balloch, that first time with Keiran. It was the same packet."

"Why have you been carrying them around all this time?"

Kevin paused. "Wishful thinking, I suppose. After that first time, I guess I was hoping for another opportunity and I wanted to be prepared."

"A good boy scout," Steve whispered under his breath.

"Thinking about it, I liked having them there, too. It was a pleasant reminder for me whenever I came across them."

"Just one problem. You told us, it only happened the once. But there was only one condom left in the pack of three."

Kevin's face turned crimson. "I can explain that," he murmured. "There was only one occasion. I was a bit over-eager and the first one I opened got ripped when I tried to put it on. I had to throw it away and use a second one."

"Is that a confession to littering?" Steve asked, breaking the tension of the moment.

"Did you ever buy that same brand on any other occasion?" Sanjay refocussed the discussion.

"No, I don't think so. Why?"

"The forensic examination on Keiran found she'd had recent sex using a condom, most likely to be of that brand. It was certainly not the stock you kept in the drawer."

"Oh, shit. Oh, Shit," Kevin repeated, tears filling his eyes. "Poor Keiran; that takes away any doubt. She was raped before she was killed."

"Yes, always assuming it wasn't consensual," Steve said.

"You bastard!" Kevin rounded on Steve. "How could it be consensual, he killed her, didn't he?"

Steve though better than to explain how alternative theories might apply.

"Are you finished with me," Kevin started to stand.

"No, please sit down. We haven't finished," Sanjay said.

"What now?"

"We've been having trouble confirming what you told us about your whereabouts on Monday."

"Not my problem."

"On the contrary. You've given us a story which we can't confirm. Worse than that, you've misled us."

"How have I misled you?"

"You told us that you left work and then went to meet your pal."

"Yes, so!"

"We now know you left your office at three thirty so that gives us another hour and a half where you can't account for your movements."

Kevin sighed before continuing. "I was given the task to hand deliver an offer document in Motherwell. One of our clients was bidding for a house. Normally we can use email, but the seller's solicitor phoned us to say their internet was down. They'd already set a closing date and time, and they'd received at least one offer already, so they didn't feel able to change the deadline. They called all parties who'd expressed a formal note of interest, so we had the opportunity to deliver by hand."

"Was there no other way?"

"There probably could have been if we'd given it some thought, but we couldn't take any chances. We were working for one of our main clients and we were up against it timewise."

"You volunteered."

"Somebody had to."

"Did you win?"

"Sorry?"

"You said your client was offering for a house; did they get it?"

"Oh, I see what you mean. I don't know. The deadline was four-thirty, so I wasn't there to see what happened. I haven't been back in the office to check. The offer went in and I've not thought about it since, not until you asked."

"It wasn't you who delivered the envelope." Seeing Kevin's hesitancy and evasiveness, Sanjay suspected he was covering and put him to the test.

"Why do you say that?"

"The receptionist didn't recognise you and we haven't been able to trace you travelling there or back on any CCTV records."

"But that doesn't mean ..." Kevin couldn't maintain the pretence under Sanjay and Steve's scrutiny. He cupped his hands over his face and sat motionless for several seconds before saying anything. "You're right, I didn't go. I started walking towards the station but didn't get that far. On my way I saw an office operating a courier service. I walked in and checked with them. They told me for thirty quid they'd send a bike rider to make the delivery and would guarantee it arrived on time."

"But why, surely you were taking one hell of a chance?"

"I guess it was stupid, but I needed a drink. I'd had a busy day and then I'd got the text from Billy. I reckoned I'd have to see him, for old times sake, but I wasn't keen." Kevin shuddered. "He'd helped me when I was struggling a bit with my studies and coached me through, so I felt I owed him. He could be a real pain in the ass, though. Mister Perfect, always got everything right and lorded it a bit. He got this mega offer from a firm in Aberdeen and I wasn't unhappy to be out of his company."

"If you didn't want to be in his company, why did you agree to meet him?"

"As I said, I felt I owed him. More to the point, he thought I owed him. I was hoping to make this one last time. I really wasn't looking forward to it, so I wanted a couple of drinks in me first. I stopped at a pub in Waterloo Street and had a couple of shots of vodka and a pint or two"

"Then you had another two pints when he didn't show." Sanjay added.

"Yeah, I was quite merry, going home. Billy didn't show, I was mildly sozzled, and I was going back to spend the evening with my girl."

"Except that's not how it turned out." Sanjay said.

"God no, if only. I dozed on the bus and I was a bit groggy when I got home. I came to sharpish when I found Keiran."

"I imagine you would," Sanjay said, "and it is a good story. But maybe you're being a bit economic with the truth."

"What are you on about? I've told you all I know."

"You've told us what you want us to believe."

"I don't know what you want."

"How about the truth, the whole truth, for starters."

"I don't understand."

"Well let's see. To begin with, the phone number you exchanged messages with wasn't Billy Marshall. Maybe you thought you were being smart, setting up your own alibi."

"No, no that didn't happen. I thought I was talking to Billy."

"Then, we can't match any sightings of you at the time you claimed, but we do think we have you arriving home more than an hour earlier." Sanjay slid him a copy of the photo taken from the CCTV."

"It can't be. That's not me."

"It certainly looks like you and we can't find evidence of you arriving later on."

"Oh Christ, no."

"So, what really happened, Kevin? Did you arrive home and suspect Keiran had been sleeping with someone else? Maybe she told you she was pregnant, and you jumped to the conclusion, right or wrong, that it couldn't be you, ergo she'd been with someone else. You grabbed her by the throat and you throttled her. Doesn't that sound more likely."

"No, no, no! It's not true. I'm innocent. It wasn't me."

"Will you not let us save a lot of time here? Just tell us what really happened."

"I have. Okay, it's true I didn't tell you where I went at first. I didn't want to admit I'd been drinking, but that's as far as it goes. I didn't kill her. I loved her. It wasn't me."

Chapter 25

Alex parked at the hospital and was accompanied by Craig, Andrew and Jenny as he made his way to Sandra's ward.

A moment's panic overcame him when he saw curtains drawn around Sandra's bed. "Wait here," he instructed the others as he charged forward. His tension was instantly released when he found Sandra calmly sitting up in bed, breastfeeding Siobhan."

"Sorry love, I didn't mean to surprise you. I got a shock when I saw the curtains closed. Is everything okay?"

There was enough of an answer in Sandra's contented grin. "We're both fine."

Alex was pensive, "Are you okay to breastfeed when you've got an infection?"

"Yes, the doctor said it would be fine. I've been given an antibiotic, but he said it's one that doesn't affect my milk."

"Give me a sec, I've left the kids outside. I'd better explain."

Alex guided the youngsters out to the corridor and told them they'd have to wait for a while.

"Can't I go in and see," Craig asked. He was sporting a broad grin.

"No, you bloody well can't," Jenny replied, walloping his arm with her fist.

"Ow, that hurt."

"Serves you right for being so cheeky." Her laughter matched his. "At least you're in a hospital so you won't have to go far to get treatment."

Alex smiled at their exchange. "Listen, I don't know how long it'll be 'til you can see them. Why don't you go down to the café and grab a cola. I'll come and get you when they're ready." Alex peeled a ten-pound note from his wallet and offered it to them.

"How about the boys go to the café as you suggested. Would it be okay for me to see Sandra and the baby just now? After all, it's something I want to learn about and it would mean Sandra wouldn't miss out on visitors for the first part of the session. I've brought a wee pressie for the little one."

Unable to think of a good reason to refuse, Alex conceded. The boys jogged downstairs.

"It means you'll be able to stay with Sandra and I'll be able to go down and swap places with Craig and Andrew when the time comes."

Alex laughed. "Okay already, you've got your wish." He pulled aside the curtain and Jenny rushed forward.

"Oh, she's so tiny. What a little cutie. Can I get to hold her?"

"Not yet, you can't." Sandra adjusted how she was sitting, trying to find a more comfortable position.

"No, I mean when you're ready. I've got a wee something here for her." Jenny lifted a small package.

"That's very kind of you. Can you open it for me please? As you can see, my hands are rather full."

Jenny ripped off the paper to reveal a small pink teddy bear, identical to the one Alex had bought.

Dismayed, Alex was about to say something, but noticed Sandra's warning look, before she said, "It's gorgeous. She's going to really love it. Thank you very much."

For the next ten minutes, Alex sat bemused as Jenny bombarded Sandra with question after question about her pregnancy, the delivery and ideas of childcare.

Finally, able to break into the conversation, he commented, "I trust your questions are for educational purposes only and you're not getting any ideas. I've just become a father again. I think it's a bit soon for me to want to take on grandfather duties."

Jenny's face flushed bright red. "No Mr Warren, you needn't worry; I'm not ready for that either. Besides, I'm on the pill, so there will be no accidents."

Her more formal method of address wasn't lost on Alex. He smiles weakly, remembering Sandra's unplanned pregnancy, the previous year which ended in miscarriage. He was also somewhat embarrassed by how forthright Jenny had been.

"I think we're ready now for the boys to meet their new sister. Could you please go down and ask them to come back." Looking at his watch, Alex added, "We'll see you downstairs soon, visiting will be over in about forty minutes."

Once Jenny was out of earshot, Sandra said, "Wasn't that thoughtful of Jenny to bring a gift. I know it's the same as the one you bought, but I wouldn't be surprised if it becomes a favourite toy, so it won't do any harm to have a spare."

"I'm a bit more concerned about the admission she made before she left. A case of too much information. What on earth am I going to say to Craig when I get him alone."

"You can't be serious. You'll say nothing. Think like a father instead of being a policeman for a moment. They're doing nothing wrong. They're both over the age of consent and they've been going out together for ages. It's not a casual relationship. What did you expect? What's more, from all accounts they appear to be acting responsibly."

"Yes, of course you're right. I find it hard to think of my kids as having become grown up."

"If it's any consolation, you've got another one here that you can keep a baby for some time to come."

"Give her here then, I've not had a chance of a cuddle yet." The baby looked even more tiny, cradled in Alex's arm. "Before they get here, a word of warning. Andrew's a bit fragile thinking he'd no longer wanted, with the new arrival and everything. It was maybe a bit insensitive of me turning the spare room into a nursery without talking to him about it first and reassuring him. It was totally my fault. I screwed up, but I reckon Helen's not helped. She's been happy to pour petrol on the flames."

"It's done, Alex. You can't turn the clock back. What's important now is to make amends, ensure he feels part of our lives and Siobhan's going forward."

"After everything you've been through, how come you're the voice of reason, when I can't get my thoughts straight?"

"It's hardly surprising. I can't say childbirth was easy, but I've not had much to occupy my mind for weeks now."

Further discussion was prevented when Craig and Andrew arrived. They were both captivated by Siobhan. Andrew was uncertain at first and slower coming forward. With some trepidation, he reached forward to touch the baby's hand and was delighted when she grasped his finger and held on. Both boys sat chatting to Sandra and cooing over Siobhan, watching her as if hypnotised.

I don't know why I was worrying; she's won him over all be herself, Alex thought. *Two days old and already she has men falling at her feet.*

With only fifteen minutes of visiting time left, Sandra's brother, Ricky, arrived.

"I'm sorry I'm late. Congratulations!" Ricky lent across the bed to kiss his sister's cheek. He extended his arm to shake Alex's hand, then slapped him, heartily on the shoulder, before moving to the boys. "Craig, Andrew, I haven't seen you for some time. Look at the height of you. You've both grown." He grinned while turning to lean over the cot for a better look. "And this young lady must be Siobhan."

"I didn't expect you to come," Sandra said.

"You're right. Sharon and I had planned to visit you at your flat this weekend. Then Dad phoned to say you may not be getting home right away, so we didn't want to wait."

"Don't think I'm not pleased to see you."

"We wanted to make sure you're okay, but I can see you look the picture of health. Sharon wanted to come too, but tonight's the night for Rainbow Guides and Tracy wouldn't miss it for anything. She's doing the taxiing, leaving me to come over. You've got all this to look forward to." He looked at Siobhan to make certain his message was clear. "We'll all come to see you on Sunday, if that's okay, wherever you are." He paused. "I should have been here ages ago but there was a foul up on the motorway and it took me forever to get through."

"Come on now, only two visitors to a bed," a nurse interrupted their conversation.

"I'm sorry, I just got here, trouble with the traffic." Ricky gave his most endearing smile.

"Tell you what, you lads go back down to the café and find Jenny. It'll let Ricky have a few moments to see Sandra and his new niece. I'll say my goodbyes and join you in a few minutes," Alex suggested. The boys said bye and left.

"Before you head away, Alex, have you wet the baby's head yet? I wouldn't want to miss out on the celebration."

"I've not had a moment since she was born. It hadn't even occurred to me."

"Aw, come on Alex. It's a tradition. We have to go for a drink to celebrate the new arrival."

"Okay, I'll give it some thought and let you know."

Alex gently kissed each of his girls and patted Ricky's arm. "I'll drop back in before work tomorrow, and Ricky, I'll get back to you about a celebration."

"Perfect," Sandra scolded. "I can do without my brother leading my husband astray."

Chapter 26

After Mary dropped Steve back at the office, WPC Beth Saunders was waiting for her.

"Have you been briefed what this is about?" Mary asked.

"No, I was only told to come here to meet you. I'm really excited to be working with CID, even if it's only for a short while."

"Don't get too excited, it's not that much different. Half of your day is spent filling out paperwork and most of what's left is carrying out research. I can't deny, it does have its moments, but when I say, *moments,* I mean the word literally."

"What is it we're working on today?"

"Hopefully this will give you a flavour of the good stuff, because it's a complex investigation. A young Asian woman was found dead on Monday and we reckon it's almost certainly murder. The correct expression for us to use is *unexplained death* until there's a confirmed cause."

"What are we going to be doing?"

"We'll be visiting the victim's family. I've called ahead and they're expecting us. In particular, I want to speak to her sister. She's young, still a schoolgirl, but we need to check whether the victim confided any personal information which might help us find the killer."

"I see."

"Because she's young and we might be discussing some intimate details, we thought it would be better if no men were present. That's why I'm doing the interview and why you're along."

"What would you like me to do?" Beth was bubbling with excitement.

"For starters, you need to settle down. This couple have recently lost their daughter. They may still be in shock but in any event, they are mourning a loss. You need to curb your enthusiasm."

"Yes, of course." Beth adopted a more sombre demeanour.

"That's better. Your purpose is to take notes and to be able to verify what I put in my report. I'll be the one asking the questions, although I may invite you to contribute. If you think I'm missing anything, then, by all means, cut in, but otherwise leave me to lead. I want you to be particularly aware of any hidden messages. It's not only the words that matter. I want you to watch expressions and body language."

"I'll do my best."

* * *

Before Mary had clicked the lock on the car, she was aware the front door of the house was open, and Mr Sharma was standing in the entrance. His face was pale and haggard, contrasting with his new-looking, crisp, dark brown tunic and trousers. They quickly walked up the pathway and Mary introduced Beth.

"Have you got any news. Have you made an arrest?" he asked.

"Can we talk inside?"

"Yes, yes. Come in. Go into the lounge and sit down."

Mrs Sharma and Jamilla were already there seated. Both looked up expectantly as they entered, they appeared tired and twitchy. Both were very sedately dressed, wearing long, skirts and high-necked tops also in dark colours.

"You didn't answer. Have you caught anyone?" Mr Sharma asked.

"We haven't, not at this point. However, we are making progress with our enquiries." Mary trotted out the stock answer.

"Tell us what you've found out. What is this progress you talk about?"

"I'm sorry, I'm not at liberty to discuss details of the case. We're still gathering and interpreting evidence. It would be wrong for me to tell you details before we understand whether they have any significance."

"This may be normal for you, but we have not experienced anything like it. It is very difficult for us."

"Yes, we understand. We are sorry for your loss. Life is very short." Mary's comment had been prepared.

"How can you say such things? You perhaps have taken two minutes to read a page on the internet and now you think you understand us and our customs." Mr Sharma blustered.

"I'm sorry you feel that way. I was only trying to show respect."

"Tarik, be silent. She is only trying to be kind. What customs are you talking about anyway? You are not religious." Mrs Sharma said.

Undeterred, he continued, "Are we able to get Keiran's body back. We need to organise her burial."

"I'm afraid I don't know anything about that. It's down to the Medical Examiner and the Procurator Fiscal. I've no doubt they'll get in touch as soon as it's okay."

"It's not right. You shouldn't be able to stop her funeral."

"I understand your concern, but I'm afraid it's nothing to do with us. I can give you a number to call, so you can find out when it will be."

"It is not acceptable. Your people have told me nothing. I have learned more from my brother than I have from you."

"That is regrettable, Sir. As you're aware, we wanted to appoint a family liaison officer, but you refused. It's not too late, we can appoint one now and then you'll be given support and you'll receive information as soon as it becomes available to divulge." Mary was becoming increasingly concerned. She realised that Mr Sharma's grief was manifesting itself in anger, but she wasn't happy to be left exposed as the target for his anguish.

"What information is it that you're talking about?" she asked.

"Ibrahim tells me that Keiran may have been pregnant."

"Yes, Sir. I can confirm that is the case."

"Why has no-one reported this back to us?"

"I can only apologise. I know that it was confirmed by the Medical Examiner, but I don't know the procedure to report such matters back to the family. As I said, ordinarily the FLO would be involved."

Sharma ignored her reply and continued to rant. "And the boy, McGowan is responsible."

"I'm sorry, Sir. I do not have any information, I can tell you."

"This is a waste of time. You know nothing. Or if you do, you are not prepared to say."

"We are doing our best. I explained when I called, my main purpose in this visit was to speak to Jamilla."

"What! You tell us nothing about Keiran's death and now you want to interrogate our other daughter."

"It's not like that, Sir. We were hoping that through talking to Keiran, Jamilla may have information which could help us."

"So, it's our help you're seeking." Sharma's tone was antagonistic.

"It's only so we can make progress in identifying what happened."

"And you want to see her alone."

"Tarik, let them do their job." Dr Sharma pleaded. "We want them to find out what happened to our girl."

"It seems what I think doesn't matter," Sharma slammed the door as he stormed out of the room.

"I must apologise for my husband. He's taking this very badly."

"There's no need to apologise, Ma'am. We can only imagine what he's going through."

"He can't forgive himself, you see. He's done nothing wrong, of course, but he needs to apportion blame to try to make some reason out of it"

Mary nodded.

"He hasn't practised any religion for years, and now he wants to observe the rituals. Perhaps he can take comfort; I don't know. I'm a doctor and I've seen this happen with patients on countless occasions.

There's nothing I can do. The pain will never go away, but over time, it will be less raw."

"You are very understanding," Mary said.

"Don't be misled. I hurt every bit as much and my heart is broken. But I am a woman of science. I can't take comfort from religion; I wish I could." Tears were running down her cheeks. "For Tarik's sake, we will do as he wishes. We shall have a religious funeral as soon as we are able. We have sat the three days of mourning and we will return to our duties tomorrow." She paused a moment before resuming. "Tarik will reopen his shop, Jumilla will return to school and I will be back in my surgery. For me, the Prophet does not give me solace. I can't accept it was his will for Keiran to die and I don't feel three days of mourning allows us to continue as if nothing had happened."

"Three days seems very soon," Mary agreed.

"The religious principle is for there to be an afterlife and because everything is Allah's will, to mourn for a longer period is to show contempt."

"Yes, I read about it."

"As part of your two minutes research on the internet." Mrs Sharma gave a wry smile.

"Something like that. Now, if I can get down to business, can you please give me a note of all of Keiran's friends that you're aware of? Along with their numbers where you have them. We're trying to match up names to each of the telephone calls and messages she received and made."

"I can tell you about her school friends and names I've heard her mention from university and work. I don't know how current or complete it will be."

"Anything you can give us will be a help," Mary replied, and Beth took notes.

"Now I understand that you want to speak to Jamilla. Would you like me to stay with you?" she asked turning to her daughter.

"No, Mum. I'm okay."

"I'll be next door in the kitchen. Call me if you need anything."

"Thank you for your help," Mary said.

Chapter 27

"Before we start, we know you're eighteen years old and able to make decisions for yourself, but you do have a right to have someone else present if it would make you feel more comfortable. It can be a family member, but you can have anyone else if you prefer."

"I understand, but I'm okay."

"Your mum gave us a very useful list. Are there any other names you think we should add?"

After some thought, Jamilla, was able to add a further three names.

"Was there anyone you thought she was particularly close to? Someone she may have been more likely to confide in."

"I think perhaps the Australian girl I told you about a moment ago, Carolyn Fletcher. She spent a lot of time with her. I'm sorry, I don't have her number. They started Uni at the same time and I think she went to the same drama club."

"Thanks, you're being very helpful."

"I don't believe they saw so much of each other after Keiran started going out with Kevin. Also, I heard she may have moved away after they graduated so I don't know if it's really much help."

"We can look into it."

"You asked me who she confided in. We were very close and spent a lot of time together. She did tell me a lot of things. I'm sure there must have been a lot she didn't say but I doubt there's anyone else she'd have said anything to which she wouldn't tell me. Other than Kevin of course."

"What sort of things did she tell you?"

"We'd share everything. I'd tell her things too and ask her advice."

"Because you were so close, it's very possible you have information which can help, even if you don't realise it."

"What do you mean?"

"We want to gather all the information we can on anyone who could have been responsible for attacking Keiran. It might be someone who had a motive because they felt she hurt or upset them."

"I doubt I could help there, there's no one I can think of."

"It may not be anything you'd normally think of as significant. Possibly as trivial as a joke she'd made where someone had taken it as a personal slight. It could be someone who'd made advances which she rebuffed. A fight or argument. Anyone who'd upset or hurt her where she may have said anything or made a complaint."

Jamilla chewed on her lip.

"You have someone in mind."

"I don't know. It was a long time ago and I don't know all the details."

"Please tell us what you know so we can decide."

"I was very young at the time, only about eleven; Keiran was fifteen, it must have been eight years ago."

"It could be important. Please go on."

"Our cousin Zahid came to Glasgow. He's actually the son of Dad's cousin. His family sent him up from Wolverhampton, so he could get some work experience. He was older. He must have been about twenty, but he wasn't very bright. I think he may have learning difficulties. He was good looking though."

"Did you see much of him?"

"Uncle Ibrahim made the arrangements for him to come here. He persuaded Dad to let him work in his shop and because we had the largest house he came to stay with us. He was given the spare room."

Mary looked around her, thinking, 'This is a big house.' "Did Keiran like him?"

"He used to show off his muscles, you know, like a bodybuilder and Keiran would laugh. She liked the look of him, but she was very shy."

"What happened?"

"One day she came home from netball practice and jumped straight into the shower. She thought no one was home. I don't know why, but Zahid wasn't at work and he heard her go in and turn the water on. He went into the bathroom after her. She had no clothes on. He told her not to scream or he'd hurt her. She was terrified but there was nothing she could do. He touched her and ran his hand over her skin. She was scared he was going to rape her, but he didn't. He was gentle only stroking her skin. She was sobbing. She tried to cover herself and turned away from him. He moved closer and started to stroke her back and her bottom. Then he saw her birthmark. You know about that?"

"Yes, we know."

"For some reason, it unsettled him. He said it was horrible and he went away."

"Just like that?"

"Yes, it seems it may have scared or disgusted him; who knows? Anyhow, when he left, Keiran slammed the door and locked it. She was still there when Mum got home."

"What happened then?"

"Keiran was in quite a state. Mum made sure she was unharmed and managed to calm her down. When Dad heard, he wanted to kill Zahid. The he said he was going to have him arrested. Uncle Ibrahim talked him out of it. There was a big row. Uncle said to do nothing as it could only harm Keiran and that Zahid had meant no harm, he was simple."

"They did nothing."

"Zahid was sent away. He left with uncle and was sent back to his parents."

"You remember all of this."

"I remember there being a big row which went on for weeks. I didn't know what it was about at the time but Keiran told me about it afterwards when I was older."

"What affect did it have on her?"

"Like I said before, Keiran had been very shy. She'd always been clever, but for a while after it happened, she seemed to go even more into herself. She'd sometimes miss school and she hardly spoke to anyone. She stopped playing sports. All she'd do was read. It went on for months. Mum and Dad became very worried. Mum wanted to arrange counselling, but then she changed."

"What do you mean by changed?"

"It was almost as if she'd woken up and was a different person. She was confident and self-assured. I've spoken to her about it on a few occasions. She told me she woke one day and decided she didn't want to be a victim. It was a state of mind. She said she wouldn't ever let anyone dominate her. She wanted to be in control of her own life."

"From what we've learned, she could be quite a forceful character."

"I think Mum and Dad got rather a shock. Maybe it was easier for them before she changed. No forget I said that. They were delighted she'd become strong even if she could be a handful."

"Can you explain?"

"She insisted on making all her own decisions. She made different friends. She liked clothes and music our parents didn't approve of. She did work hard at school and she got brilliant results in her Highers. Mum and Dad were delighted. Mum wanted her to study medicine to become a doctor like her. She would have got a place, but Keiran insisted she wanted to do pharmacy instead. She lost any interest in religion and she read up on atheism, Richard Dawkins and the like. Dad didn't know how to deal with her. He couldn't argue with her because she was so smart, she was always able to run him around in circles."

"It can't have been easy for them."

"It wasn't, but it made life much easier for me. I was regarded as the *good* daughter." Jamilla laughed. "No, seriously, she didn't do anything actually bad, but she was unorthodox and didn't conform to what was expected of a teenage Moslem girl."

"I thought your family weren't religious."

"They're not, but they still follow a lot of the conventions. Also, Uncle Ibrahim is very involved in the Mosque and he made it known that he didn't approve. Because of his involvement in bringing Zahid to Glasgow, they weren't prepared to listen to anything he said."

"All the same, they couldn't have been very happy when she started going out with Kevin."

"That's an understatement. It caused terrible rows and even more so when they moved in together. Dad refused to let her in the house. Mum was upset. She felt caught in the middle. She didn't agree with what Keiran was doing and she tried to talk her out of it, but she didn't want to lose her. They still spoke often and met occasionally, but she respected Dad's instruction that she wasn't allowed back in the house."

"What about you, did you still see her?"

"Oh yes, very often. We spoke most days and saw each other at least once a week. Sometimes we'd go shopping or out for a coffee or a lunch. I was invited to their flat several times. Mum knew I was seeing her and was pleased we were close. I'm sure Dad knew too but he wouldn't acknowledge it."

"You must have met Kevin, then."

"Yes, many times."

"Did the two of you get on well?"

"We did. I liked him. He was kind and funny and he seemed to make Keiran happy. That's what was most important to me."

"Did Keiran tell you much about him or about how he treated her?"

"She did a bit. Like I said before, Keiran liked to be in control. She told me about how they first got together. She told me other things about their relationship. She liked to try new things, but he wasn't complaining from what I heard."

"She pretty much led the relationship, from what you're saying."

"Yes, I think so. Keiran was always very determined. If she decided she wanted something, then ninety-nine times out of a hundred, she'd get it."

"And she wanted Kevin."

"Yes. I can't say I know why. He's not the most gorgeous bloke in the universe. He's not particularly sporty or brilliant, and there are times when he has too much to drink."

"Does he get violent?"

"No, no nothing like that. He's more prone to fall asleep. Now, don't get me wrong, he's smart enough and he's not painful on the eye either, but Keiran could have had anyone."

"You thought she could have chosen better."

"I'm not saying that either. Well, I suppose I was, but I wasn't being fair. Thinking about it, Kevin was probably a good choice. He was kind and he adored her. He'd have done anything she asked."

"I wouldn't mind a man like that," Mary said.

"I remember before they were going out. Keiran told me she'd met a boy and she planned to pick him up. I'd no idea who he was, but she said they were both acting in a play at her drama club. She said I should go and see the production if I wanted a laugh."

"Did you go?"

"I did, and she was right. It wasn't a comedy or at least it wasn't meant to be. She kissed him onstage right in the middle of the show and he didn't have a clue what was happening. I knew to expect it, but none of the audience realised anything unusual had taken place. She pranced off and he was standing stunned, centre stage. It took me all my time not to fall off my seat, I was laughing so much. I got some strange looks, I can tell you."

"I guess it got her noticed."

"She knew he'd come looking for her and she led him around for hours before she let him catch up. He was completely captivated."

"I guess it worked then,"

"Well the result was they started going out. As I said, she knew how to get what she wanted."

"Had she done anything like that before?"

"Not that I'm aware of. She had dated other boys, but Kevin was her first serious boyfriend. She genuinely cared for him. I think he was the first man she truly trusted."

"I noticed you used the expression *cared for*. Do you not think she loved him?"

"I suppose she must have. I don't know how you can judge. He was the first man she had sex with."

"She must have been what, twenty or twenty-one by then."

"Yes, I think so. After the Zahid incident, Keiran was very careful about men. She didn't like being touched. It took a long time for her to trust anyone and it always had to be on her terms."

"So, you're telling me that she had to feel in command of any physical relationship."

"Yes, I'd say so. Even though she'd decided she wanted Kevin as her boyfriend, it was a long time before she let him touch her. After the first time, I think she felt released; she wondered why she had waited so long. Like I told you before, she'd always been controlling but she became more confident."

"You don't need to explain. We've seen their private photos."

"Photos? What photos? What's that about?"

"I'm sorry. I shouldn't have said. It was only I thought you already knew. Keiran and Kevin had an album of intimate photos they'd taken of each other."

"Right. Maybe she had told me, and I'd forgotten." Jamilla tried to regain her status of appearing to be entrusted with all her sister's secrets.

"A moment ago, you said 'Kevin was the *first* man she had sex with'. Does that mean there were others?"

"N' n' n', no that's not what I meant. I don't think there was anyone else. I don't know."

"There's something you're not telling us."

"I don't know, it may be nothing."

"Please tell us. It may help in discovering what happened."

Jamilla's voice became a whisper. "As I said, it's probably nothing. But there was a time, a few weeks back when Keiran went a bit strange."

"What do you mean by strange?"

"For a number of days, she didn't talk to me and didn't return my calls. I was very worried. When she did call me back. She said it hadn't been important. I wondered if it perhaps had something to do with Kevin's drinking, if they maybe had a row or even split up. I told her, I knew her better than that and something must be badly wrong. She said everything was okay but admitted she had been worried because she'd done something stupid. She wouldn't tell me more. It wasn't like her. Then everything seemed to be back to normal, so I thought no more about it."

"What did you think she meant?"

"I didn't know. I thought of all different theories, but as she wouldn't say it was pointless to speculate. Then she called me on Monday to tell me she thought she was pregnant. I put two and two together and assumed that's what it must have been she'd worried about – she'd probably had unprotected sex."

"You mean with Kevin?"

"That's what I thought but I don't know."

"How did she sound? Was she happy about the prospect, or worried? Was she considering a termination?"

"No, she didn't mention it. She was excited and nervous. She said she planned to tell Kevin that evening."

"So, she told you first?"

"Yes"

"Did she tell your parents?"

"God no!"

"And you didn't say?"

"No, it wasn't my place."

"When Ibrahim said to your parents, that must have been the first they knew."

"Yes, and I had to pretend it was news to me too."

"Is there anything else you can tell us which you think could be at all relevant."

"No, that's it."

"Beth, can you think of anything else to ask which we haven't covered?"

Beth jumped, shocked by the question. "No, nothing I can think of."

* * *

Once back in the car, Beth was bubbling with excitement. "That was incredible, just like on the telly. You were brilliant, the way you got her to tell you everything."

"Thanks, but now comes the fun part. We need to get the whole thing written up, so we can brief the rest of the team."

"We? You mean I get to take part?"

Chapter 28

"What did you think of our wee darling?" Alex asked proudly.

"She's gorgeous," Jenny replied.

"I'm sure we'll get used to her," Craig answered, unsuccessfully trying not to grin.

"She doesn't do much yet, but I suppose that will change as she gets older. Maybe I can teach her things," Andrew offered.

Resulting from his previous apprehension about Andrew, Alex was delighted his sons were accepting their step-sister into the family and he wanted to reward them. "I was going to drop Jenny home first, but how about we all go to the Derby Café for an ice cream; then I can take you home afterwards."

"Okay by me," Andrew said.

"We'd being planning to ask you to drop us at the chippie. We thought we'd grab a bag and have a quiet walk together." Craig replied. "I quite fancy an ice cream though." He turned to Jenny and she nodded. "Then you could leave us there; we'd only have to cross the road to get our chips."

"Yeah, no problem. You haven't changed. You always did want to eat your dessert before your main course."

"Yeah, yeah. You're only trying to embarrass me."

Alex's phone buzzed. Looking at the Parrot screen, he didn't recognise the number but saw the area code was for Birmingham. His brow furrowed as he pressed the accept key for the hands-free device.

"We understand you've been involved in an accident which wasn't your fault." The voice was bright and cheery.

"How did you get this number?" Alex demanded.

Ignoring his question, the caller continued, "We need to take all your details and then we'll be able to get you compensation."

"This is an unlisted and protected number. You are committing an offence under data protection legislation by making unsolicited calls. Do you understand?" The line went dead.

"*You* might be involved in an accident which *is* my fault," Alex muttered under his breath. "Bloody conmen and vultures."

"I get them phoning me all the time, too," Jenny said. "It's really annoying."

"I don't know how they get away with it," Alex said. "If you register your phone number with the Telephone Preference Service, it helps, but a lot of them still manage to get through. Whenever I remember, I put a complaint into the ICO, that's the Information Commissioner's Office. It's easy to do online and they're meant to act against the rogues. I'm not convinced it works because the calls continue, usually from a different number, but I suppose it helps."

"I didn't know. I must try it. Thanks Alex," Jenny said.

"See the old man does have some uses," Craig said.

"Less of the *old,* you cheeky bugger," Alex replied.

A moment later the phone rang again.

"Who now? Yes!" he answered brusquely.

"Hello Sir, this is Stuart Black, from Craigie Street station."

Alex took a moment to place the name. Then he remembered the robbery. "Yes, Stuart."

"I've been trying to call you for the last hour. I have some news."

"Give me a moment." Alex drew the car to a halt and switched off the engine. He lifted his phone and stepped onto the pavement."

"Sorry about that. The phone was switched off while I was visiting, inside a hospital. I had been driving, with passengers, so I wasn't able to talk until I got out. What can you tell me?"

"No problem, Sir. I said I'd keep you updated. I wanted you to know that we now have the search warrant for the electrical repair company. We're planning to hit the place tomorrow morning when they reopen. I'll be about nine-fifteen, nine-thirtyish. They have an office, showroom and workshop in Tradeston. Would you like to be there?"

"It's kind of you to ask and I'd love to be in on the raid, but I'm afraid I've got too much on. Please let me know how you get on."

"Will do. As soon as I have anything, I'll give you a call."

Alex was smiling as he got back into the driving seat.

"What was that all about?" Andrew asked.

"Just business. I'm trying to find out what happened to your games. It's a long shot, but it could possibly pay off."

"Don't you ever switch off, Dad," Craig asked.

Albeit jocular, Craig's words made Alex feel guilty. He knew his commitment to work had been a significant ingredient in his marriage break-up from Helen. He'd sworn he wouldn't repeat past mistakes but wasn't convinced he knew how. He made a conscious effort to think of family matters.

"I just thought. You told me you were going, last night, to watch your school play in the regional tournament for rugby sevens. I forgot to ask you, how did they get on?"

"It was a disaster," Craig replied. "We got cuffed by Barrhead. We'd beaten them the last half dozen times we met, and we were odds on to do it again. We played rubbish; it was painful."

"What went wrong?"

"McGowan, our best player, didn't turn up. He's normally really solid and the team just fell apart without him."

"That's a shame. Was he ill?"

"He wasn't in school on Tuesday or yesterday. I don't think there was anything wrong with him. I heard something about a family crisis."

"The name you mentioned was McGowan. Would that be Robbie McGowan?"

"Yeah, how did you know that?"

"I know about the family crisis. It was his brother's girlfriend; the brother came home from work on Monday and found her dead."

"Oh God! That's awful. No wonder he couldn't play. What happened to her?"

"It's under investigation. You know I'm not able to talk about it."

"I suppose something really bad must have happened if your lot are looking into it."

"Not necessarily, but it creates the possibility. I can't say any more."

"They must be going through hell," Jenny said.

"How well did you know Robbie?"

"He's in our year, but he's not in any of my classes," Craig said.

"Me too," Jenny added.

"What can you tell me about him?"

"Is this part of a police investigation? Surely you're not trying to exploit your own son to advance your career?" Craig smirked.

"Very funny. No, I'm not trying to exploit anyone, and it certainly won't advance my career. It is a serious matter though, and it can sometimes be a real help to us to better understand the people we're dealing with."

"Sorry Dad, I was only joking. I'm not sure what I can say. Like me, he's in sixth year, so he must be seventeen or eighteen, and he's big. I don't just mean tall, he's broad. Well you would expect that of a rugby player."

"It's not so much what he looks like. I'm more interested in his character, how he gets on with people."

"Isn't he the one who was given a week's suspension for fighting? What was it, about six months ago, not long after the previous term started?" Andrew said.

"Yes, that's right. I'd forgotten. How did you know about that?" Craig asked his brother.

"My pal, Chris. It was his big brother, Derek, that Robbie hit. I don't know what was behind it, but Derek thought he was a bit of a nutter. He warned us to stay away from him," Andrew said.

"If I remember correctly, it wasn't only the fight which got him into trouble. There was some talk of verbal abuse. I don't know the details, whether it was homophobic or racial. It might even have been both. Anyhow, it's all hearsay," Craig added.

"I'm impressed you knew to qualify your comment," Alex said. "Maybe you want to consider a career in law enforcement."

"No way, Dad. I want to go into banking or accountancy. I want to go where the real money is," Craig replied.

With a laugh Alex replied, "You've been spending too much time talking to your mum." Although spoken as a joke, there was an edge of seriousness to his comment.

"I can't say I know him myself," Jenny said, "but I've heard some of the other girls talk about him."

"Was he liked?" Alex asked.

"Mixed opinions, I'd say. Some of the girls thought he was a bit of a hunk, but others thought him arrogant and boorish."

"I suppose they're not mutually exclusive. Did he have a girlfriend?" Alex asked.

"No, I don't think so, not in our school anyway," she answered.

"What about boys?"

"I haven't heard any suspicion that he's gay," Craig replied.

"No, that's not what I meant. Do you know which of the other lads he's friendly with?"

"Yeah, I understood the first time." Craig laughed. "Truly, I don't know. He does a lot of sport and he mixes with other players in the school teams, but I'm not aware of him having any close friends."

"Okay, thanks. You've all been very helpful. I'll pass on the information to whoever's working with it. Now what ice cream would you each like, and do you want to carry it out or eat in?"

"I'd like to sit in and have a chocolate fudge sundae," Andrew said.

"A knickerbocker glory for me," Craig added.

"I'll just have a large cone, please," Jenny said. "I have to watch my figure."

Alex glanced in the rear-view mirror. "I don't think you've got anything to worry about."

"It's more a case of anyone else watching your figure which bothers me," Craig said.

Chapter 29

An early start on Friday morning was Alex's plan, intending to visit the hospital before travelling into work. It hadn't turned eight when he arrived at Sandra's ward.

"Hush, talk quietly," Sandra whispered. "She's had her feed and only dropped off to sleep a moment ago."

Alex, the proud father, stood gazing at Siobhan, watching her covers rise and fall with each breath. Only after some time did he turn to embrace Sandra, then sat next to her on the bed with his arm around her shoulder. "How are you this morning?"

"I'm still tired but otherwise I feel fine. I hope I'm given the all clear when the doc does his rounds. If so, I could be out before lunchtime."

"That would be good. I'm going into a meeting, but I can come away to get you if you call. I'll leave my phone switched on in case you need me."

"There aren't regular rounds at the weekend. I'm concerned if I don't get out today then it might not be until Monday. I couldn't stand that. I'm desperate to get this wee one home and I want to sleep in my own bed."

"Fingers crossed. You know I'll be there to help whenever it is. I've reserved my paternity leave. The Sharma enquiry is the only big case we have ongoing and I can trust Sanjay to handle everything in my absence. I'll only have to take the odd call."

"No, no, no. You're not getting away with that. Don't forget, I know what it's like and I know what you're like when you're in the middle of an investigation."

"But…"

"No buts. You have your leave booked and that's what it will be, time for only the three of us. If you start taking calls, your mind will be on the case for half the time and our lounge will likely be turned into an incident room with your team coming and going at all hours."

Alex was about to protest, before he realised the wisdom of her words. He'd been promising to change his ways and put family ahead of work and this seemed like a good place to start. "You're absolutely right. I'll brief the team when I go in and I'll tell the bosses too. I'll keep my mobile switched off and I don't want anyone calling the landline or arriving at the door. Not for work reasons anyway."

"How about I allow you one concession? I know you'll go crazy, wondering what's going on in your absence. Let Sanjay send you one text each evening, say about eight o'clock, to let you know of developments."

"Now be honest, Sandra. Your suggestion isn't to stop me from going crazy; it's because you're desperate to know what's going on."

Sandra's face darkened. "How can you suggest such a thing?" She burst out laughing, before turning to hug and kiss Alex. "Yes, guilty as charged."

They drew apart to look at each other. "Ow, what was that for?" Alex rubbed his arm where Sandra had punched him.

"You're keeping me hanging on?" Sandra said.

"What do you mean?"

"I'm waiting for the latest instalment. What else has happened?"

Alex smiled. "I wanted to be up to date before going into the team meeting, so I had all of the interview reports emailed over to me last night. I read through them after taking the kids home. Believe it or not, I managed to get a good night's sleep. It's the first one I've had in a while."

"Now you know the magic formula. If you could just bottle it, you could make a fortune selling it as an insomnia cure. Seriously though, you're probably catching up after missing out on so much earlier in the week."

"That and Donny's scintillating writing style." Alex chuckled. "Okay, let me fill you in." Alex summarised the contents of all the latest reports.

"What leads are you chasing?" Sandra asked.

"As you'd expect, we're trying to locate Keiran's friends to see if they can fill in any gaps or tell us about anyone else we haven't considered. Although it seems unlikely, just for completeness, Donny's following up on this Zahid character. Phil's testing Ibrahim's alibi; he knows to tread carefully, but it needs to be done."

"And that leaves the families."

"Exactly, it's always the first port of call," Alex said. "I just realised, I haven't told you what I learned from the kids, last night." Alex repeated the discussion about Robbie McGowan.

"I don't suppose you've had a chance to check that out yet."

"I thought I'd give Brian Phelps a call."

"You mean your old drinking buddy."

"Why not? As deputy head of Eastfarm, he'll know if the stories are true, and he's sure to know a lot more. The only problem is he may not feel able to talk about it over the phone. You'll remember the last time I wanted some info, I met him for a pint at the Bank."

"You know you don't need to ask my permission to go out for a drink with your mates. However. if your motive is to work on your case during your paternity leave, well that's another matter."

"I had no intention. I'm hoping I'll be able to speak to him this morning because he's less likely to be as open if I send Sanjay or Phil."

"What's your next move? Give me a rundown,"

"We need some more solid information. As things stand, Kevin has to be our prime suspect. We could do with some reliable evidence which will either clear him or point the finger. Robbie gives me a problem; something doesn't smell right. I can't say I'm too comfortable with the parents either. They're too churchy. I can't believe they were as comfortable as they make out accepting a Moslem into their family. Perhaps they thought they were being missionaries and trying to convert her, but I don't buy it."

"Yeah, it sounds unlikely."

"Then we have the Sharmas. Ibrahim's made no secret of his hostility and I can't be too comfortable about Tarik either. There's more remote family too who must have been uncomfortable about Keiran embarrassing them, particularly if they knew about the pregnancy. And then there's Zahid. Dr Cartwright looks to be in the clear, his DNA wasn't a match."

"You're spoiled for choice. If you could trace the mobile, the one on Keiran's phone log, that Kevin claimed his friend had texted from, well that would help."

"Nothing on it yet, I'm afraid. I was wondering if we had enough to order a search on the McGowan house. You never know what that could uncover."

"It would be worth a try. Perhaps have a word with the fiscal."

"Have you established any relationship between Keiran's last sexual experience and the strangulation?"

"I've no doubt they're connected but that doesn't mean it was the same person."

"No, I suppose."

Alex looked at his watch. "I'll need to make a move. It doesn't look like this little lady is going to honour me with her attention."

"Don't worry, you'll see her later. Wasn't that kind of Jenny to bring a gift for Siobhan. She's such a sweet kid. I hope Craig appreciates her."

"I still can't get used to the idea of them being grown-ups."

"Get used to it Alex. If he gets the results he needs, Craig will be off to university after the summer and Andrew won't be too far behind. You need to let go, for their good and yours."

"I know. I only hope Craig and Jenny don't ask if they can come and stay over with us, together, I mean."

"It's hardly likely now we have Siobhan. But what's your problem? What age were you when you had your first serious relationship?"

"Okay, I was younger than Craig is now, but it wasn't the same."

"Don't you think you're being a bit hypocritical?"

"Isn't that every parent's prerogative, 'do as I say, not as I do'." Alex was grinning.

"Yep, and then you wonder what creates teenage angst."

Chapter 30

Alex's schedule had been to arrive early, wanting to check for updates and have a chat with Sanjay prior to the team meeting. However, his plans were thrown into disarray because of a minor accident on the Clydeside Expressway, not far from the Exhibition Centre, which held up the early rush hour traffic and caused tailbacks affecting all the trunk roads. Despite his best efforts, the meeting had already convened by the time he arrived.

"Okay everyone, let's settle down," Alex interrupted the hubbub of conversation bringing the meeting to order. "We've all had a chance to read the interview transcripts; what more do we have?"

"I've checked Ibrahim's alibi," said Phil. "It's got more holes than a sieve. It's true he was at a meeting in the mosque, but his meeting was finished by four. There were other groups which went on until seven, but he had no reason to attend them."

"Is that it?"

"No, Sir. He gave two names, he claimed would confirm his story. They both backed him up. Fair enough, one of them must have been in the late meeting, but the other was a sham. I've got evidence confirming he was in the town centre not long after five. If he wasn't at the Mosque, then Ibrahim's alibi is meaningless. More to the point, why were they both lying?"

"Good work, Phil. Let's keep Ibrahim on hold for now. Bring in the friend and put him under pressure. You know the routine. We want to find out why he lied. We want to know what Ibrahim was up to."

"Do you really think it could be an honour killing, Sir," Phil asked.

"My gut feel is no, and I'm praying that's not just wishful thinking," Alex replied. "Before I say more, I'd like to hear your thoughts, Sanjay."

"I don't think we can rule him out and he's certainly not done us, or himself, any favours by holding back information and by lying to us. However, I feel the same way as you, Sir. My gut feel is he's not involved. Let's look at what we know. On the one hand, he's religious and has fundamentalist links."

Heads nodded in agreement.

"He was unhappy about Keiran's relationship and wanted her disassociated from the family. On the other hand, he maintained links with her. We only have his word for what they spoke about, but it rings true to me. How embarrassed he might have been by her, we can only guess. If he didn't take action when she moved in with Kevin, and maybe even tried to win her back, would the discovery of her pregnancy have been enough to tip the scale? Personally, I don't think so. I don't think we'll get anything from him, bringing him in. Not unless we have some leverage. No, I agree the best way forward is to pressurise his witness."

"What else?" Alex asked.

"I've been doing some checking on Zahid," Donny said.

"In the interview notes, Jumilla said he went back to his family in Wolverhampton," Alex said. "What have you learned?"

"The girl was right, he was sent home and from what I can gather he's been in and around the Midlands for the last eight years. He doesn't have a criminal record, but that's not the whole story. He's been investigated on a number of occasions, on suspicion of sexual assault. At no time has he been prosecuted. It seems every time they've got close, the complaint had been dropped."

"That's odd," Sanjay said.

"I spoke to a sergeant who appeared to know all about him. He said a couple of times they were on the verge of court action and then their prime complainant or witness withdrew their evidence. He's certain they were either bought off or had the frighteners put on them."

"Did you get any details?" Alex asked.

"I did get some. Each *alleged* assault was an opportunist attack. Girls walking home on their own, down a dimly lit street or through a wood. Every one of the *victims* was a Moslem girl, between the age of fifteen and twenty-five."

"What was the nature of the attacks?" Alex asked.

"That's the most worrying part. It's been getting more severe. From what he told me, the first few cases must have been scary for the girls, but they were relatively trivial. Zahid would detain them and maybe touch or stroke them through their clothes, before he let them go. It appears he's become bolder over time, ripping clothes and sexually assaulting them. The latter cases can only be described as attempted rape and maybe the word attempted could be superfluous too. It's also likely that many incidents wouldn't have been reported."

"Bloody hell!" Steve blurted. "He's been a nasty piece of work. Kieran seems to have got off lightly. How did he get away with it, did his family have influence?" Steve asked.

"Moron!" Mary replied. "Sorry, Sir. I was attacking the statement not Steve."

"It's okay, go on, Mary," Steve said.

"I mean, how can anyone think Keiran got off lightly. From all accounts, her encounter with Zahid has tainted her entire life. We've only had Jamilla's second-hand version of her attack and it could well have been played down, by her, or her family, to avoid it affecting Keiran's future prospects. We don't know what impact it had on the circumstances leading to her death."

"Fair comment, but to answer your question, Steve, as far as family influence goes, they own a large wholesaling business. To me, that suggests they've got lots of money and often it's in cash. Two of them also hold positions on local councils, which gives them some political clout. Mind you, you haven't heard the best bit yet," Donny said, sporting a broad grin.

"As if that wasn't enough, what else do you have?" Alex asked.

"Zahid's no longer in the Midlands. Three weeks ago, he moved up to Edinburgh. He's got a job labouring for a building materials, delivery company and it's active throughout the Central Belt."

"Oh shit," Phil said. "So, we've got a known sexual predator, on the prowl in our area, and nobody's told us. Worse still, he's got history with Keiran."

"When he moved up, unofficially he was reported as a risk, through to Edinburgh." Donny advised. "No bloody use to us though."

"Thanks Donny, you've done well. Have you been able to check Zahid's whereabouts on Monday,"

"I tried, Sir. The company couldn't help. He took the afternoon off."

"We need to track him down. Better have a responsible adult available for the interview if learning difficulties might be an issue. One further question, Donny, on the attacks you spoke about, in the Midlands, did he wear a condom?"

"I don't know, Sir. I never thought to ask. Why?"

"We know Keiran had sex before she was killed and her *partner* was wearing a condom which was a different brand to the ones she and Kevin had a stock of."

"Ah, I see where you're coming from, I'll check."

"Okay, what do we have on Kevin McGowan?" Alex asked.

"We've got motive, whether genuine or not," Sanjay replied. "As he thought Keiran was pregnant and believed himself to be infertile, he'll have concluded she'd been screwing around. That gives him motive. He's misled us on his movements on Monday and we haven't been able to verify the whereabouts he's told us about. We've had to drag information out of him and even now, it doesn't all stack up."

"He's definitely in the frame," Steve said.

"Can we get a search on the parent's house. We don't know what he might be hiding." Mary suggested.

"Get it organised," Alex replied, looking at Sanjay.

"Yes, Sir."

"What about the brother? What have you got there?" Alex asked.

Nobody answered.

"It's come to my attention that Robbie has a history of racial antagonism. He's Kevin's brother and there's at least an element of sibling rivalry. He seems to have had a thing about Keiran; call it lust or whatever you like. I think you need to consider him as a suspect, too. The house search can be used to catch two birds with the one stone."

"I'll get onto it," Sanjay said.

"Make that three, or even four birds," Alex added. "I'm not convinced by the parents' story. They might have wanted Keiran out of the way, particularly if they knew she was pregnant. If they truly believed Kevin was infertile it would give them one motive, but if they thought the baby could be Kevin's they could have been afraid she was going to trap him. Either way, they have a reason to be rid of her."

"You can't believe they would have been capable of killing her, knowing she was expecting," Mary said.

"We've come upon poorer reasons for murder," Steve said.

Noting the looks of surprise on everyone's face, Alex smiled then continued, "You can thank my sons and Sandra for the lead on Robbie. Do we have any others?"

The question was met by stony silence,

"What about the lists of friends and contacts?" Alex asked.

"We've made a start, but we've not had a chance to follow up on many of them yet," Sanjay replied.

"Jamilla spoke about a particularly close friend, a Carolyn something," Alex said.

"Fletcher, Sir. Carolyn Fletcher," Mary said.

"Have you got hold of her yet?"

"No, Sir. She's moved away, so we gave her lower priority," Mary replied.

"Where did she go?"

"Perth, she went there not long after graduating."

"Why should that make a difference? It's only ninety minutes away."

"No, Sir. It's Perth in Western Australia. She doesn't have the use of the same mobile and there weren't any international calls on Keiran's log. They used to talk regularly up until she left."

"Okay, I can see your point. Mind you, if they were close, it's odd there hasn't been at least some contact. Have you checked FaceTime, Skype and WhatsApp? They may have used one of those to communicate as it would have been much cheaper."

"Sorry, Sir. It didn't occur to me. I'll get onto it now," Mary said.

"Everyone press ahead. I've some calls to make and then I'm out. If Sandra gets the okay, then I can take her and Siobhan home this afternoon. If so, you won't see me for the next fortnight, so Sanjay will be in charge. Sanjay, I'd like a word in private please."

"Before you go, Sir, Can I have a quick word," Donny asked.

"Come through now, Donny. Sanjay, come in straight after."

Alex settled at his desk and Donny stood next to the chair opposite.

"Sit down, Donny. What did you want to say?"

"I'll only be a second. I just wanted to let you know things have settled down a bit at home."

"I'm pleased to hear that. What's changed?"

After we spoke, I felt a bit better and I talked it through with Steve. He suggested I talked to Ben about the kids. Anyhow, when I went home, I got talking to Ben and he was receptive. I mean we were really talking. He was saying how much he missed his kids. I told him we missed them too. I suggested we all went down to London together, Ben, Cath and me. It's the first time I'd seen him smile since he's been home."

"He must have been too scared at the idea of facing them on his own."

"Yes, Sir, that's exactly it. Anyhow, we're planning to take a long weekend in a fortnight's time and we'll all get to see the kids. I'm due time off then. Ben phoned his wife and it's all arranged. I just have to make the hotel and travel arrangements. He's even been talking about phoning round the agencies so he can make work enquiries while he's there. I think he's starting to come to terms with it."

"It won't be easy, but it sounds like he's over the worst. I reckon he's had a terrible shock and he's been in denial."

Chapter 31

It only took two minutes for Alex to brief Sanjay on the contact arrangements he'd agreed with Sandra.

"No problem, Sir. Good luck."

Alex reached for his phone to call Brian, but his mobile rang first.

"It's Stuart Black again, Sir. I promised to call you back." His voice sounded excited.

"Yes, Stuart. What news have you got?"

Stuart couldn't get the words out fast enough. "Well, Sir. I've got some good news and some bad news. We went into the electrical place as planned. It's quite a big operation and on first glance it all looked legit. They have a large workshop and they have two employees solely to carry out repairs"

"Slow down Stuart, I want to follow what you're telling me."

"Yes, Sir, okay. They also have a small showroom for retail customers but their main business is selling second hand electrical appliances and accessories. They use the internet. They have their own sales webpage but most of their sales go through auction sites, local community groups or social media pages."

"So far, it all sounds like a proper business."

"It is, Sir, and their paperwork all stacks up. The employees are through their payroll; they're VAT registered and they pay their taxes. They even got an enterprise grant when they set up."

"Was that the good news or the bad news?"

"Neither, Sir, I thought I ought to give you the background. As I said, it all looked legit on first sight; it was only when we probed deeper we found out how they got a lot of their stock."

"Tell me more."

"Like it says on their flyers, they do repairs and they buy used and unwanted items. However, they use intermediaries to deliver the leaflets and these same intermediaries will buy or collect goods and sell it to them."

"*Collect* being the operative word."

"Yes, Sir. I'll get to that in a minute. They have purchase invoices showing what they've bought and who they bought it from, but a lot of the time it's the one supplier – the same one who they use for the flyers."

"Yes, I understand, but so far there hasn't been any wrongdoing."

"We found that an awful lot of the stuff they bought matched items we had listed as stolen, and more often than not, the dates tied in too. They might have got away with claiming coincidence, but a small number of the victims had taken the precaution to security label their appliances."

Alex chuckled.

"You weren't the only one, Sir. However, we did find a couple of items you'd told us about, and they had them included in their stock."

"What action are you taking?"

"There are two joint owners of the company and we've charged them with receiving stolen goods. We have the names, addresses and phone numbers for the people they've been buying from and we've issued an arrest warrant. We managed to get one of the owners to phone them and ask them to come into their office. So, here's hoping."

"You must be really pleased."

"I sure am, Sir. Because I was the one who first identified the link to the advertising flyer, my sergeant said I might be in for a commendation."

"Well done, Stuart. Now you said there was good news and bad news."

"Yes, Sir, I'm afraid so. It's about your television. We found it in their workshop. It was one of the items we identified. Someone must have dropped it because there's a crack all the way across the screen."

"That is a pity, Stuart. I guess it won't be worth taking back, which means I'll need to claim my insurance for a new one." Alex faked a soulful voice,

"I'm sorry about that, Sir."

"You didn't happen to come across any computer games?"

"I was going to tell you. Yes, we have the ones you reported."

"My son will be delighted. Any chance you found my whisky?"

"Sorry, Sir, not a trace.

"My luck had to run out sometime. Thanks for letting me know."

When Alex hung up, he noticed a voicemail had been left while he was on his call. He clicked on the icon and within seconds received Sandra's recording. "Hi Alex, I guess you're busy at the moment. I'm afraid I've a bit of bad news, but don't worry, it's not too bad. - My consultant's been round and said the infection's clearing up but not fast enough. He wants to keep me in a bit longer. He's going to check on me later this afternoon. If I'm not clear then, he did say someone would be available to release me tomorrow if there's further improvement. Anyhow, while I've been sitting here, feeling sorry for myself, I've been thinking about your case. Something occurred to me. It may be a longshot, but I thought I'd mention if you want to check it out. From what you told me, Keiran was worried her mum, being a GP, might have had access to her medical records. What I wondered, - would it be possible that Dr Sharma accessed Kevin's records, unofficially I mean. I haven't thought it all the way through, but if she had researched him, what could she have found - maybe the infertility. And how might she have reacted if she found out Keiran was pregnant. I felt there was something funny about the reports when she and her family were interviewed. She sounds too good to be true. It's probably just my addled brain trying to do *what if* exercises, but I though I'd say to you."

Alex tried phoning Sandra back, only to discover her phone was switched off. He dialled Phil's number. "Phil, can you please check if a log is kept whenever someone accesses a patient's medical record. If so, I want to know if anyone has checked out Kevin McGowan, then find out who, and when."

"I'll get onto it, Sir. What's the thinking?"

"It's a theory Sandra had. It may be a long shot but best to be sure."

"With his phone now free, Alex thought he'd make another attempt to call Brian Phelps.

Chapter 32

"Hi Alex, how are things? Sandra must be due any day now." Brian was quick to answer when he recognised Alex's number.

"I'm now the proud father of a two-day-old girl. Sandra gave birth on Wednesday and we've called her Siobhan."

"Congratulations, great news. I trust they're both well."

"They're both fine, although Sandra has a mild infection so she's not home yet."

"Look on the bright side, the sleepless nights haven't started yet. Take advantage while you can."

"It won't make much difference; I have sleepless nights for a whole number of reasons."

"If you're calling to enrol Siobhan into Eastfarm, then you're far too early." Brian laughed. "I know our school has a waiting list, but she needs to go through toddlers, nursery and primary first. It's likely to be another eleven years before you need to apply. Even then you're out of area. Unless you move back into the district then we can't give Siobhan a place."

"Very funny. But listen, Brian, this isn't just a social call. I wanted to ask you for some information."

"If I can help, I will."

"This is off the record. I wanted to know if there's anything you can tell me about one of your pupils, Robbie McGowan."

Brian gave a low whistle. "I can't talk from here. How about we meet up for a pint this evening."

"Much as I'd like to, I need to stay available in case Sandra gets out."

"Henpecked already, I don't know." Brian laughed. "No, seriously, I understand. As it happens, I don't have a class at the moment, because my lot are away on some field trip for Geography. It means I'm free until after lunch. If you can get over here quickly, we could go for a coffee."

"I'm on my way. I should be with you in about twenty minutes. I'll pick you up at the front gate."

* * *

"Where would you like to go?" Alex asked.

"Nowhere too close, I wouldn't want to bump into any pupils, or parents for that matter."

"I'll cross the boundary then. How about the Costa in Darnley? Albeit only by a few hundred yards, it will take you outside of East Renfrewshire."

A few minutes later, they were sitting at a corner table, well away from other customers.

"Thanks Alex, this is a treat. Much as I enjoy their caramel lattes, I seldom indulge because they're so sweet and I need to watch my sugar level."

"I didn't know you had a problem."

"Not yet really, but I'm a borderline diabetic. I'll be okay so long as I'm careful what I eat and drink. Anyway, enough about me. What's this all about?"

"I was hoping you might be able to give me some background info on Robbie McGowan."

"He's been off school since Monday. We heard there was some family issue, something about his brother's girlfriend and a sudden death. I guess that's what you're investigating."

"Spot on. At present we're treating it as an unexplained death. I'm trying to accumulate as much information as I can about the families."

"We've got Robbie in sixth year. I know of him, but he hasn't been in any of my classes. I did teach his older brother, Kevin. He left, four, maybe five years ago."

"It was Robbie, I came to ask about, but anything you can tell me about Kevin would be welcome too."

"Where can I start, the two boys were like chalk and cheese. You asked first about Robbie, so I'll start there. He's very strong and sporty."

"Yes, my boys told me."

"He really is quite an athlete. The school tries to encourage sporting excellence. As you must know, we don't only push academic subjects. We have several accomplished kids who take part in national competitions. We even have a couple who are already in the G.B. squad for their sports."

Alex waited patiently.

"Robbie is a top quality rugby player. He's good at football, basketball and cross country too, but he's quite exceptional at rugby. We hadn't realised how much the school team relied on him until he was absent from the game on Wednesday." Brian shook his head.

"Craig told me; he was there."

"Sorry, this isn't what you came to hear. Outside of sports, he's a fairly average pupil, probably a below average achiever, actually. It's not that he lacks intelligence, but he doesn't try."

"Do you think that's because he gets his accolades in sport?"

"To some extent, but it's not the whole story. Many of our sports stars are high flyers academically. I'd put Robbie's attitude more down to him wanting to differentiate himself from his brother. Kevin was a good student and a hard worker. He had a determination to do well so he could go to university. He didn't care about subjects which didn't contribute to that aim."

"And Robbie is the opposite?"

"As far as I've heard, he has no ambition and no real focus. Yes, he excels at sports and he's happy to do so, but he does it without really trying."

"What is he interested in?"

"Good question. I don't have an answer. I reckon the parents could be the problem. I met them at Kevin's parent teacher meetings and they lavished attention on him; they wanted to be involved in every decision. From what I've heard they didn't show the same interest in Robbie. They've attended very few of the meetings for him and I don't believe they've ever been to see him compete. I think it's very sad."

"I understand that Kevin had some health issues when he was younger," Alex said.

"Yes, it was before I knew him. Although he needed occasional time off for medicals, he didn't have any ongoing problems which affected him that I was aware of. But I take your point. It's not unusual for parents to dote on a child after they've had serious medical issues. In Kevin's case, I think he was badly spoiled. I don't think it did him any good. I always felt he was troubled."

"What do you mean by troubled?"

"We come across many troubled kids and it often results from lack of attention. This certainly wasn't Kevin's problem, quite the reverse in fact. I used to get the impression he was fragile. I don't mean physically. He seemed strong enough that way, more like emotionally fragile. I thought he seemed to be on the edge of a breakdown."

"Have you any idea why?"

"I put it down to the parents. The way they treated him must have been quite claustrophobic, added to which they are deeply religious."

"Would that make a difference?"

"I don't know. I'm an atheist, but I feel it might have increased the intensity."

"What about Robbie?"

"Although I don't agree with it, I can understand them wanting to cosset Kevin. It doesn't excuse them ignoring Robbie though. From what I can gather, he's troubled too, but in a different way."

"Can you explain?"

"Robbie gives the impression of being fiercely independent. I believe it's an act to cover for his insecurity. A result of feeling unloved. Beneath the surface, I think he's quaking. I'm afraid he's a powder keg, a timebomb waiting to explode."

"I heard he got into a bit of bother a few months back."

"Ah, you know about that."

"None of the details, I heard he was suspended for fighting. Can you fill me in?"

"You're partially correct, but there's more to it. It was about six or seven months ago. Something set him off and he started shouting and screaming at a couple of Asian girls. He ranted about them coming and taking over his country and about them not being wanted. His language was choice. I won't repeat the words, but suffice to say, they were unacceptable and racist. He was twice their size and he was being aggressive; the girls were terrified."

"I think that may have been around the time Kevin's girlfriend, Keiran, moved into their house. She was given Robbie's room and he was made to share with Kevin."

"That explains a lot. Anyhow, one of the fourth year boys stepped in and told Robbie to back off. Robbie hit him. He might have done him serious damage if some others hadn't stepped forward and pulled him off."

"What did the school do?"

"Once he'd calmed down, Robbie was very apologetic. He said he'd been upset about something and it wasn't like him. He claimed he hadn't meant what he'd said. We spoke to his parents, one of the few times they did come to the school on Robbie's behalf. They said they would discipline him at home and pleaded for nothing to go on his record. The head, you already know Harry Forrester, he dealt with it, himself. He thought the parents were being sincere. As punishment from the school, Robbie was given one week's suspension, but only the fighting was put on his formal record. Forrester spoke to the parents of the girls and the boy who was hit. He got their agreement, although he arranged to keep a close eye on Robbie."

"There have been no more incidents?"

"Nothing."

"Thanks, I really appreciate you helping. I'd better get you back to the school before you're missed."

Chapter 33

"Mary, have you had any success looking for Carolyn Fletcher?" Sanjay asked.

"I was about to come and tell you. The boss was right. She and Keiran have been talking on Skype. They used videocalls and they've been in regular contact. I used my mobile so I could send her a message, to ask if she'll speak to me, and I received a reply. They're seven hours ahead of us in Perth. She's on her way home from work but expects to be back in half an hour or so. She said she'd take my call then."

"What did you tell her? Who did you say you were?"

"I haven't told her anything yet. I wanted to clear it with you first. All I've given her is my name, and I told her it was to do with Keiran Sharma."

"Good, you can use the computer in the meeting room, so we can record the conversation, and I'll sit in with you."

Sanjay and Mary took the next forty minutes setting up equipment and discussing their approach. "I'll leave you to do the talking and only come in if needed," Sanjay said. "Ready?"

Mary nodded and pressed connect. The distinctive electronic, almost musical, ringtone played for several seconds. Mary was on the verge of hanging up when the call was answered. The screen flickered a couple of times, then she could see a suntanned, heavy-set young lady with shoulder length hair, tied in bunches.

"Are you Carolyn Fletcher?" Mary asked.

"Yes, you must be Mary, the one who messaged me earlier. You said you wanted to talk to me about Keiran. Who are you, and what's this all about?"

"My name is Mary Mackenzie and I'm a police officer. I'm a detective constable with Police Scotland in Glasgow; sitting beside me is Sergeant Sanjay Guptar." Mary swivelled the webcam so Carolyn was able to see Sanjay, then moved it back and presented both their warrant cards to the camera."

"Now you've got me worried."

"We believe you may have information which can help us with our enquiries, but before we start, I must caution you that this call is being recorded."

"I hope that wasn't designed to make me feel more comfortable? If it was, you failed? I'm frightened to ask …"

"We have some bad news, I'm afraid. It's about your friend, Keiran Sharma. I'm sorry to have to tell you, she's dead."

"Oh my God, no." The colour drained perceptibly from Carolyn's cheeks. "I spoke to her on Monday; she was okay then. I've tried to get hold of her since and was starting to become concerned. Oh no. What happened, did she have an accident?"

"We're investigating to find out what happened; we'd like to ask you some questions."

"You didn't answer. If it wasn't an accident, what happened?"

"Kevin reported that he came home from work on Monday and found her dead. It's too early to know all the details, but there are indications to suggest she'd been murdered."

Carolyn looked as if she might faint. "Poor Keiran, do you know who did it? Was it Kevin?"

"Why would you jump to that conclusion?"

"I don't know. I just thought…"

"As I said, we're trying to find out what happened, and we'd like to ask you some questions."

"I suppose that would be okay. I'd like to help if I can, but give me a minute first. I need to get some water. It's hot in here and the aircon hasn't tripped in yet."

"Yes, no problem."

A few moments later, Carolyn returned. She sat down in an upright chair at a table in front of her camera. She placed a glass in front of her and covered her face with her hands. "I can't believe it," she whispered. "She was so vibrant and alive. She was my best friend."

"We're sorry for your loss. We're trying to get some background and we hoped you might be able to help. To start with, can you tell us how long you have known Keiran?"

Carolyn moved her hands away and dabbed at her tears. Punctuated by sobs, she began speaking, "We started Uni together; we met at Freshers Week. We had the same interests and got along right from the start."

"What were those interests?"

"We both love theatre and cinema. We wanted to preform, not just watch, so we joined the amdram group. We have a similar taste in music and we'd go to the gym together too."

"What about boyfriends, did you like the same ones, or did you ever double date?"

Carolyn chuckled. "I said we enjoyed films and there were some superstars we may have fought over, but not when it came down to real men. We had different taste. I guess that was lucky."

"Can you please explain? How did you differ?"

"I don't know how much you already know. I found the sort of boys Keiran was attracted to, were the sensitive arty types. Do you know what I mean? I'm more into the rugged physical ones."

"And you regard Kevin as falling into the first group."

"Yes, definitely. He wasn't puny by any measure, but I doubt if he'd have known the difference between basketball boots and hiking ones. I remember, well; Keiran noticed him early on. It must have been back in first year. He seemed a nice enough lad, but I didn't understand what she saw in him."

"Don't get me wrong. I was happy she fancied him. Keiran had the looks and figure to turn heads. Because she had designs on Kevin, it meant I had less competition to worry about."

"Tell me more."

"Keiran was quite complex. She decided right from the off that she wanted Kevin, but I don't think she was ready for a relationship at that time. She flirted a bit, made sure he noticed her. And boy did he notice her. His eyes followed wherever she went, all the time."

"You're telling me he was fixated on her."

"I hadn't thought of it that way, but maybe, yes. He was shy, too shy to approach her, and he wasn't too great an actor to hide his feelings. Anyhow, during second year, our director had a play he'd written and wanted to produce. He invited Keiran to play the lead and she agreed, but she insisted he cast Kevin in one of the main male roles. It brought them into much closer proximity."

"You're telling me Keiran was responsible for him getting the part."

"Yes, absolutely."

"And he didn't realise."

"No, not then and probably not now either. She didn't want him to know that it wasn't on his own merit."

"That's' kind of cute."

"I suppose so. He was keen on her before, but working on the part and rehearsing together, I reckon he became besotted. He was too shy to do anything about it and I think Keiran was a bit reticent as well. I challenged her. I dared her to kiss him on stage for a laugh. We worked out this plan. She would take him by surprise when in mid show and in front of a whole audience."

"Yes, we already heard Kevin's version."

"He was completely dumbstruck. He didn't know what to do."

"So, your plan worked."

"If Kevin wasn't hooked before, which I doubt, he was then. He was ready to chase after Keiran like a puppy dog."

"We've heard it said that Keiran was determined. If she wanted something, she got it."

"You could say that, but I don't think Kevin was complaining."

"I guess not. From what you're telling me, they were both keen on each other for a while and it took a long time for them to get together, but once they did they were very close."

"Not exactly, but we're getting into some very intimate stuff, I don't know if it's right."

"These details may turn out to be very important if we're to find the truth. We need you to tell us."

Carolyn looked somewhat uncertain but seemed to come to a decision before continuing. "Do you know about the incident with her cousin?"

"Yes, Zahid, we've heard."

"Good, I don't need to explain then. Before getting together with Kevin, although Keiran played about a bit with boys, she was still a virgin and deep down she was terrified. That's why she always felt a need to be in control. With Kevin she felt relaxed, probably because she was in control. When it came to it, she was the one who seduced him."

"We've heard about the day out in Balloch, but we'd like to know what Keiran told you."

Carolyn's version was almost identical to what Kevin had divulged. "Afterwards, she became bolder and was eager to try new things."

"Was that with other men, or women for that matter?"

"No, No, she was most definitely heterosexual, and she didn't show interest in anyone other than Kevin. Not for a long time anyway."

"You're getting at something."

"Let me take it in order. Keiran had this thing about not wearing clothes. Often when no one was around she'd walk about her flat stark naked. If someone came to the door, she'd quickly throw on a dress before answering. Sometimes, she'd go out wearing no underwear. It gave her a thrill knowing she was naked or only partially dressed when no-one else realised."

"That's a bit kinky."

"In second year, there was a day she went to all her lectures wearing only a short skirt and a top. It really gave her a thrill and because of the tiered lecture theatre it might well have given some others a thrill too."

"Wasn't it a risky thing to do?"

"I don't know if she'd even thought about it until I said to her. I'm sure no one saw anything, but I had some fun winding her up and she got quite embarrassed when she realised. We had quite a laugh." Carolyn smiled at the memory.

"Was that before or after she got together with Kevin?"

"It must have been before, but not much. Anyhow, Kevin thought the *no underwear thing* was something special she did for him, just to turn him on. She used it that first time when she seduced him on the day out in Balloch, and he assumed she only did it to mark special occasions."

"I suppose it made it a special occasion for him."

"Yes, fair point. Everything went well for them for a while, but Kevin had a bit of a problem with alcohol. Don't get me wrong, he's a lovely guy but often when he starts drinking, he doesn't know when to stop."

"How did Keiran feel about it?"

"At first, it didn't bother her, but more recently, I think, she started to worry that it might be getting out of control."

"I take it something happened."

"There were a number of occasions, she told me, that troubled her, and she was becoming increasing anxious."

"Had she spoken to him about it?"

"Yes, of course. He'd promise to be more restrained and he did try. He'd control it for a few days. or even weeks, and then he'd be as bad as before."

"Did they seek help?"

"Not that I'm aware of."

"You're leading up to something, I can tell."

"Yes, about a month back. It was Kevin's birthday. They had a big evening planned. They went out for cocktails and a meal. They shared a bottle of wine and, by shared, I mean Keiran had a glass or two and Kevin had the rest. On their way out, they bumped into Kevin's brother, Robbie, and he insisted on buying both of them more drinks to celebrate. By the end of the evening, Keiran was quite tipsy and Kevin was out of his face. They ordered a taxi and Robbie helped Keiran get Kevin home and into bed."

"And then," Mary asked, suspecting the answer.

"This is really difficult. I feel I'd be betraying a confidence. She doesn't deserve that."

"It's information we may need if we're going to find out what happened to her."

"From what she told me, they went to the door for Robbie to leave. Keiran touched Robbie's face and thanked him. He leaned in and kissed her. She told me she resisted at first but then succumbed. I ... I can't say more." Carolyn covered her face with her hands.

"You must," Mary urged.

Carolyn drew in a breath. "They had sex there and then in the hall."

"Did Kevin realise?"

"No, although he must have been only a few feet away, he was asleep throughout. Afterwards they went into the lounge. She told me she started to cry and told Robbie she was sorry, and it shouldn't have happened. She said Robbie took her in his arms and kissed away her tears ... they had sex again. This time he was very gentle and loving. She told me she felt powerless to stop him."

"All this happened, a stone's throw from where his brother lay unconscious."

"When she'd fully sobered up, Keiran was very upset realising what she'd done, but at the same time she was exhilarated. She said she couldn't understand why she did it; she was confused. Her words to me were, *he's little more than a boy but it was the best sex I've ever had.* As I said, she was confused. She hadn't intended to cheat on Kevin, but the experience thrilled her. She truly loved Kevin and she knew any relationship with Robbie meant nothing, it was only physical, but she couldn't stop thinking about it."

"Did she blame it on being drunk?"

"No, I think she suspected it may have lowered her inhibitions but she when she opened up to me, she took responsibility."

"And afterwards."

"She was in a quandary. She did love Kevin, but she had concerns about the relationship. I don't believe she even liked Robbie; she didn't trust him, yet she lusted after him. She was also frightened about Kevin finding out and she pleaded with Robbie not to say anything."

"It appears she talked to you quite a lot about this."

"We always tried to talk on a regular basis, but those first few days, she needed someone, she could bounce things off, someone who she felt wouldn't judge her. She called me at all times of day and night. I didn't mind of course."

"I take it the sex they had was unprotected."

"Yes. It had been unplanned by them, and that was another worry for Keiran."

"She had quite a dilemma." A thought occurred to Mary. "After that night, how did she communicate with him?"

"By mobile I think. Wait a minute. I remember her saying. She was worried about anyone else realising they were talking to each other more than might have been considered appropriate. She bought him a pay-as-you-go phone. One that he was only to use for talking to her and to keep hidden."

"Bingo! Now we've an explanation for a lot of the unexplained calls on her log. Do you know what they talked about?"

"She told me some of the things and they didn't always make sense. One minute she'd tell him they could never see each other again and the next she would talk about him needing to carry condoms with him in future because she couldn't use the ones bought by Kevin."

"It sounds as if she was very confused."

"She was. She was trying to keep everything normal with Kevin whilst in her mind she was in total turmoil."

"Not only her mind."

"Yes, you're right. After the time with Robbie she knew there was a chance. She suspected she might be pregnant for a while and was too frightened to check. I told her she must find out as soon as possible so she could make a decision."

"Did she not agree?"

"In a way. She knew she was being a coward, putting off finding out. However, she said even if she was pregnant, she'd wouldn't consider a termination so what did it matter. I talked her into taking a test. Oh my God; could this have anything to do with her death? Am I to blame?"

"Don't torture yourself. If may have had no bearing, but even if it did, she had to find out sometime. Rest assured, you're not to blame. I assume she told you the result."

"More than that. She bought the test and called me before she used it. She kept me on hold while she checked it."

"How did she react when she found out?"

"Hardly at all. I think she already knew herself and all it did was confirm her suspicions."

"Did she say what she planned to do?"

"She was going to tell Kevin that evening. They had a special dinner planned for their anniversary and she was going to tell him and see how he took the news."

"Was she planning to tell him about Robbie?"

"God no! Although it was less likely, it could have been Kevin who made her pregnant and he wasn't to know differently, not as long as Keiran didn't let on and of course, Robbie would need to keep quiet."

"Was she going to talk to Robbie?"

"She hadn't decided. She knew she'd have to talk to him at some point and maybe she wanted to get it out of the way. She was worried about how he might react. When I last spoke to her, she was indecisive about what she would say and when."

"And you didn't hear from her after that."

"No. I was desperate to find out how it went, and I didn't hear anything. I thought her computer might be broken or something. I was thinking I might have to try and locate her sister. I hadn't dreamed she'd be dead."

"Earlier on, after I told you murder was suspected, you asked me if it was Kevin."

"I guess I wondered if he'd heard about Robbie and lost it."

"I'm sorry to have given you the bad news. What you've told us could prove very valuable. We may want to come back to you for further information and we may need you to sign a formal statement. Would that be okay?"

"Yes, Keiran was like a sister to me. I'll do anything I can to help."

Chapter 34

"Mr Hussein, thank you for coming in. We need to talk to you about the statement you gave us, earlier this week," Steve said. "May I remind you that you're still under caution."

"You phoned at the right time. I was passing nearby on my way to visit one of my properties. It wasn't too much of a detour and I wanted to get this out of the way. What I don't understand is why you wanted to see me again. I already told you what you wanted to know."

"Perhaps you told us what you thought we wanted to hear. However, we'd much rather know the truth."

"I don't need to listen to this. I came here to do you a favour and all you can do is insult me."

Steve opened the file he had waiting on the table. "I have a signed statement from you saying you were in the company of Mr Ibrahim Sharma in a meeting at your Mosque throughout Monday afternoon. You said this was from approximately two o'clock through until seven."

"Ye…e.e.s," Hussein's reply was more hesitant.

"We now know you were lying. The meeting you spoke about ended at four o'clock."

"Pah! You're playing with words. The first meeting ended at four, but there was a series of meetings which ended at seven."

"I don't doubt it. However, where I take issue is that neither you nor Mr Sharma attended the later meetings."

Hussein looked more nervous. "That isn't true. How can you say such things? Nobody can say that we weren't there. You are talking rubbish."

Steve made no verbal response initially. Instead, in slow and deliberate fashion, he lifted two photographs from his file and placed them in front of Hussein. Each was taken from a camera at different points in Buchanan Street and each showed Hussein. Steve tapped each photo, pointing to the time and date mark which showed he'd been there late afternoon on Monday. "Given your assertions, how would you explain these?"

Hussein became even more agitated. "They are fakes. You're trying to confuse me."

"The photos I'm showing you are stills, taken from official security surveillance footage. I must make you aware that providing false evidence in a murder investigation is a criminal offence and can lead to a custodial sentence. Do you want to end up in prison? Now tell us the truth."

Hussein looked downward, unable to maintain eye contact. He sat with his head in his hands, elbows propped on the table. "I have responsibilities. You can not send me to prison. I meant no harm."

"The truth, now. If you cooperate then we'll see what we can do."

"It is true. I left after the meeting ended at four o'clock."

"And Sharma?"

"He came out of the meeting at the same time. I don't know if he went back or what he did."

"Why did you give evidence that you and he both stayed at the Mosque?"

Hussein's words came interspersed with sobs. "He asked me. He said he needed me to cover for him and it was easiest just to say we were together in the Mosque."

"But why did you agree?"

"I owed him. He has done many favours for me over the years. It was my chance to do something for him."

"Why did he need a false alibi? Did he tell you where he had actually gone?"

"I don't know any details. All he said was that he needed to attend to family business."

* * *

Steve updated Sanjay on the interview with Hussein.

"The boss will be pleased. We're making some real progress now. "Sanjay said. "Let's get Ibrahim back in and see what this *family business* is all about."

"Excuse me, Sarge. I've got an update for you," Donny interrupted.

"Yes, what have you got?"

"Nothing much, I'm afraid. I checked with my contact in Birmingham, as the boss asked. There are no indications of Zahid wearing a condom in any of the reports."

"Thanks, Donny. Will you give Fitzpatrick a bell and ask if he has anything else for us?"

"Will do."

"Where's Phil?" Sanjay asked.

"I'm not certain," Donny replied. "The last I saw of him, he was making enquiries about medical records; I think he was getting fobbed off. He may have gone to try to get a face-to-face with someone at the Heath Board."

"What's next?" Steve asked.

"I'm waiting to see if Mary has a result from the search warrant application," Sanjay answered. "If so; we go in. I want to check first with the boss, but my plan is to bring in both McGowan boys. From what we learned from the Carolyn Fletcher interview, they both have a lot of explaining to do."

"A bit more progress," Donny called over. "Fitzpatrick has more matches, again not too clear, but it is something. He's sending us the photos."

"What's he got?" Sanjay asked.

"He'd already given the sighting at five-thirty in Minard Road. He has another which just might be Ibrahim. It's from the same camera but it's about an hour earlier, around four-thirty. He has two more, both in Pollockshaws Road. One was heading into town at six thirty and the other coming towards the flat at about seven. Both would be consistent with going to or from the bus. Neither of them is clear, but both have a resemblance to McGowan and all appear to be wearing a dark jacket, quite possibly leather."

"I'm not convinced that helps too much," Sanjay said.

"There's another in St Vincent Street, not much before five. It's consistent with McGowan's story about leaving the pub in Waterloo Street and going to meet his friend at Wetherspoons."

"Where precisely in St Vincent Street?"

"Let's see, ... approaching the corner with Renfield Street."

"He might just as well have turned into Renfield to catch his bus home from there, or for that matter to get the wine and flowers and jump on at Union Street."

"In the photos, was he carrying anything?"

"I don't know, never thought to ask. I'll check once they come through."

"I was hoping the cameras might have given us something more concrete. From what you've said, all the images are poor quality."

"Fitzpatrick was having a moan about that. He said he was getting really pissed off. Everyone was criticising him, when it wasn't his fault. He said he'd had enough and was thinking of packing it all in. When I asked what he meant, he said a new company had taken over the equipment maintenance and they were crap by comparison. In his words, *Tens of millions of pounds worth of equipment not worth a damn because some asshole moneyman at the Council was trying to save a few quid.*"

"Maybe, he's got a point. Let's wait and see what he sends."

Chapter 35

"Hello, Sir. It's Stuart Black again."

"Yes, Stuart. This is starting to become a habit." Alex replied.

"Oh, I'm sorry, Sir. I didn't mean to be a nuisance. I can call you back if you tell me when, or I can leave a message at the office."

"No, it's okay Stuart. I was trying to be funny. It's only my unique brand of humour. Please go on."

"I've got more news for you. I thought you'd want to know."

"Yes Stuart. It's okay. Please tell me."

"We've made the arrests. Two young men; both aged nineteen. One's from Possil, the other's a Romanian from Govan. They've both got form. They met each other whilst they were each serving community service for past misdemeanours. They struck up a friendship and decided to go into business together, so to speak."

"A right couple of entrepreneurs."

"Yes Sir. They tried to deny doing anything wrong, at first, but when they saw some of the evidence, they folded. We have full confessions."

"Well done, Stuart. That's good police work. Now I don't suppose there's any sign of my whisky?"

"Well, there's the thing, Sir. We have recovered it, but we're a bit late."

"You mean it's empty."

"Not quite, Sir. There's about a third of the bottle left. Beattie, the Possil lad, said he thought it had tasted really good, smoothed down with some cola."

"Bloody hell! That's a worse crime than the thieving. It's sacrilege, poisoning good scotch with cola. It was a twenty-five-year old, single malt, for God's sake, a collector's item. Forget a trial, you want to lock them up and throw away the key."

"I'm sorry, Sir. Are you being serious?"

"I'm deadly serious, but I didn't mean it literally."

"I'll mark down for the bottle to be returned to you the moment it's no longer needed."

"No forget it Stuart. It wouldn't be the same. I appreciate your efforts though."

"There's something else, Sir, something I wanted to ask you about."

"Yes, Stuart. What can I do for you?" Alex was apprehensive, expecting to be asked for a favour."

"It's about the murder, Sir. The one I first met you at on Monday."

Alex was now intrigued. "Go on."

"I remembered when I was hanging around waiting in the close; I saw a flyer for the electrical company sticking in a letterbox. I reckoned it was hand delivered on Monday."

How did I and any of my team manage to miss that? Alex thought.

"I just thought, if the same lads put the leaflets through those doors, maybe they saw something suspicious which could help your investigation."

"Makes sense."

"I asked Beattie and he confirmed they leafletted and knocked doors in Waverley Gardens, late on Monday afternoon. He complained it had been a waste of time with not a single bite. When I asked if he'd seen or heard anything suspicious, he told me that he was walking along when he was practically knocked off his feet. Someone in a hurry, wearing a leather jacket ran straight into him, scattering his flyers. Apparently, he just rushed off; no by your leave or apology."

"Did you ask if he'd be able to recognise the person?"

"I did. He wasn't certain."

"I'm going to get one of my officers across to your station. I'd like Beattie to look at some photos. Stuart, you're a genius. Have you ever thought of applying to CID?"

"Yeah, sure, some chance of that ever happening."

"Seriously, I'm aware there's going to be an opportunity coming up next month. It's for a six-month secondment. I think you'd be an ideal candidate if you're interested."

"I'd love to have the chance. Thanks for telling me about it. I'll definitely be applying."

* * *

Alex phoned Sanjay. "I'm on my way to see Sandra but wanted to let you know a few things."

"I've got some interesting news for you too, Sir. Things are starting to come together a bit."

Alex told Sanjay about his discussions with Brian Phelps and Stuart Black. Then he arranged for Steve to take a selection of photos, including the two McGowan boys, for Beattie to look at.

Sanjay gave Alex a run down on the interview with Carolyn Fletcher. "I've got more," he added.

"What else?"

"Ibrahim's alibi broke down under pressure from Steve. At first, he tried to hold out, but when he was shown Hussein's new statement, which proved he was lying, he fell apart."

"Make sure Steve also has Ibrahim's photo to show Beattie, and better have one of Zahid too, for good measure."

"Yes, Sir. I'm planning to bring Ibrahim in. I'll charge him with obstruction for starters; then we'll see where it leads."

"Good plan. What about the McGowan boys? After what Mary found out this morning, I reckon they both could have strong motives."

Sanjay told Alex about the CCTV sightings.

"Let's think this through," Alex said. "Fitzpatrick's good at his job, the best in fact. If he thinks there's a reasonable match, we have to run with it."

"He wasn't certain, Sir. Young men with ginger hair wearing dark jackets may not be two a penny, but neither are they particularly rare in Glasgow."

"True; we won't get a conviction, solely based on it, but I just want to consider the possibilities."

"Okay, Sir. If we have Kevin in town before five, he could be the one in Minard road at half-past. Then the other two sightings would be irrelevant."

"Not necessarily. If he was the culprit, then maybe he left the flat. Who knows, maybe to dump evidence or just to escape from the scene. He might have caught a bus town-ward and then taken another one back. Perhaps he wanted to be seen arriving at the later time as an alibi."

"If that's what he was trying. He didn't do a very good job of it; he wasn't noticed by anyone we could find."

"If it was Robbie, does the timeline fit?" Alex asked.

"That could work too. Perhaps, he arrived at five-thirty and left an hour later. Then Kevin arrives back as he'd said."

"And if it was Ibrahim?" Alex said.

"Again, Kevin arrives back as he'd said, but the earlier sightings wouldn't mean anything."

"Right, it's time to bring both boys in, separately of course. We can afford to lean on them quite heavily as we know Kevin's already lied to us and we've the new information about Robbie, all of which he's withheld. We'll need to see what the search brings up too, if anything."

"Yes, Sir."

"Okay, go for it."

Chapter 36

Alex was in a state of excitement. He sensed the investigation was close to a breakthrough and was keen for the result to be uncovered.

However, once in the atmosphere of the hospital, his thoughts quickly transferred to family matters. His long legs taking them two at a time, he bounded up the stairs to Sandra's ward. Seeing her brilliant smile, he anticipated good news.

"Test results just came back and I'm clear. There are a few formalities to go through, but I'll be able to get out in about an hour or two."

"Terrific news." Alex hugged and kissed Sandra, then turned to see a contented looking Siobhan, lying in her cot. Unable to resist, he reached in to lift her and cradle her in one arm. "Before you can come out, I'll need to get the baby seat out of the boot and see how easy it is to fit. The instructions appeared fairly straightforward; even so, it could take me a while."

"Did you bring spanners and things?"

"I have my toolbox in the boot but according to the instructions, I shouldn't need them."

"Did you remember to bring some biscuits or chocolates for me to leave the nurses? They've been very kind and I want to give something as a small thank you."

Oh sh... , I forgot. Never mind, I'll be able to pick something up in the shop in reception when I go down to sort the seat. I'd better give Sanjay a call, so he knows he's taking over as from now."

"Before you do, why don't you update me on what's happened this morning."

"I'm happy too, but it could take a while. We've made a lot of progress." Alex told Sandra about all the morning's developments.

"What a betrayal of Kevin; his brother and his partner having sex, quite literally, behind his back." Sandra said.

"Not a bad motive," Alex said. A crime of passion. If I remember correctly, it used to be considered a justified homicide in France."

"You think it's him, then," Sandra said.

"Not necessarily. He has to be the prime suspect, but we can't rule out the other contenders."

"I've not been idle. I made some of my own enquiries." Seeing Alex's confused look, she continued. "About the medical records. After I spoke to you, I thought about it. What better place can there be than a hospital, to ask about medical record administration."

"Ah right. Phil was trying to look into it, but the last I heard, he hadn't got anywhere. What did you find out?"

"From what I've been told, every GP's surgery has their own database, and it's not part of a national network. As a general rule, records are very well protected and secure. A GP from one practice ought not to be able to access anything, other than their own patients. Hospitals are different, but the same principles apply."

"What about hacking?" Alex asked.

"Nowadays it seems an accomplished hacker can get into anything. If NATO, the Pentagon and the MOD can be hacked then nothing is 100% secure, but it would take an expert. It wouldn't be easy."

"Could someone get access if they broke into the premises?"

"I'd say it's unlikely. You would need to know both the system and have the sign in codes. From what I've been told, even a locum or nurse working in a practice wouldn't be able to get into the system without an authorised account holder signing them in. Even then, they'd be logged out after a time and need someone to sign them back in."

"It sounds a secure system," Alex said.

"It should be, but as with everything else, it's down to the diligence of those using it to observe the rules so that it works."

"So, in summary, we can discount the risk of Dr Sharma having a sneak look at Kevin McGowan's records, or Zahid's for that matter."

"Yes, sorry for starting a wild goose chase," Sandra said.

"Don't apologise. It was important to check as, had the answer been different, we'd have had a whole new set of possibilities to consider. Anyhow, its Sanjay problem now."

Sandra smiled. "Times going on, you'd better go and get the car sorted. And don't forget to buy something for the nurses. I'll get dressed and pack my belongings."

Alex laughed as he settled Siobhan back into her cot. "Yes, your majesty; any other requests?"

As a reply, Sandra aimed a packet of paper tissues at Alex. Although her direction was good, the range fell considerably short and Alex was smirking as he left the ward.

Before long, Alex had returned, carrying a large, gift-wrapped box of Thornton's Continental Selection. "All set."

Chapter 37

Ibrahim sat squirming in his chair, waiting for Mary and Phil to get set up. Seeing Mary settle into the chair facing him, he said, "I don't want to speak to a woman."

"You have no right to dictate who interviews you," she replied.

"Then I will say nothing."

"That of course is your prerogative," Mary replied. "If you're not going to be cooperative, we can remand you in custody until your case is called in court."

"What case? I know nothing of any case."

"Did you not understand that you were formally charged with obstructing the police? My notes say it was clearly stated to you when you were read your rights."

"It will never come to court. You can not do this to me. I have done nothing wrong."

"You told us you were in the Mosque on Monday until seven in the evening. We know you were lying and your alibis have withdrawn their statements."

"Rubbish!"

Mary presented a copy of Hussein's revised statement.

Ibrahim pushed back his chair and stood. "I will leave now."

"You don't have that option," Mary replied. "Either you can answer my questions, or we can lock you in the cells."

"I've done nothing wrong. What do you want to know anyway?"

"We want to know what you were doing on Monday afternoon."

Ibrahim said nothing.

"We understand you were attending to family business."

A surprised look shot across Ibrahim's face.

"And this business involved you seeing your niece Keiran." Mary decided to take the risk. She slid a copy of one of Fitzpatrick's photos across the table.

"Yes." Ibrahim's voice was a whisper.

"You strangled her."

"What? No, of course not."

"She was alive and well before you went. She was dead after you left."

"No, you're being ridiculous. She was fine when I left. I didn't go to harm her. I went to protect her."

"Protect her from what?"

"I can't say."

"Now you're the one being ridiculous. You come out with a statement like that and refuse to say more. Then you expect us to believe you."

Ibrahim shrugged.

"Is this to do with Zahid?" Mary asked.

Ibrahim reacted as if he'd been slapped. "What do you know about Zahid?"

Mary ignored the question. "You said you went to protect Keiran. Were you protecting her from Zahid?"

"You don't understand."

"Why don't you help me to understand?"

Ibrahim looked frantically around the room. He found no inspiration or escape. "He's not a bad boy. He doesn't mean to harm or upset anyone."

"Yet he does."

"Yes, it's not his fault."

"Tell us what happened to Keiran."

"He didn't harm her. He only looked and maybe touched her."

"He half scared her to death. She was terrified, it changed her whole life."

Ibrahim turned his face to the wall. "We sent him away."

"That didn't solve his problems."

Ibrahim looked back at Mary, his expression pained, "No, it didn't."

"He's back in Scotland."

"Yes, he's living with a cousin in Edinburgh."

"Tell me what happened on Monday."

"As I said I had a meeting at the Mosque."

"We've already been through all of that. I want the truth."

"No, be patient. As I said, I was at the Mosque and I had planned to be there until into the evening."

In exasperation, Mary tapped the witness statement. Ibrahim held up his hand in a gesture to wait. "During my meeting, I received a call from my cousin. He told me Zahid came home for lunch but did not return to work. When he looked, he was not in his room, but he found an open train timetable. It was for the inter-city to Glasgow."

"You suspected he was coming to see Keiran."

"I didn't know; it was possible. The boy sometimes has strange ideas."

"Would he have known how to find her?"

"Maybe not. I couldn't be certain. Although Zahid is not smart, and he has problems, he can be surprisingly resourceful when there's something he wants to do."

"What did you do?"

"I went to see Keiran. We'd talked in the morning and I knew she was at home. I thought it best to be there in case Zahid turned up."

"And did he?"

"No. He did take the train to Glasgow. But I had other family looking for him. They found him on his way out of Queen Street Station and they've taken care of him."

"Taken care of him, how?" Mary was apprehensive.

"They took him to their home and kept him until his parents collected him. He is back in Wolverhampton now. They are arranging for him to go to Pakistan."

"Surely that's only shifting the problem somewhere else; it isn't solving it."

"You know nothing." Ibrahim's response was angry.

"I know this," Mary said, 'Zahid is not a boy; he's a man now and a dangerous one at that. Even you must think so, or you wouldn't have rushed across to protect Keiran. Tell me though, did you inform Tarik and Nadia about Zahid being in Glasgow?"

"No, why?"

"Zahid wouldn't know where Keiran lived without research or someone telling him, but he did know Tarik's house. Surely there was greater risk of him going there. Jamilla could have been in serious danger."

"Ibrahim's jaw dropped, his eyes opened wide, "I never thought."

Mary released Ibrahim. She told him she would send her report to the procurator and it would be up to him whether he'd face prosecution.

As she walked back to her Office, Steve caught up with her. "Too late to be of use to you now, but Beattie looked at the photos. He thought the one he bumped into looked like one of the McGowan boys. He couldn't tell which, but he ruled out Ibrahim and Zahid."

"It helps a bit," Mary replied, to place one of them in the right location at the right time. It doesn't prove anything, nor does it completely release the others from suspicion."

* * *

A few minutes later, as Ibrahim was leaving through the police office reception, he hardly noticed the couple sitting on the bench seat before he was accosted.

"You're the father, aren't you?" Lizzie McGowan challenged. Frank was standing by her shoulder.

"What? What are you talking about?" Ibrahim stepped back from their menacing approach.

"You're Keiran's father. My poor boys are in there," she said pointing, "being given the third degree all because of your slut of a daughter. You should be ashamed."

"You stupid woman. I am Keiran's uncle, not her father," Ibrahim replied. "The poor girl is dead. If the police are questioning your sons, then they have a reason. It is most likely because they are stupid and evil like their parents." The irony of his own words was lost on him, having only been released from questioning moments before.

Further interaction was averted when the desk sergeant stepped in to break up the argument, ushering Ibrahim out of the door.

On his return, he addressed the McGowan's, "You can sit there quietly if you wish. If I get another outburst like that, you'll be out the door. Either that or I'll charge you."

Chapter 38

"We've put Kevin into interview room 1 and Robbie into number 3. We'll be ready to start as soon as you are," Donny said.

I'll come with you to see Kevin. I'd like to keep Robbie on hold for a bit," Sanjay replied.

Kevin was hardly recognisable from the last time Sanjay had seen him, He'd aged considerably in the very short space of time. Sat slumped over the table, his skin was like parchment and his eyes were sunken and surrounded by deep, dark rings. His hair was lank, and he looked as lifeless as a scarecrow. Sanjay didn't shake hands fearing Kevin might crumble if gripped too hard.

"You've not slept." More a statement than a question.

"I've not done anything. There's no point. There's no reason to go on."

"Have you been drinking?" Sanjay suspected binge drinking may have worsened Kevin's condition.

"I haven't touched a drop since Monday. Keiran had wanted me to cut down, but it's too late now."

"You were drunk on Monday. Were you out of control?"

"No, I said to you before, I'd had a few, but I wasn't drunk."

"You claimed you arrived home on Monday about seven, is this you?" Sanjay presented the photo taken in Pollockshaws Road around that time.

Kevin glanced at the image. "Yes, I think so."

"What about this one?" He presented the image in Minard Road.

"Yeah, yeah."

"This photo was taken at five thirty."

Kevin blinked a couple of times as the message permeated. "No, it can't be. Let me take another look." He studied the image more intently and compared it to the first one. "I'll grant you they look similar, but it can't be me."

"You'll need to do better than that."

"The photos aren't clear. True they look a bit like me, but they're fuzzy. You don't have a clear picture and I'm telling you categorically that it isn't me."

"We also have an eye witness who identified you leaving the flat at about six-thirty."

"How many times do I have to say? It wasn't me." Kevin sighed, "I don't know why I'm bothering. I don't care what you do to me. But I won't have anyone saying I hurt Keiran."

Sanjay decided to try another approach. "You may say that but didn't your drinking affect Keiran. Didn't that hurt her?"

"Yes."

"You said she wanted you to cut down."

"I had; these last few weeks; I tried."

"Please explain."

"Over the last few months, she'd suggested I cut down, to look after my heath better, but it didn't really bother her too much." Kevin paused. "It was only after the last real bender, she…, she seemed different."

"What happened?"

"It was over a month ago. We'd gone out to celebrate my birthday. We went into town for a meal and we had a few. It was a good night. It started to go wrong when we happened to meet up with Robbie and had a few more drinks. I'll admit it myself. I overdid it. I was out of my face. Robbie had to help Keiran get me home to put me to bed."

"Go on."

"It should have been a great night, but I spoiled it getting drunk. Keiran was annoyed."

"What do you mean?"

"She just seemed different. There was something, I can't explain. We didn't seem to be as comfortable together."

"From your earlier statement, you continued to have sex."

"Oh yes, that didn't change at all. Well maybe it did. It became more physical, less loving. … Why am I telling you this?"

Kevin looked pensive.

"What are you thinking?"

"It was only after what you told me this week … about Keiran being pregnant. It got me thinking… maybe she was different because of the pregnancy. Perhaps it affected her hormones."

"I don't believe that's what you were thinking."

"Yes, it was."

"Be honest, Kevin. Haven't you been thinking there was someone else? Isn't it true that for the last month you've thought that's why Keiran had been behaving differently?"

"No," there was less assertion in his voice.

"When you heard she was pregnant, you were convinced someone else was the father."

"But…"

"You came home on Monday and Keiran told you she was pregnant. Because you thought you were infertile, you thought the baby had to be someone else's. You'd suspected she'd been cheating for some time, but her pregnancy gave you the evidence." Sanjay paused, "And because of that, you killed her."

"No, it's not true."

"You held her by the throat and you squeezed, and you squeezed, until she was dead."

Tears trickled over Kevin's cheeks. "No, I didn't. You mustn't think that. It wasn't me."

"It all adds up."

"No, it doesn't. Keiran wasn't unfaithful. The baby was mine."

"You thought you were infertile. It was only after we ran our tests when you found out otherwise."

"Yes, you're right. I didn't know until you told me. But I didn't kill Keiran. Why would I. I loved her. I didn't know she was pregnant. I was in the dark until you told me that too. She phoned me at work to say she had something to tell me, but I never got to hear. She was dead when I got home. It wasn't until you said that I knew. You have to believe me. Keiran was good and true and I wasn't the one who killed her."

"Much as we'd like to believe you, we know you're mistaken. Keiran was not faithful to you."

"You're only saying that to upset me. It's a trick. You want me to admit to something I didn't do. I told you. I don't care what you do to me, but I'll not have you speak badly of her. I won't let you spoil her memory and I will never admit to hurting her. I didn't do it."

"It's no trick, Kevin. We know Keiran had sex with someone else and we know who."

"I don't want to hear it."

"The same night you passed out drunk. The night Keiran and Robbie carried you home and put you to bed."

"You can't be serious."

"We are very serious. You said it yourself; she was different after that night."

"It was because I let her down. It was because I spoiled the celebration."

"Have you not thought it could have been because she was the one who let you down."

"No, I don't believe you." In frustration, Kevin banged his hands on the table, his tears now in full flow.

"I think we should adjourn for a few minutes for you to calm down. Would you like some water?"

Looking thoroughly miserable, Kevin shook his head.

* * *

"You were a bit brutal in there," Donny said.

"How else could I be? I needed to get a reaction from him and the boss said to lean heavily, so I did. I must say, he held up better than I expected," Sanjay replied.

"He did. I can tell you, I feel sorry for him whether he did it or not. He's suffered enough."

"Not our decision to make," Sanjay replied. "It's our job to get the answers; someone else can dispense the justice. But you are right; he's had a rough deal."

"Much as he had the strongest motive, there are some things about the evidence which bother me," Donny said.

"Me too. I'm not happy about what the scene-of-crime specialists told us about the different brands of condom."

"He did have a packet of them in his jacket," Donny replied, and we only have his word about them being there since Balloch, and his explanation of why there was only one left."

"Yes, it doesn't rule him out but why would he have used them on Monday?"

"He's a lawyer. If he had an understanding of forensics, maybe it was to mislead us into thinking someone else was responsible," Donny suggested.

"Could be," Sanjay replied, sounding unconvinced, "but it would have taken pretty quick thinking. If the murder was triggered by her cheating, which he suspected only after she told him about the pregnancy, it seems unlikely he made a snap decision to create misleading evidence before he killed her. Creating a diversion like that would suggest some level of premeditation."

"I see that. Maybe he knew before he came home. Perhaps she told him on the phone, or he had other reasons to be suspicion. We can only guess how long he may have been planning."

"Thanks for being devils advocate. What were you unhappy about?" Sanjay asked.

"This whole business with the phone messages from the friend. Now we know the texts came from the phone Keiran bought for Robbie.

Why would Robbie have wanted him to come home late?" Donny asked.

"Yes, fair point," Sanjay replied.

"Sarge, I'm glad I've caught you," Phil interrupted. "Some important information has just come in from the techies."

"What is it?"

"They've had a look at Kevin McGowan's bank transactions. He made a purchase from Sainsburys in Union Street on Monday."

"Yes, he told us he bought the wine and flowers there. What good does that do us?"

"He paid by bank card, a contactless one. They were able to trace the exact time the purchase was made. It was six twenty-four."

"If it was a contactless card, anyone could have used it," Donny replied.

"True," Phil said, "but the purchases tie in with what Kevin says he took home. Besides, there's more. He withdrew forty quid from the hole-in-the wall."

"They've checked?"

"Yes, it was timed a few minutes before the shopping. What's more the ATM has a camera. There's a clear, date and time stamped picture of him collecting the money."

Chapter 39

After a short discussion and briefing, Sanjay instructed Phil and Donnie to interview Robbie as they'd been the ones who'd seen him before. Sanjay watched and listened from outside.

"Do you know who did it?" Robbie asked, as soon as they entered the room.

"As a matter of fact, we think we do," Donny replied, "although there are gaps we need to fill."

"Before going any further, I want to check with you one last time; you were given the option to have someone accompany you. You could have a member of your family or a friend or you could ask for a solicitor," Phil offered.

"Why would I want that? You may want to know things I don't discuss with my family and I haven't done anything I consider wrong. No, I'm happy to handle things by myself." Robbie's attitude was smug.

"Just so long as it's clearly your choice and we have this on record," Phil replied. They'd prepared for Robbie's attitude to be antagonistic and confrontational. Phil already knew their expectation wouldn't be disappointed.

"We asked you last time if there was anything else you wanted to tell us. You said there wasn't anything at the time. Have you thought any more about it?" Donny asked.

"I haven't really given it any thought," Robbie replied. He pondered for a few seconds, before adding, "As I suppose you must know, Kevin's been in quite a state. He's hardly eaten or slept for days. Mum's been really worried."

"I assume this is not at all like him," Phil said.

"What do you think? Something's eating away at him."

"Are you suggesting it's anguish or guilt?" Donny asked.

"It's not for me to say."

"You don't appear to be unduly concerned," Donny observed.

"I explained the last time, we tolerate each other but we don't get on well."

"Please leave us to deal with anything to do with your brother," Phil said. "We're here today to speak to you." He nodded to Donny to indicate he wanted to lead the questions.

"I was only trying to be helpful," Robbie said.

"Yes, I'm sure. Now let's start off with your whereabouts on Monday. Please tell us where you went."

"I told you last time. I went into the West End to meet friends for a drink."

"It was a school day."

"Yes, I am eighteen after all. I don't stay out late when I have an early start. It shouldn't make a difference whether I'm at school or in work. It's not as if I wear my uniform into a pub."

"Please give us details. We would like times and places."

"Okay. I had a full day at school. I must have got home the back of four. I made myself a sandwich. Do you need to know what I put in it?" The question came with a sneer.

"I don't believe that will be necessary."

"Okay. I had a lie down in my room, played some computer games, and then went for the bus into town. The number 38."

"Was anyone else in your house when you got home, or up until the time you left?"

"No, I was just by my lonesome."

"Did you speak to, or text, your brother or Keiran at any time during the day?"

"No, why should I?"

"We'll park that one just now."

Robbie frowned in consternation.

"What time did you leave the house?"

"I dunno, maybe six or seven."

"Can you be more specific?"

"Not really, I don't wear a watch." Robbie exhibited his bare wrist. "It would be earlyish because, as I said, I don't stay out late. Anyway, I got off in Hope Street and jumped on another bus out to Partick. I walked up Byres Road to the bar."

"Do you know what time you arrived?"

"I guess it was around seven-thirty. It was a loose arrangement and my pals were already there before me. You could always check with them, but I'm not certain they'd be able to help."

"Yes, we'd like their details."

Robbie identified the information on his mobile and narrated four names and numbers while Donny took notes.

"Thank you for being so helpful." Phil tried to disguise the sarcasm he felt ought to accompany the words. "Now, I'd like to take you back in time a little. About six months, I think. We understand you had a bit of bother at school."

Robbie sat back, feigning shock. "What are you on about? What does my performance at school have to do with any of this? Have you nothing better to do with your time?"

"We're talking about your behaviour, not your performance. Please answer the question."

Robbie smiled. "Okay, I had a little bit of bother. I had a fall out with one of the other boys and it led to some fisticuffs. So what?"

"Your skirmish with the other boy is not our concern. We want you to tell us about the racial abuse of the girls."

Robbie swallowed hard. "There's no record. You can't …How do you know?"

"We're waiting."

Robbie inhaled deeply, regathering his composure. "It was nothing. A storm in a teacup. That's why it wasn't recorded."

"We're still waiting."

"I was angry. I said stupid things."

"What made you angry?"

"I was moved out of my room at home because Keiran came to stay. Another case of my parents not caring about anything else, as long as Kevin's whims were taken care of."

"You were angry with Keiran."

"No, not really. She was the only good part of it. I was angry with my parents and I was angry with Kevin, for going out of his way to make my life a living hell."

"What about the girls you shouted at."

"They wandered into my path while I was training. I nearly fell over. They meant nothing to me. They were a convenient target."

"The comments you made were racist and Islamophobic."

"Maybe, yes. It was because they reminded me of the why I was suffering at home."

"Were you not echoing your parents' views on religion and immigration?" Phil didn't know for sure but thought it worth the risk.

"I suppose. I never thought of it that way."

"Maybe you share some of these feelings."

"No, I'm not like that, not with Keiran anyway."

"You were infatuated with her."

"Maybe, I don't know; she was beautiful; anyone would have wanted her."

"You wanted to get back at your brother for all the torment."

"What do you mean?"

"You told us before. He kept goading you and belittling you. He was horrible to you. You wanted to get your own back."

"Well yes, I suppose."

"That's why you wanted to have sex with Keiran. You thought it would be a way for you to get back at him."

"No."

"He taunted you that you couldn't find someone as good. So, what better way to prove him wrong than to take her from him."

"What? No, what are you suggesting."

"On your brother's birthday, you had your chance and you took it."

"What are you saying? You can't know?" Robbie's eyes were wild.

"We do know, but we want to hear your version."

"Robbie sat thinking what to do. After a lull, he seemed to relax, coming to a decision and he smiled. "He bullied me all my life. When I grew bigger and stronger than him, he couldn't push me around any more. But he did and said other things to hurt me and make me feel small. My mother let him do it. For years, I dreamed of getting my own back."

"Tell us what you did."

Robbie was looking up at the ceiling. He became detached, as if he was in another world. "I had it all planned. I knew Keiran liked me from the times we'd spent chatting. I was aware of how she'd looked at me at times when she thought I couldn't see. I just had to create the right opportunity."

"Kevin's birthday."

"Being his special day made it even sweeter."

"Tell us."

"I had a plan. I knew where they were going for dinner, because my folks had bought them the restaurant voucher as part of his birthday present. I expected Kevin would have a few drinks. I waited outside, so I could bump into them on their way out of the restaurant. I made it look like a coincidence. I insisted on taking them for a drink to mark Kevin's birthday. I was sure they wouldn't refuse. Once Kevin had a few, he didn't take a lot of persuading."

"Very clever, you set him up."

Robbie chuckled. "Yes. Keiran was rather merry and Kevin was quite far gone. I had to be sure though, so I crumbled a tab of Demerol into his drink. He was pretty much out of it after that."

"Where did you get the Demerol from?"

"I'd been prescribed it as a painkiller after an injury I'd had playing rugby, some time back. I'd read the warnings and knew it shouldn't be taken with alcohol because of the way they reacted together."

"It made him ill?"

"Mostly it knocked him out."

"You helped him home."

"Keiran didn't know how she'd get him back. She was grateful to me for helping. Between us, we bundled him into a cab and I helped him upstairs and into his bed. He was unconscious by the time his head hit the pillow."

"You didn't leave, though."

"No chance." Robbie laughed. "I went to the door, as if to go. Keiran said thanks and kissed my cheek. Instead I held her and kissed her properly. She didn't resist, so I put my hands under her hips and lifted her up. When she wrapped her legs around me, I could feel they were bare and realised she had nothing on under her skirt. The feel of her skin was exquisite. I dropped my pants and fucked her standing up against the wall. She loved every minute. The real bonus for me was knowing that Kevin was lying sleeping, just on the other side of the bedroom door."

"You weren't afraid he'd wake."

"At that time, I don't really know if I'd have minded, but there was no chance. He'd have slept through an earthquake." Robbie grinned. "The way the earth moved for Keiran, I suppose in a way he did." Robbie was clearly proud of his own joke.

"Did Keiran regret it?"

"She was a bit confused and rather tearful afterwards. I tried to sooth her. I took her into the lounge. We sat and talked for a bit then we had sex again on the couch."

"You must have been happy. You achieved what you'd set out to do."

"Yes, but it wasn't how I planned."

"You'll need to explain what you mean."

"To start with, I was doing it for revenge. I wanted to get my own back on Kevin. I thought once he found out, it would break them up. It would break him. But it didn't turn out like that."

"What was different?"

"I guess I cared for Keiran and she pleaded with me not to say. I didn't want her to get hurt. I suppose if I'm truthful, I wanted her for myself and I knew if I told Kevin what we'd done, she'd never forgive me. I wanted to keep seeing her you see."

"You said you wanted her for yourself. Was that because you truly cared or because it would have given you even more satisfaction to steal her from Kevin?"

Robbie thought about the question. "To be honest, they both played a part. I have to admit that I felt good in these last weeks, knowing what we'd done, and that Kevin didn't have a clue."

"In the time since Kevin's birthday, did you see Keiran again?"

"Not much, two or three times, but we spoke a lot on the phone."

"Did you have sex again, after that night?"

Again, Robbie paused before speaking. It was clear he wanted to think about how much to say. "Keiran gave me mixed messages. Her head was all over the place. Sometimes she'd say it was all a terrible mistake and others she'd say I had to bring protection for the next time we got together, because she thought it would be wrong to use the condoms Kevin had bought." Robbie sniggered then continued, "I thought it funny, she thought it was okay to have sex with me, but she thought it would be wrong to use Kevin's condoms."

Conversation stopped when they heard a knock on the door.

"Let's adjourn for a few minutes," Phil said. And he and Donny left the room.

They followed Sanjay along the corridor and found an empty room for a quiet word.

"Is something wrong? Have I missed anything important?" Phil asked.

"Not at all, you're doing a great job. He's one crazy, mixed up kid. We need the doc to give a proper diagnosis, but I reckon there's definite sociopathic tendencies," Sanjay said.

"Why did you stop us?" Phil asked.

"I've received some material, you'll be able to use. I thought you'd reached a good point to break."

"What have you got?"

"The search on the McGowan house; let me tell you what we found. Robbie had a hiding place in his room. There's a fire surround with a slot-in electric fire. He kept his special stuff in the void behind the fire."

"Nice," Donny said.

"We've got the pay-as-you-go mobile he used to communicate with Keiran, the one she bought for him, according to Fletcher. It proves the message he sent to Kevin, and we can see the call log where he phoned or heard from Keiran. We also have the pack of Demerol, he used to drug Kevin and we have the missing photos, the kinky ones from Kevin and Keiran's collection. We're getting them checked for prints, but I think you're safe enough using them."

"Right, I'm ready for round 2," Phil said.

"Okay, let's pick up where we left off," Phil started. "You were telling us, Keiran had sent you mixed messages."

"It's like I said, one minute she was talking about us hopping into bed together and the next she would say we couldn't see each other again."

"I want to take us back up to this week. We asked you about your movements on Monday, but quite frankly we don't believe you."

"I told you what I did." Robbie smiled. "If you don't believe me it's your problem."

"No Robbie, you've lied to us and that makes it very much your problem."

"How have I lied? Show me."

"You went to see Keiran."

Robbie shook his head. "No, I didn't."

"We have evidence."

Robbie looked more uncertain. "You're just saying that."

"We have a logged call of you talking to Keiran on Monday afternoon."

"No, you haven't; you're bluffing. Here, check for yourself." Robbie held out his mobile.

"You didn't use that phone. You used the pay-as-you-go mobile which Keiran bought for you."

"How did you know about that? It means nothing, anyway. I told you Keiran was good to me. She gave me the phone, so nobody would know we were talking to each other. It wasn't me who spoke to her on Monday. I lost the phone a while back. I don't know where it is."

"Don't worry, we found it, you kept it hidden behind your fire in your bedroom."

Robbie was visibly shaken. "Oh, that's where I left it. I'd forgotten." His show of bravado was unconvincing, even to himself.

"You did speak to her."

"Yes, I must have forgotten."

"Mmm, more memory problems. Did you also forget going to see her?"

"How can you know that?"

Phil presented the photograph taken in Minard Road and then the townward one, taken in Pollockshaws Road. "These were taken on Monday afternoon and show you coming to and going from her flat."

Robbie studied it. "Is that the best you've got," After a moment's thought he added, "Even if it was me, it doesn't mean I went near the flat."

"So, you admit it was you."

"I didn't say that."

"We also have an eyewitness account from the man you bumped into when you were leaving. He recognised you and said you were in a real hurry."

Robbie sat upright in his chair. One leg started to shake, his foot tapping on the floor. "What if it was me? I'm not saying it was. But even if, … it doesn't mean anything."

"For starters, it proves you've been lying to us even more. Now tell us what you were doing there."

Robbie said nothing.

"Let me tell you what we think. We think, just maybe, you went around to see Keiran hoping for another of your little personal liaisons.

You'd sent Kevin a message from your private phone, pretending to be from his friend, to send him on a fool's errand. You wanted to make sure he came back late."

"But, but, how can you know?"

"We can't be certain exactly what happened when you were there. We've got enough to go on to believe you raped her and after that you strangled her before you left. We'd like to know why. Had she rejected you or maybe she told you she was pregnant. Then, as if nothing had happened, you caught a bus into town for a night out with your chums."

"It's not true. I didn't rape her. I didn't kill her." Robbie was becoming frantic.

"You're telling me you were there, and you did have sex."

"I don't have to answer."

"I think you just did."

"Can I have something to drink, please?"

Donny filled a plastic cup and handed it to him.

Robbie gulped down the water.

"Are you ready to answer now?"

"We talked for a bit then we went to bed."

"You had sex."

"Yes."

"She didn't want to."

"She did, she encouraged me; then she changed her mind and said no. Then she changed back."

"You were rough with her."

"It's what she wanted."

"You used a condom, one you'd brought with you."

"Yes."

"Afterwards you argued."

"No, we didn't."

"She told you she was pregnant."

"No, she didn't. I didn't know. Be reasonable, if I knew, there would have been no point wearing a condom."

"She didn't tell you until afterwards."

"It's not true. You can't know these things. You can't think these things."

"And then you killed her."

"No, it wasn't me. It must have been Kevin."

"You tried to set Kevin up, didn't you?"

"I don't understand."

"You had it all planned, just like the birthday."

"No, it isn't true."

"You made sure Kevin would return late and unable to account for where he'd been."

"That was only so I could have some private time with Keiran."

"But it didn't go as you planned."

"I told you already."

"She resisted your advances."

"It wasn't like that."

"You held her down."

"It's what she wanted."

"You held her by the throat."

Silence.

"You did. You held her by the throat."

Robbie cupped his hands over his face. "She asked me to."

"And you squeezed."

"Only a little, it's what she wanted. I was so aroused, I wasn't in control. Her body convulsed. I hadn't expected it and I didn't let go. I heard a noise, a crack and she went limp. I thought she might have been fooling around at first. I didn't realise she was dead."

"You killed her."

"I didn't mean to."

"You killed Keiran and wanted Kevin to be blamed."

"I didn't want her to die."

"Wasn't that your perfect solution? Keiran dead and Kevin arrested."

"I didn't plan it that way. I cared for Keiran."

"She served your purpose."

"What do you mean?"

"You didn't really care for her."

"I did."

"To you, she was another Moslem, a pretty one, but someone of no value."

Robbie sobbed. "I didn't mean it to happen."

"But you did want Kevin to be blamed."

"The damage was done. It was as well to serve some purpose."

"You rearranged Keiran's dress before you left."

"Yes."

"And hid any evidence you'd been there."

"Yes."

"You took away the condom and dumped it."

"Yes."

"Then you went off to meet your friends and left Kevin to arrive home and report her dead."

Chapter 40

Alex and Sandra arrived home with Siobhan. Alex transferred the cot into their bedroom. After he'd set up the video monitor, so they'd be able to keep an eye on her, he settled the baby down to sleep.

"Are you ready for a coffee?" he asked Sandra, while flipping on the kettle.

"Could you make mine a tea, please, Sandra replied. "I know it's still afternoon, but I think I'm going to need an early night. I'd be better to avoid the chance of caffeine buzz."

"Not a problem, although I read somewhere there's more caffeine in tea than coffee."

Alex busied himself in the kitchen and further debate on the subject was prevented when their doorbell rang.

"Who on earth can that be?" Sandra reached for the entry phone.

"It's Sanjay. I know you're just home and Alex gave me instructions about communicating, but I have some important news and I've brought a pressie for the wee one. I promise, after this, I won't bother you at all for the next two weeks."

"You'd better come up," Sandra pressed the remote entry.

Alex had the door open before Sanjay had climbed the stairs and ushered him into the lounge. "I just made a pot of tea; would you like a cup?"

"Thanks, I'm just ready for one." He sat down and removed a shoulder bag. "I won't stay long; I just wanted to tell you in person that the case is broken. We have a confession."

"Robbie," Sandra and Alex both called out in unison, then looked at each other in surprise.

"Yes, how did you know?" Sanjay asked.

"Too much didn't add up for it to be Kevin," Alex said. "Even if he'd been a good actor, which it appears from his stage record - he wasn't, then I don't believe he could have faked the grief he showed."

"Your other suspects had motives and they did cloud the waters a bit, but I didn't buy into any of them killing her," Sandra added.

Alex brought in the tea and Sanjay gave a detailed account of the day's events. "We charged him and then he asked if he could go home."

"We have the confession, but what do you believe?" Sandra asked. "Do you think he could be telling the truth that he didn't mean to kill her?"

"You mean, as opposed to the whole thing being premeditated," Sanjay said. "I truly don't know. There's definitely something wrong in his head but I don't know just how much he might be capable of."

"From everything I've heard, Keiran appears to have been sexually adventurous," Sandra said. "It's not too outrageous to consider she may have been up for a bit of non-consensual role play. You know what I mean, being pinned down or gripped in a strangle hold. It could have happened that way and just got out of control with tragic results." She paused for a moment before continuing, "On the other hand, Robbie could have made up the whole story. Not the sex, we know that happened. Perhaps, she was willing at first and then changed her mind or maybe he forced himself on her from the start. In any event, he's held her down and choked her to death, whether he meant to or not. He's admitted as much. What's also in no doubt is that after she died, he's seen an opportunity to set Kevin up as the murderer."

"The minimum we can prosecute for is culpable homicide. We'll need to see how the fiscal wants to play it. He could go all the way to first degree murder," Sanjay replied.

"One thing's fairly certain," Alex said. "His lawyer will try to go for a diminished responsibility plea, try and get him of on psychological grounds."

"We've done our bit. Thankfully, it's not our problem to solve. The fiscal will get psych assessments done and then decide how to prosecute." Sanjay said.

"It's the Sharma family I feel sorry for," Alex mused. "I hope the prosecution can be tied up quickly and simply without going to a public trial. It's bad enough they've lost their daughter, without having intimate details of her relationships bandied about on the front pages of the tabloids. Cab you just picture the headlines?"

"It will be pretty hard on Kevin, as well, although I don't feel too much sympathy for his parents," Sanjay added.

"Anyhow, I'm glad that it's tied up before my leave starts properly. Thanks for letting me know the details, Alex said. "Thanks for letting *us* know," Sandra corrected.

"I'd better go and leave you to it," Sanjay said. "Can I get a peek at the little lady first? I've brought a present."

"Of course you can, just so long as you don't wake her, but what's this about a gift. You've given us one already," Alex said.

"This wasn't ready the other day. My wife's been knitting like mad and she's just finished it." He lifted out and opened a mass of tissue paper to reveal a white-coloured shawl, made of the finest texture of wool.

"It's beautiful," Sandra said, running her hands across the fabric, "and so soft. It must have taken her hours. Please thank Seher very much from us."

"That's not all." Sanjay said. "When the team heard about your losses from the break in, they held a whip round. In here, I have a bottle of twenty-five-year-old Benlochy and, so Sandra didn't feel left out, a Caorunn gin."

Alex was speechless. When he showed off his daughter to his friend, it was unclear whether the tear in his eye was from gratitude or pride.

Minutes later, closing the door on Sanjay and the rest of the world, Alex slipped his arm around Sandra's waist. Completely content, they both walked into the bedroom to check on Siobhan and then returned to the lounge, settled onto the couch and switched on the television.

"Nooooo," Alex cried in dismay, not another medical drama." The screen focussed on an operation. A gloved hand was steady, confident and sure. Controlling the razor-sharp blade, it smoothly sliced through skin and flesh...

Dear reader,

Thank you for taking time to read *Offender of the Faith*. If you enjoyed it, please consider telling your friends or posting a short review. Word of mouth is an author's best friend and much appreciated.

To find out more about Zach's books, link to - http://author.to/zachabrams

Or to contact the author emailto: zachabrams@authorway.net

Also by Zach Abrams

Made A Killing (the first novel in the Alex Warren series)

Scott Stevenson was a despicable character and nobody mourns when his bloody corpse is found with an ivory tusk driven through his torso. DCI Alex Warren and his team are given the challenging task of discovering his killer. They investigate the numerous people Stevenson has harmed and their enquiries reveal a host of related crimes, motivated by sex and greed. They struggle to close the case before more lives are lost.

A fast moving, gripping novel set in the tough crime-ridden streets of Glasgow.

To purchase. Use link - http://mybook.to/madeakilling

A Measure of Trouble

A cold, bleak February morning in Central Scotland commences with the discovery of a body. Chief Executive, Hector Mathewson is found dead within the cask room of his own distillery. DCI Alex Warren needs to balance his own turbulent personal life while directing the hunt for the murderer. There are suspects aplenty with motives ranging from greed, nationalism, adultery and revenge.

To purchase. Use link - http://mybook.to/ameasureoftrouble

Written to Death

DCI Alex Warren and his girlfriend, DI Sandra McKinnon, return from a short holiday, but hardly manage to step off the plane before he is called to investigate a suspicious death. Sheila Armstrong.a member of a Eastfarm Writers' Association has been stabbed to death, on stage, in a school, while rehearsing. The death mimics the plot of the play they'd been rehearsing. Within hours Sandra is roped into investigating a series of crimes which appear to be mob related. Both their enquiries run in parallel as they each struggle to make progress while supporting each other professionally and emotionally.

To purchase. Use link - http://mybook.to/ameasureoftrouble

Ring Fenced

If you think your life's complicated then spare a thought for Benjamin who obsessively juggles and controls his five independent personae, until ... Ring Fenced is Zach Abrams first novel. A story about power, control and obsession.

One man, five lives, ring-fenced and separated,

Bennie, loving husband and father,

Benjie, youngest son of orthodox Jewish parents,

Ben, successful corporate banker,

Benjamin, millionaire author and publisher of pornography

and Jamie, part-time lover of a beautiful musician.

Relying on his Blackberry to keep all his personae separate, his life is perfect.

But what if holes begin to appear in the divisions?

When a sequence of events throw his life into chaos, his separate words collide with explosive consequences.

[This book contains content of an adult nature with use of sexual swear words and depictions of sexual encounters. It is unsuitable for young readers and it may be offensive to some readers of all ages.]

To purchase. Use link - http://mybook.to/ringfenced

SOURCE, A Fast-Paced Financial Crime Thriller

A novel investigating financial crime and sabotage within the banking sector

Tom is an accomplished journalist and lead features writer at Global Weekly's London office. He's an unhappily married workaholic seeking to advance his career.

Sally is single, ambitious and independent. Visiting from Australia, she's chasing the same story.

Each is eager to research alleged wrongdoings at Royal National Bank, exposed by a series of whistleblower revelations. RNB is one of the largest and strongest financial institutions in the world, or it was. There have been several incidents within a period of weeks. The effect has rocked the bank to its core, causing its share price to tumble and world stock markets to ripple. International economic stability is at risk.

Both Tom and Sally suspect something or someone must be behind it. It couldn't just be coincidence. They think it inconceivable for such rapid decline to result from merely incompetence and a series of blunders. It must be sabotage. Yet the timing and diversity of location make it improbable. Has someone been powerful and ingenious enough to mastermind such demise? If so who, and why?

Tom and Sally become reluctantly twinned in the investigation looking for the "source' and their trail leads them from London to Glasgow, Manchester, Barcelona and Collioure.

They tread a dangerous path as Tom's life and wellbeing becomes imperilled by strange and cryptic warnings. Through this, Tom struggles to hold everything together. He's hoping to restore his crumbling marriage and uncertain personal finances, yet is distracted by an irresistible attraction to Sally.

They feel daunted by the prospect of an unknown enemy, who seems to have unlimited power and connections. With great fortitude, they tackle the most challenging investigation of their lives, facing threats and hostility countering their every move.

To purchase. Use link - http://mybook.to/source

Released by Zach Abrams together with Elly Grant
Twists and Turns

With fear, horror, death and despair, these stories will surprise you, scare you and occasionally make you smile. *Twists and Turns* offer the reader thought provoking tales. Whether you have a minute to spare or an hour or more, open *Twists and Turns* for a world full of mystery, murder, revenge and intrigue. A unique collaboration from the authors Elly Grant and Zach Abrams

To purchase. Use link - https://www.amazon.co.uk/dp/B00818C16O/

About the author

After a successful career in business and finance, Zach Abrams has relatively recently started writing fiction.

His first novel *Ring Fenced* was published in November 2011 and this is a crime story with a difference as the underlying theme is obsession tinged with power, control and how they are used and abused.

This novel was followed by a collaboration with Elly Grant to produce *Twists and Turns* a book of short stories and flash fiction.

Zach's second novel *Made a Killing* was the first of a series of Alex Warren murder mysteries (published in November 2012) and this has been followed by *A Measure of Trouble* (August 2013) and *Written to Death* (February 2015).

First published in 2013, *SOURCE, A Fast-Paced Financial Crime Thriller*, is an easy-read adventure story following three investigative journalists as they travel across Europe researching manipulation and corruption in the banking sector.

IN 2017, Zach published the first of his planned series of business books It's an easy read guide book aimed at people interested in the property market, titled, *So You Think You Want to be a Landlord?*

Alike his central character in *Ring Fenced*, (Benjamin Short), Zach Abrams grew up within an orthodox Jewish family. He completed his education in Scotland and went on to a career in business and finance. He is married with two children. He plays no instruments and has an eclectic taste in music, although not as obsessive as Benjamin.

Unlike Benjamin, he does not maintain mistresses, write pornography and (sadly) he does not have ownership of such a wealthy company. He is not a sociopath (at least by his own reckoning) and all versions of his life are aware of and freely communicate with each other. More in keeping with Alex Warren, he and his family reside in the south side of Glasgow.

41433272R00146

Printed in Poland
by Amazon Fulfillment
Poland Sp. z o.o., Wrocław